Garden of Eldrich Delights

Published by Raw Dog Screaming Press
Bowie, MD

First Edition

Cover: Daniele Serra
Book design: Jennifer Barnes
Printed in the United States of America
ISBN: 978-1-947879-08-9

Library of Congress Control Number:
2018952195

www.RawDogScreaming.com

Garden of Eldritch Delights

Lucy A. Snyder

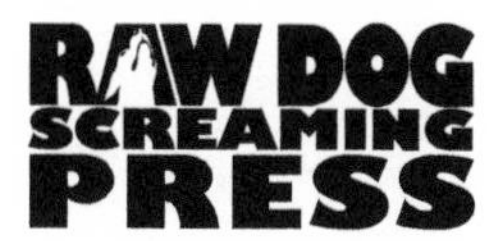

Contents

That Which Does Not Kill You

It's odd how the pain doesn't register at first. You wake to an ill stickiness coating your arms and belly, the sheets dark and stiff, the sour stink of copper in the air. Mind blurred and eyes bleary, you wonder where your girlfriend Ashley is. Why are you awake so early on a Saturday? Has something happened? Is there something you're supposed to do?

A neuron fires: you have a morning coffee date with Brenda. You two first met at the fencing club in college and kept discovering friends and interests in common. She became a steadfast bestie. But lately, you've been too busy with Ashley to keep up with anyone else.

There's an itch between your breasts so you sleepily try to scratch it. Your cold fingers find slashed skin, the ragged hardness of your broken sternum, and the torn cavity beyond. Your sliced aorta and pulmonary vessels feel like calamari, fleshy cannelloni in congealing Bolognese.

And then, as your fingers trace the severing, *that's* when the pain hits.

Agony is too small a word for what you're feeling. You try to scream but your lungs are deflated balloons, pierced by the same angry gashes that took your heart. Collateral damage. Your lover was not exercising a surgeon's precision last night. Nothing but bile rises from your throat.

Wordless, weeping, you throw off the sheets and stagger to your feet. You're certain that you should be dead–the pain is so horrible you *want* to be dead–but you're still moving. Still alive? You stare down at your trembling gray hands and your blood-smeared naked body in wonder. What kind of life is this? How long can you possibly go on like this?

There's a trail of blood on the carpet leading out of the bedroom, and your only thought is that if you can just find your heart, maybe everything will be okay. Maybe the pain will stop. You follow the blood down the hall, down the stairs to the living room.

Ashley is there. So is her boyfriend Kurt. They don't see you right away. He's kneeling by the bookshelf, stacking her movies and hardcovers into a cardboard box. Ashley's put on her Cornell University tank top and the old jeans she usually wears to pottery workshops. Kurt's wearing his usual weekend outfit of track pants and a tee shirt advertising some brand of protein powder. He works at a gym supply company and has a million tees. You can't remember if you've ever seen him wear anything else. He must have *some* nice clothes; he travels to health clubs around the country to pitch new products, and the upscale fitness centers probably expect a salesman to wear a suit. Besides, Ashley likes the kind of restaurants that don't admit men without their ties.

Ashley met him at her gym, and she likes to go on business trips with him. They were just travel and workout buddies, at first. At least that's what she told you. But she also told you on your second date that she doesn't do monogamy, so Kurt was never much of a surprise.

The living room is full of moving boxes. Most are open and only half-filled, and you spot the vase of shells the two of you beach-combed in the Bahamas, the ukulele you bought her in Maui, the shot glasses from Vegas, the red scarf from Montreal. Five years of mementos. For the first time, you realize you were best together when you were far from home. But no relationship can cruise at 30,000 feet forever.

She's pacing beside her boxes, nervously flicking a gray box cutter's blade in and out. *Click. Click. Click.* Her hands are covered in dried gore all the way to her elbows. It looks like she's wearing ragged brown opera gloves. And then you're remembering your third date when you went to a fancy-dress ball in a downtown loft and you both got tipsy on the host's $100 champagne and then went up to the roof to make out like a couple of schoolgirls. Her lips were so soft. You feel a reflexive pang of worry: has she cut herself? But no, she hasn't. It's all your blood.

That mild epiphany makes you dizzy, and you stumble on the stairs and nearly fall. The couple startles at the thumping of your unsteady feet. For a moment, they both look shocked to see you standing there. Kurt blushes uncomfortably at your nakedness and looks away, but Ashley grimaces in frustration.

"Damn it, Emily, can't you just stay out of the way like I told you?" she snaps.

You don't remember her telling you anything. You gesture toward the gaping hole in your chest and manage a strangled moan with the little bit of air left in your lungs.

"Well, what else was I supposed to do?" Ashley crosses her arms, still clicking the box cutter's blade. "I *told* you I can't sleep with your heart beating so goddamned loud all the time. You have the fucking loudest stupid heart I've ever heard."

You want to ask her why Kurt's heartbeat doesn't bother her. Maybe his broad weightlifter's chest muffles the sound better than your skinny tomboy body does. Maybe he's got a teeny-tiny heart in that mighty rib cage and it's far too petite to disturb her delicate ears. More likely, his heart beats just the same as yours does. But he's new and you aren't, so he hasn't gotten on her nerves yet. After all, your heartbeat didn't seem to be a problem until your trip budget dried up.

"I'm a sensitive person. I have *very* acute hearing." Ashley uncrosses her arms and points the box cutter at you. "I told you to do something about it but you *didn't.*"

She's cut the truth from your mutual history. You *did* do something, in fact you did *many* things, for months. First you tried sleeping with a pillow over your chest. Then you moved downstairs to the sofa at night. But she complained she could still hear your heart through the wooden floor, so you bought her a white noise machine for the bedroom. For a while, that seemed to satisfy her, and she often let you sleep in your own bed with her again.

On your birthday, she bought you a very sharp pocketknife, a pretty little thing with a pearly handle. The surgical steel blade was etched with the words "*Quies et Pax*". You laughed, thinking the inscription was a joke. You'd have done almost anything to make her happy, but silencing your own heart was not one of them. Ashley always did like to take matters into her own hands.

"You're a complete disaster." She's staring at the ragged, leaky hole she put in your chest. "You're a *monster.*"

Standing there in mute torment while she harangues you isn't getting you your heart back, is it? The blood trail leads through the living room to the kitchen and patio doors so you stagger after it, weaving along the rusty dotted line like a drunk.

"Oh, Christ, don't go out there," Ashley says as you fumble with the handles of the French doors. "Have some self-respect. The neighbors will *see* you like this."

Trying to ignore her, you push on into the back yard. It's a cool, sunny late September morning, and the leaves are just starting to turn yellow and orange. Your heart is out there, still beating. You can *hear* it but no matter where you look, you can't see it.

Ashley seems to hear it, too, and shudders. "God damn that thing."

You follow the sound to an old apple tree near the fence. Someone–Kurt, maybe, or Ashley if she dragged your stepladder out there–has impaled your heart on the broken stub of a small branch jutting high on the trunk. Despite all the damage it's beating loudly, vainly pumping air, the valves clacking as if they're mahogany castanets. Maybe it's absorbed some of the tree into itself. It's covered in tiny black ants that have marched across the bark. If you concentrate very hard, you can feel the sting of their bites and the itch of their crawling legs.

You reach up to try to rescue your heart, but it's well beyond your grasp. You jump for it, but your knees buckle and you collapse onto your back at the bottom of the trunk, exhausted. All you can do is stare up at your speared, severed flesh.

"This is exactly why I can't live with you." Ashley stands over you, her fists on her hips. "You're so fucking dramatic about these things. You're just *broken*."

Tears well up in her eyes. "I can't be around all this negativity. Good-bye."

She turns on her heel and walks back across the yard. You continue to stare up at your clacking heart as you distantly hear them load her boxes into Kurt's truck. The agony has faded into a dull, hollow, all-consuming ache. Your strength is gone; you can no more stand up than you could sprout wings and fly into the sun. In the periphery of your vision, you see the neighbors peek over the fence like nervous prairie dogs, then duck back down. Nobody calls out to see if you need help, or offers any. You wonder how long it will take the tiny stinging ants to devour your body.

A little after noon, you hear the fence swing open and then the grassy swish of footsteps approaching you.

"Well, *shit*." It's your friend Brenda's voice. You remember that you were supposed to meet her for coffee.

With great effort, you raise a hand to wave at her.

Brenda comes closer and leans over you, concerned. She's dressed casually in a light grey sweater over dark denim leggings, but she's got on a pair of nice red leather pumps and a pretty turquoise necklace. It occurs to you that while she's not dressed up for a *date*-date, she's put thought into her ensemble. Her care might mean something more, or not. You're just glad to see her.

"Wow," She says. "She really tore you up, didn't she? Is this the second time this month?"

You raise three fingers.

"Damn, girl."

You mutely point up at your heart.

"Oh. Yeah. That would help, wouldn't it?"

Brenda kicks off her nice shoes, pushes up her sleeves, and nimbly scales the trunk. She used to be a gymnast. Everybody needs a friend who used to be a gymnast, you think. Soon she's back on the grass, and she takes your heart over to the garden hose to rinse off all the ants. You feel a bracing chill as the water washes over it.

She returns, and you accept your damp heart with cold, quivering hands. You awkwardly pack it into your chest and pull your flesh back together. After a couple of minutes, you feel warmth spreading back into your chilled limbs, and you can finally take a breath again.

"Thank you," you gasp.

"De nada," she replies.

"How did you know I'd be back here?"

"Ashley posted an Instagram of the bloody box cutter. When you didn't show at the coffee shop, I had a hunch."

"I didn't mean to stand you up. Sorry about that."

"Don't apologize. Just promise me that you won't hook up with her again, okay?"

"Third time's the charm." You cross your scarred heart. "Never again."

Have you just told a lie? What will you *really* do when Ashley inevitably severs Kurt and comes back to you with her soft champagne lips?

Brenda's holding out a strong, steady, gentle hand, and so you take it and pull yourself to your feet. You meet her eyes, and find yourself surprised that in all the years you've known her, you never noticed the flecks of gold in her hazel irises.

Brenda blushes a little under your wondering gaze and bashfully looks away. At that moment, you know in your aching core that you've told no lies. You are done with Ashley. If she comes back, you won't be home.

"So, do you want to get dressed and go get that coffee?" she asks. "I don't mind waiting if you need to shower first."

You smile. And remember that she only likes coffee shops because you do. "How about we hit the Barcade for pinball and whisky and breakfast burritos instead?"

Now she's smiling, too. "Deal."

Sunset on Mott Island

Mom had another bad night; she kept waking up and calling for my father, who'd died when I was only five. Sometimes, she called for her own father, and sometimes, she called out strange names in a language I didn't recognize. For hours, she refused to take the sleeping medicine Dr. Olmstead had left us, but shortly before dawn I finally convinced her to swallow a pill with a sip of water. As the sun broke over the horizon, her mouth went slack, and she drifted into what I hoped would be a dreamless sleep.

I climbed the creaking stairs to the rooftop deck to watch the sun rise over the ocean. It was gorgeous as it always was this time of year, the clouds lit in different shades of scarlet and orange. *Red sky at morning, sailors take warning.*

Miles away, I could see a dark speck moving across the dune-covered southern causeway. Dr. Olmstead on his beat-up beach cruiser bike pedaling in for his weekly house calls. I knew he was a good man when I first met him, but that was before the world went insane. Lots of people could be good upstanding citizens when it didn't cost them anything, and most pillars of the community abandoned the city the moment things got difficult. Dr. Olmstead stayed to do what he could for the people who needed it despite the toll it was taking on him. He had just three patients still alive out here on the island, my mother among them. He visited us every week. I didn't know how many people he was still trying to help in the city.

I gazed out at the city skyline beyond the causeway. Allstate Tower was still burning, but the smoke was much less than it had been even a day ago. When the panic started after the monsters came up from the sewers, Dr. Olmstead said practically every building downtown suffered some kind of arson. He'd been busy at the hospital and it took him three days to find out that his apartment building had burned to the ground.

Fortunately, the looting and monsters never reached the island, and Dr. Olmstead found a safe place to stay with a friend who'd since fled. I watched the doctor's progress up the road; I had maybe twenty minutes to shower and put on some fresh clothes. I knew Dr. Olmstead had seen far worse than a sweaty thirty-year-old woman with bed head, but I didn't *want* him to see worse. I wanted him to be in a place where people were glad to see him and didn't stink. A place with comfortable furniture and cold drinks and cookies. Well, I couldn't offer much in twenty minutes besides boxed gingersnaps and lemonade, and my mother's sofa was sagging pretty hard from all the nights I'd slept on it, but I'd do the best I could out of respect for him always doing the best he could. At least we had a working icemaker.

I headed downstairs, pulled some fresh clothes off the rack I'd set up in my mom's laundry room, and went into her cramped bathroom to bathe. We'd lost natural gas service when the city burned, but the weather had only just started to turn cool and the water wasn't unbearably chilly yet. For now, I still had enough fuel for the generator; I knew the family that owned the Main Street gas station and they let me stock up when they abandoned it. The island's power grid was flaky at the best of times, and I wanted to make sure that Mom always had ice when she needed it in the summer. I'd almost had a newer gas stove installed, but was glad I'd stuck with the old electric that came with the house. If Mom lasted into the winter, I could heat up water for her bath on the stove.

I soaped up and started to give my breasts a once-over. It had been weeks, maybe months since I'd remembered to examine myself. When you're busy watching your mother die, little things can fall by the wayside. I pressed my slick fingers into the side of my right breast and made a circle. My index finger found something that felt like a shard of pottery a half-inch beneath my skin.

The water suddenly seemed a whole lot colder. I probed the lump more carefully. It was hard, all right, maybe the size of a broken shooter marble, and it hadn't been there before.

"God dammit," I whispered.

Mom had found a lump just like this one when she was 60. Same breast in nearly the same spot. Her doctors took her breast and gave her radiation treatments, but the malignant cells had lain in wait and sprouted in her brain and spinal cord ten years later. Long enough for her to be a statistical breast cancer survivor but not an actual one.

I took a deep breath to try to calm myself. Turned off the water. No sense in borrowing trouble when there was so much already at hand, was there? It could just be a cyst. I'd ask the doctor to take a look after he'd checked on Mom. I toweled off, combed my damp hair into a ponytail, got dressed, and went into the kitchen to mix up some lemonade.

Soon I heard footsteps on the wooden stairs outside, and shortly thereafter came a rattling knock on the screen door.

"Land shark!" Dr. Olmstead called. "I mean, uh, Candygram!"

I laughed. "Come on in. Want some lemonade?"

"Just water, please, with a pinch of salt in it."

Dr. Olmstead stepped inside with his leather physician's satchel, carefully pulled the screen door closed behind him, took off his windbreaker and hung it on the white antique hook rack. He left his knitted multicolored scarf on; it was a handmade Doctor Who replica, though at most a third as long as the one the Doctor wore.

I got his salted water from the kitchen and smiled at him, remembering the first time I'd seen him wearing that delightfully nerdy neckwear...and in that moment I realized that he looked *terrible*. His clothes were neat as always–well, *nearly* neat as always–but his body had changed for the worse. When I first met him a year ago he was very fit, with a nicely muscular frame and a full head of dark curly hair. But now, his blue polo shirt hung loosely on bony shoulders. His bare scalp gleamed. He'd been buzzing his hair short since the city burned, and I'd always thought it was just for the sake of hygiene, but looking at him now I wasn't sure that his hair hadn't fallen out.

And his face...had his face always been that narrow? Had his eyes always bulged out like that? When had he gotten so damned *pale*?

"Are you feeling okay?" I asked.

He shrugged, took a long drink from his water glass, and gave me a tight-lipped smile. "Right as could be expected, considering. How's our lovely lady?"

I shook my head. "She had a bad night. Nightmares, hallucinations...I can't tell."

"Probably a little bit of both." He tugged at the scarf around his neck as if it itched, but he didn't try to unwind it. "Let's go take a look."

My mother was so groggy from the sleeping pill that she was barely able to sit up and open her eyes when the doctor asked her to. He spent time peering into her eyes with a penlight and gravely listening to the sounds of her body with a stethoscope. When he was finished, he tucked his instruments back into his bag and gestured for me to follow him back into the living room. Mom was asleep again before he'd gotten up from the chair beside the bed.

"How is she?" I asked.

"Not good. Her heart is failing. The sleeping medicine is hard on her body, but insomnia will kill her just as quickly and be a whole lot less pleasant. And her breathing doesn't sound right; I suspect she might have a mass pressing on her lungs, or the beginnings of pneumonia."

"Jesus." I rubbed my eyes. I didn't want to cry in front of him. "How much time does she have?"

"Days. Maybe hours. It's hard to know."

"Can you stay?" I blurted it out before I could stop myself. "I…I don't know what to do after she dies."

He gently touched my shoulder. "I have to check on the others, but I will come back and stay, yes. And I'll help you bury her someplace nice, okay?"

"Before you go…can I get you to look at something?"

I explained what I'd found. Dr. Olmstead had me lie down on the sofa and he performed a breast exam. His hands were cold and clammy, but gentle. When he found the shard-like lump, his expression turned grim.

"That feels like a problem, but even with your family history, I can't make a definite diagnosis one way or the other." He offered me a hand to help me sit up. "Normally I'd refer you for a mammogram and biopsy, but…"

He trailed off, gesturing helplessly toward the city.

"Is there anywhere else I could go?" I refastened my bra and buttoned up my blouse.

"You could go inland, but from what I hear on the shortwave radio, what happened here happened along every coast. There are so many refugees that the hospitals and clinics are completely overwhelmed. I'm not sure you could get care in time for it to make a difference if it *is* an aggressive cancer."

I shook my head, wondering if I was going to start weeping, but instead I started laughing. "When it rains around here, it really pours, doesn't it? Mom always said I was an early bloomer."

"For what it's worth, I'm really sorry. If you start getting sick, I can give you something to make it easier." He tugged at his scarf.

"What's going on with your neck, Doc?"

"It's nothing." He looked away, embarrassed.

"Liar. C'mon, you just saw me naked. There's no reason to hide whatever it is if the wool is making you itch."

He sighed, gave another tight-lipped smile, and started to unwind the scarf. "You're not the only one with unfortunate family genetics. I, however, seem to be a *late* bloomer in that regard."

He pulled the scarf free, and I saw a series of purple slashes running horizontally along both sides of his neck. At first I thought they might be scars from a suicide attempt. But no, if he'd done that he'd have been terribly injured. I couldn't make sense of what I was seeing.

"What…what are those?" I asked dumbly.

"Gills. Not open yet. Probably they'll open in a few days and I'll have to go in the water after that. I think the flood's coming before then, though."

He flashed me another smile, this one with teeth. Too many teeth. I'd seen the same grin on a piranha once.

"Flood?" I stammered.

He looked at me, sad and earnest. "Haven't you had the dream?"

I shuddered. I didn't know if it was the same one he'd had, but for the past five nights running I'd dreamed that I was standing on the rooftop deck watching an enormous tsunami roll green and cold and massive toward the beach. Five times taller than the burning Allstate skyscraper and utterly unstoppable. Here I'd been thinking it was all a metaphor for what my mother's death would do to me, but a look at the doctor's expression told me he was sure it was literal prophecy.

"But…but what could possibly cause a wave like that?" I shivered.

"Great Cthulhu rises, and Father Dagon, too." Dr. Olmstead gazed reverently toward the sea. "Mother Hydra. They all rise, and the world will be theirs. Until then, they still sleep, and live in our dreams."

The watery nightmares I'd tried to forget came back to me, vividly, and I realized everything he was saying was true. I should have been terrified. I should have been so frightened I was falling to the floor, babbling in madness. But I wasn't terrified. I was *furious.*

"Fuck that, and fuck *them.*" I balled my fists in my lap to keep myself from hurling the reading lamp across the room. Mom loved that stupid lamp; it was a lopsided, wobbly orange thing I'd made in art class when I was 15 and she'd prized it like a Tiffany original.

"The *only* thing I've wanted for the last goddamn year was for my mother to enjoy her final days as much as she possibly could." I was yelling, and the doctor was flinching away from me, looking worried. I wanted to feel bad about that, but I didn't. "She wanted to live on the beach in the little town where she spent her summers as a child, so I found this place and bought it for her. Quit my job and helped her move because *goddamn it* she's my mom and I could do it so *goddamn it* I should. And here I find out some fucking…fucking fish gods are depriving her of the sleep she needs to have anything resembling a good quality of life? *Fuck cancer, and fuck them*!"

We just stared at each other for a moment.

"But…she won't have to see the worst of it," the doctor finally said. "She won't be here for the rising. That's a silver lining, right?"

"Right. It is. *Clearly.*" I took a deep breath, trying to calm down. Me raging around the house wouldn't do anything but scare Mom.

"What do I do now?" I asked quietly.

"Do what you've been doing. Make things pleasant for her. If she wants potato chip casserole, make her a casserole. If she wants ice cream and bourbon, ditto. No restrictions. Doctor's orders."

Mom woke up later that afternoon and tottered into the living room with her walker, her eyes bright and some rosy pink back on her hollowed cheeks. I couldn't help but remember the fancy tropical fish we had when I was a kid; their colors seemed to grow so much brighter a few hours before they died.

"I'm hungry." She sounded like a little girl.

"What would you like to eat?"

"Pie and cookies and ice cream."

Jesus. That would send her blood sugar straight into orbit. "We're out of ice cream, but there's a key lime pie in the freezer. What kind of cookies do you want?"

"Chocolate chip."

"Okay." I went into the kitchen and surveyed the contents of the pantry. I had enough chips left for a decent batch. We were out of real dairy butter but Mom never minded cookies made with butter-flavored shortening. "You want anything to eat while the pie thaws?"

"No, thank you. Can you put on a show for me?"

The local TV stations had disappeared into static since the city burned, but I'd bought mom a brand-new Betamax player as a housewarming present, and in the year since we'd gotten a nice little collection of mail-order movies. I briefly pictured the expensive tape cases scattered and covered in barnacles under a hundred feet of seawater, then put in her tape of *The Day the Earth Stood Still* and started baking.

Dr. Olmstead returned soon after I pulled the cookies out of the oven. Mom had polished off two slices of pie and was snoozing on the sofa while Bobby and Klaatu searched for Professor Barnhardt onscreen.

"Wow, it smells great in here," Dr. Olmstead said.

"How are your other patients doing?" I asked.

"They're hanging in there." He stepped closer, lowering his voice. "For better or worse. I gave them all opiates to take in case things get bad. I've heard drowning can be a painful way to go."

I nodded and moved some gooey cookies onto a plate. "Good idea."

He helped me mix up some glasses of instant milk and I carried the drinks and cookies in to Mom on a bamboo tray.

"Oh!" She sat up, her eyes red and her voice slurred. "Can I have one of those?"

"As many as you like," I replied.

The doctor and I settled down on the sofa on either side of her. We all drank well-water milk and ate warm cookies as the tape played on. Mom soon nodded off again, and I became engrossed in the movie, even though I'd seen it a half dozen times.

"I think she's stopped breathing," the doctor said a little while later.

"Are you sure?" I looked at my mother. Her mouth hung open, and her filmy eyes were half-closed. She didn't look asleep. She looked *gone*.

Dr. Olmstead pressed two fingers to the side of her neck, feeling for a pulse. He met my gaze and shook his head.

"Oh."

I'd though I would cry when she finally died, but it all just seemed so surreal. I mostly felt numb, and didn't quite know what to do, so I said the Lord's Prayer.

"Were there any places she liked to walk?" he asked. "We can find a pretty spot and bury her."

I suddenly felt anxious when he said the word *bury*. I tried to not think of maggots burrowing into my mother's flesh…and failed.

And then another problem occurred to me. "If it floods, her grave will wash out, won't it? I mean, we probably can't get it deep enough in this soil, and the dirt above her will be too loose to hold."

He blinked. "Yes, that will probably happen."

"And then crabs will eat her. Maybe sharks." Tears finally started welling in my eyes at that. "I…I don't want my mom eaten by sharks. Even if she's dead and can't care about it."

"Well." The doctor was silent for a moment. "We could make a pyre?"

We wrapped my mother in a sheet and carried her down to the beach. Dr. Olmstead started gathering driftwood and dry brush while I went back up to the house to search for an accelerant. I found a bottle of bourbon and an unopened bottle of Everclear in the liquor cabinet behind my mother's stash of chardonnay. I put them both in a picnic basket with a couple of shot glasses and went back down to the pyre.

We gathered a decent amount of wood and a few bags of charcoal, set my mother atop it, soaked it down with the Everclear and lit it at sunset. Dr. Olmstead and I sat on the sand upwind, drinking up the bourbon and watching the flames. When it started to get gruesome, I closed my eyes and tried to listen to the waves instead of the pop of burning fat. Tried to pretend it was any other fall bonfire.

I was starting to drift off to sleep when there was a sudden roaring *whoosh* from the ocean.

The surf had abruptly sucked far out to sea, leaving piles of algae and fish flopping on the wet sand for hundreds of yards, a completely unearthly scene in the dying light.

"I read about this," I said. "This happens before a tsunami, doesn't it?"

Dr. Olmstead nodded, looking upset. "It does. It's happening. I left my bag up at the house…I don't have time to give you anything. I'm so sorry."

"It's fine. I'm a big girl and I'm not scared to drown. Just…"

I trailed off.

"Just what?" he asked quietly.

"Would you hold my hand?"

"Of course."

He took my hand in his, and I nestled against his cold, gaunt shoulder and watched my mother's bones glow amongst the driftwood embers.

The Gentleman Caller

My back and ribs screamed at me as I leaned out over the armrest of the motorized wheelchair and slapped the round steel button again, harder. An eternity later, the front door of FoneLand swung open and I rolled out of the biting January air into the warm lobby.

The old man at the security desk peered out over his trifocals at me.

"Oh, sorry, didn't see ya, Janie. Woulda got the door for ya," Pete wheezed.

"S'okay." I forced my cold-numb cheeks into a smile as I drove down the beige carpet. Pete was a sweet old man, but God help us if anyone nefarious tried to sneak into the place.

The motor whined like a sick dog; rolling through all the snow outside was hard on the chair. Hell, it was hard on me. Even when I was healthy, if the temperature dropped below 20, the separation scar that ran the length of the left side of my body did nothing but ache.

Today, the cold made everything from my toenails to my teeth ache. I'd carefully folded my legs up and wrapped them in part of the sheepskin rug I rode on to keep my butt free of pressure sores, but even so my thighs and feet burned something fierce. Normally I didn't have any sensation down there at all, except for a dull, phantom itching when I had been moving around a lot. Probably something to do with my veins, which were bad enough that the doctors were always bugging me to get my legs amputated. They told me I could get a blood clot and die suddenly when I got older. I hadn't yet decided whether that would really be such a bad thing.

I still felt lightheaded and weak from the viral encephalitis that had laid me up for the better part of two months. Coming to work was probably not the smartest thing I'd ever decided to do...but I was so damn sick of watching TV in my assisted living facility apartment I could cry. I wanted to be out around people, *young* people, not the eternally sick and dying.

Tooling around the snowbound parks and overcrowded malls weren't pleasant options, though. Going to my parents' house would have been even worse. So, that left work.

"You take care now." Pete's smile held an ample measure of pity.

Pity. I stopped the chair beside the elevators and stared up at my reflection in the round security mirror as I waited for the next lift. My face was as pale as the belly of some undersea creature. I supposed I looked normal enough from the neck up but no amount of blankets could completely hide that I was a deformed dwarf from the neck down: torso twisted and permanently hunched to one side, arms stunted. My legs looked like nothing more than useless spindles of flesh and bone, but they did help me keep my balance in the chair. And stylish baby shoes fit me fine. Today I had on a pair of glittery red ones just like Dorothy's magic slippers.

If only I could click my heels.

To the outside world, I looked like an eternal virgin. Nobody knew I'd been jilling off since I was twelve. The best present I ever got was a little battery-powered vibrator one of the young nurses' assistants gave me surreptitiously when I was spending an otherwise lousy sixteenth birthday in the hospital. She was just a few years older than me, full in the flush of hormones herself, and I guess she felt bad that I was never going to get laid.

Thing was, I *could* get laid. I *could*, dammit. If I was careful and saved up enough money, there was a local place that could rent me a pretty boy for a few hours. Word was it was a classy business with a no-theft, no-disease guarantee; the city had some of the best rehab hospitals in the country, so there were plenty of disabled girls and pent-up old ladies who wanted their services.

And, if I were willing to risk my safety, I wouldn't even have to pay for sexytimes. I'd been lurking on the BDSM FetLife site for a couple of years, more than long enough to know that people got turned on by the strangest things. If I started posting photos, I'd get a zillion meetup requests. Probably some of the pervs would even be nice. But it would be difficult finding anyone who saw me as a person and not a niche fetish.

But when you came down to it, I really didn't want a gigolo or a BDSM scenester. My ever-growing collection of toys did me fine. My rent-a-boy fund had taken a serious hit there, but thank God for discreet mail order. The biggest challenge was keeping my parents from finding my stash of schtupperware.

Neither they nor old Pete would *ever* imagine that I worked for FoneLand's fantasy line.

Once I got to work, I became Lady Rayne, a popular telephone mistress who got dozens of men creaming in their jeans each day. Some of my regular callers even sent gifts to her through FoneLand. Gifts to me, rather, but of course Rayne's fans didn't know that.

About a week before I got the encephalitis, a regular who said his name was Brandon sent me a real jade necklace. It was a gorgeous piece, but strange. The beads were etched all over in a strange pictographic language that none of my Internet searches could decipher. The curvilinear carvings looked positively ancient; it *had* to cost serious money.

Brandon never wanted to talk about anything raunchy. He behaved like a perfect gentleman during our sessions, and he mostly just wanted to chat about movies and theatre. As our sessions went on, I had a hard time figuring out why someone as articulate and seemingly urbane as him needed to pay for conversation. And I was simultaneously intrigued and frustrated that nothing I said to him seemed to turn him on, yet my occasional attempts at dirty talk never offended him, either.

So, I'd considered sending the necklace back. I did feel a little like a fraud, even though I'd never asked for the present. But ultimately I decided to keep it. I felt...special when I wore it. Prettier. More important. I'd worn it every day since I got it, except for when I was in the hospital and worried someone might steal it while I was asleep.

And, I told myself, why not keep it? Even if I had committed a kind of fraud, I figured that Brandon could never find out who I really was. The company had a strict information security policy, and nobody creeping around the parking lot was likely to picture me as the source of anyone's fantasies.

My callers were probably picturing a woman like my twin sister. Linda was a genuine beauty: tall, green eyes, deep red hair, long legs and an ample bust. Our parents were rich enough to afford the endless series of plastic surgeries Linda had needed once the doctors at Johns Hopkins removed me from her back a couple of days after we were C-sectioned out of our mother.

Linda got the ribs and kidney we shared. I was six months old before I even got a name. No one expected me to live, and when I lived, no one expected me to be anything more than a retarded cripple. Not that my parents would ever use ugly, demeaning words like those to describe their own daughter. Not out loud, anyhow.

Maybe I'm being unfair, but I think Mom and Dad would have been happier if I'd been a vegetable. Then they could simply institutionalize me and forget that their lovely Linda had ever been two-thirds of a monster they'd spawned. They probably secretly wanted to give me up for adoption, but that would have been a faux pas of epic proportions for a family that made a big thing of donating to the March of Dimes each year.

Abnormalcy is not something my family suffers gladly. My father's life revolves around stocks and fancy cars and golf, and my mother gets freaked out if the silverware doesn't all match. If they ever found out I was working phone sex...wow. I was saving that little tidbit for a general announcement at the next family reunion so that they'd be most optimally mortified.

Linda would *act* horrified but I thought she would be secretly amused. And maybe, just for a moment, a little envious. We were born with essentially the same brain, after all, but her weird side would forever remain in the closet hidden behind the pink taffeta prom dress of the Good Girl image our mother had thrust upon her.

I smiled to myself as I rode the elevator up to the tenth floor. Maybe I wouldn't go through with my plan for the reunion...but it was an awful lot of fun to think about. Pity I could never dress the part; neither nasty boots nor corsets would ever fit me. Not without causing me a hell of a lot of pain, anyway.

I got off the elevator and rolled onto the fantasy line floor. Zoe, a gangly rivethead who was one of my closest friends, was making herself some green tea at the coffee nook. She was dressed relatively conservatively in shiny black vinyl pants, tall Doc Martens and a black cardigan over an old Misfits tee shirt.

"Hey, Jane, how you doing? Didn't expect to see you back today." Zoe pushed her electric-blue bangs away from her eyes.

"The cabin fever got to me," I replied. "Figured I'd see if I could get through a half shift."

"So you're all better now?"

"Eh, sorta-kinda. Light still hurts my eyes."

I wasn't planning to mention the petit mal seizures I'd had since I left the hospital. The doctors assured me they would pass. I'd also had unusually vivid dreams ever since my feverish delirium; in some of them, I was a creature swimming through a sunken stone city in a deep ocean trench. I found that dream terrifying, and didn't want to talk about it. But most of my real-as-life dreams had been far too mundane to mention. Why bore poor Zoe by telling her I'd dreamed I was a night auditor at a hotel going over stacks and stacks of receipts? Or that I was an insomniac watching terrible late-night TV?

"But don't worry, I'm not contagious any more," I added.

"I wasn't worried." Zoe blinked slowly and smiled, her cheeks dimpling over her deep blue lipstick. "Just don't push yourself and relapse, ya know? It's been boring here without you around. No one to be rude with but the boys on the gay lines."

I threw a hand up against my forehead and pretended to swoon. "Oh, woe!"

Zoe giggled. "Get on in there, girl. The sweaty masses await their audience with the sultry Rayne."

I smiled and punched in at the time clock, then rolled down into the phone pit. Taking my place at an empty carrel, I put on my headset, logged into the computer, and tapped in my personal ID code to make myself available for calls.

I genuinely enjoyed working FoneLand's fantasy line. It was far, far better than telemarketing in every way. Sure, I sometimes got the occasional abusive freak, but we were allowed to terminate a call whenever we felt uncomfortable. And I did sometimes feel sorry for the guys who called...many of them seemed sad and lonely. But I enjoyed the attention, and the challenge.

It wasn't just the acting–to be *really* good, you had to figure out how to keep them coming back for more. You had to get inside a guy's head and figure out what he wanted to hear. I could size up a caller within the first ten seconds, and I regularly logged the longest calls in the center.

The phone buzzed, and I picked up.

"Hello, this is Rayne," I breathed. "What's your pleasure?"

"I...I wanna do something really dirty," the guy stammered earnestly. He sounded pretty young, maybe just barely old enough to be making the call. "I wanna do it...doggy style."

"Ooh, you want me down on my knees? But what if I want *you* down on *your* knees?"

Who the hell still thought doggy style was any big deal? The kid had to have led a massively sheltered life. I could practically imagine him sitting on his bed in his old church camp T-shirt and gray boxer shorts, heart pounding and sweat trickling down the groove of his back, his cock already hard from the excitement of doing something his Pentecostal minister father would never *ever* approve of....

I suddenly felt dizzy, and had to shut my eyes against the vertigo. The jade necklace felt heavy and cold against my flesh.

When I opened my eyes a moment later, I was no longer in my phone carrel. I was sitting in the middle of an unmade bed in a messy bachelor apartment bedroom. Clothing littered the floor, and the walls were covered with Christian rock band posters. An old-fashioned phone handset was tucked uncomfortably between my chin and shoulder.

I looked down...and realized I was *in the guy's body.*

Am I having another seizure? I wondered. *Is this a hallucination?*

I stared down at the erect cock bulging beneath the thin fabric of his boxers.

I shouldn't do this, I thought.

But I laid the receiver on the pillow, reached down and started doing what my caller had probably been told his whole life was a sin worse than touching a woman against her will.

The flesh was more than willing. In just a few strokes, I came in a sweet hot shuddering spurt. I groaned loud in the guy's voice, and felt the come spatter against my chin and neck–

–the sudden dizziness was intense, and when I came to I was back at my phone in the call center. Zoe was gently shaking my shoulder.

"Jane? Jane, you okay?" Zoe asked.

The call was still live. Through my headset, I heard the rustle of sheets, and then the guy's disoriented voice.

"What–what just happened?" he stammered. "I was in a dark place. It was so cold. I couldn't see anything."

"Everything's fine," I replied, trying to recover my composure as best I could. "Take a nice warm shower, and call back soon."

I clicked the call termination button on the computer screen, put myself on break, and turned to Zoe.

"What happened?" My voice shook. "What did I do?"

"You zoned out on us, girl. You started talking, and then you just sort of froze."

I winced, remembering how I'd moaned when I came. When *he* came. "Did–did I make any noise?"

Zoe shook her head. "Nope, not a sound until you came out of it just now. Don't know why the guy didn't hang up."

"Shit, I'm sorry. I–I still have little seizures." I knew full well that whatever I'd just had, it wasn't a seizure. "I thought I'd be okay. I think I need to go home."

After the shuttle bus took me back to Oakwood Tower, I went up to my apartment and hid under the covers of my bed with my cell phone. I stared at the bright screen in the muffled darkness. What had really happened at work? Surely it was some kind of hallucination…but I heard the guy's confusion. I *heard* it.

I wanted so desperately to know if it had been real. Wanted to know if I could do it again.

Could I enter the bodies of other people, live inside them? Experience life as a fully functional human being whose every waking moment wasn't a fight against pain? I knew it wasn't right to hijack somebody else's body. It might be a kind of rape. But if I had that power, would I be stupid to refuse to explore it? Stupid to refuse to take advantage of what little pleasure and escape the universe had offered me?

But how had this happened? Had my brain fever triggered something inside me? Or was something else going on? I couldn't be sure it was real, not yet. I had to call someone. Who?

An image of Linda immediately rose in my mind, followed by a complex wash of emotions. If anyone would understand my predicament, surely it was my own twin sister. I tried to ignore the tiny dark voice that told me that she owed me. She'd gotten everything in life that I'd been denied. If I called her, and if my new power worked, I'd finally be able to spend a few hours in the body I *should* have been born with. I could know what it was like to have a handsome, successful husband and a beautiful home in the country. To have parents who loved me and were proud of me.

I felt bitter tears welling in my eyes. Could I really do it? Did I dare? After walking in Linda's body and life, could I ever be happy again when I inevitably came back to *this*?

I finally decided that if I didn't do it, I'd spend the rest of my life wondering. Better to regret what I'd done than what I hadn't.

Two hours later, my sister finally answered her cell phone.

"What's up, Janie?" Linda sounded faintly impatient. "Is everything okay?"

"Everything's okay." I rolled my necklace's irregular jade beads between my fingers and closed my eyes. I could feel my sister's tall fine body, smell the perfume on her tailored clothes, feel the gold earrings bumping warmly against her neck....

"I just wanted to know what I should get Mom for her birthday," I finished. In Linda's voice. Linda's throat. My perfectly-manicured hand rested on a glass-topped coffee table, and I was sitting on a cream-colored leather couch. I disconnected the call on the new iPhone and surveyed my sister's domain.

"Holy shit. I've done it."

There'd been no dizziness, no vertigo. It was as if my consciousness were made for this body. I stared at her toned, perfect legs in their cream-colored tights. In my own body, I'd never been able to stand up, ever, much less walk... and I wasn't sure how it was done. Could I make her body do it? Or would it remember how on its own through muscle memory?

I got my feet under me and slowly stood. The bones and muscles acted in practiced concert; the body *did* seem to remember. After my first tottering steps,

I realized that the trick was to simply let the flesh do its thing and not think too hard about it. I went from room to room, touching the beautiful furniture, admiring the expensive art. I crossed through the airy, vaulted living room to the glass doors of the pool and Jacuzzi room.

The steamy blue water sparkled in the late afternoon light filtering through the fogged glass walls. Linda was an excellent swimmer. She'd competed in the butterfly and freestyle in high school and college, and had even gone as far as competing in an Olympic trial. I'd only ever learned how to float in case I fell into a pond or pool; I hoped Linda's body would also remember how to swim.

Had Linda ever gone skinny dipping? If I had a great pool like this, I'd do it every day. And if I had a hot husband like hers, I'd do *him* in the Jacuzzi twice a day. At least.

I kicked off my sister's black patent leather flats, unbuttoned the hunter-green linen dress suit, shimmied out of the satin slip and peeled off her tights and lace panties. I carefully laid the clothes across the sailcloth seat of a nearby lounge chair and then stretched, enjoying the feel of my sister's supple joints and toned muscles.

There was a full-length mirror set into the wall beside the towel hamper. I stepped up to it and turned to look at Linda's back, tracing my fingers down the place where I thought my body had been removed from hers. There was no visible scar, only the faintest of indentations in the ribs beside the spine and a slight granularity and numbness to the flesh above the bone. I pressed my fingers into the indentation; no pain.

Feeling deeply envious, I abandoned the mirror and walked down the pool's steps into the water. I pushed off from the edge of the bottom step with her toes, her outstretched fingers slicing neatly through the cool blue water. Linda's body remembered perfectly well how to swim.

And it was glorious. Swimming in her body was every bit the pleasure I'd imagined it would be. I could walk, I could dive, I could push myself until I was gasping and still felt no pain.

As I backstroked the length of the pool, I heard the door click open. Linda's husband Richard stood in the doorway to the living room. Wisps of steam curled around his Italian loafers and the hem of his gray wool Armani suit. His hand went up to straighten his already perfectly straight red power tie, a gesture I recognized as a sign of nervousness.

"What are you doing?" he asked, his voice betraying more confusion than his courtroom-neutral expression did.

"Swimming. Want to join me?" I flicked some water in his direction.

The water droplets landed a yard away from him, but he took a step back as if he were afraid I'd ruin his loafers. Or as if he were afraid of *me*; he was staring as if he thought I'd gone slightly mad.

"Uh, no." He gave his tie another tug. "I have an important case in a couple of days, and one of the junior partners is here to go over the court documents with me. Please see that we're not disturbed. And *please* get some clothes on."

His cold tone and annoyed look told me that I should be ashamed of myself. Ashamed of my body. I felt a mortified blush spread across my face. Richard averted his gaze and stepped out of the room, pulling the glass door shut behind him with a stern click like a disapproving tongue.

What the hell? Linda was *hot*. Most guys in the city would jump off the north bridge to have a chance at getting wet and naked with her.

But my inner protestations did nothing to dispel the anxious lump in the pit of my stomach, the same lump I'd felt throughout grade school when the other kids taunted me. *Dwarf. Freak. Ugly.*

I splashed out of the pool and got a fluffy white towel from the hamper by the lounge chairs. *Dwarf. Freak. Ugly.* Tears stinging my eyes, I toweled off and got back into Linda's expensive clothes.

I looked around the beautiful pool room and felt disoriented, disconnected. This was all wrong. This was not my beautiful house, nor my beautiful life. Maybe Linda had everything I thought I'd always wanted, and maybe she didn't, but at that moment I mostly wanted to be back in my own bed.

"Get in, get off, get out," I muttered to myself.

I headed into the half-bath adjoining the pool room and locked myself in. Hiked up my skirt, slipped a hand down the front of my tights and ran my fingertips over the softly curling pubic hair. Nothing; not so much as a happy tickle. I circled my index finger over the hooded clitoris. The flesh was numb, unresponsive. Nerve damage. Jesus.

This is what our separation had cost her. I explored further to confirm my sweating fear: everything was too numb to feel pleasure. She *couldn't* come, at least not by any means I knew. I was stuck inside her. And where was she? If I stayed in her body, what happened to her consciousness? Was she trapped in that frightening cold, dark place the caller spoke of? And what would happen to my own body? Would it die?

I leaned against the sink, swallowing against my anxious nausea. No. I couldn't let myself panic. There had to be a way to get back into my own body. What was *like* an orgasm, but wasn't?

I'll take electric shocks for $500, Alex.

One of Linda's memories bloomed: Richard carried a stun gun. It was probably in one of the pockets of his winter overcoat. Supposedly the thing was powerful enough to knock a 300-pound man flat on his back but would cause no permanent damage.

I straightened my clothes and hurried through the house to the coatrack in the foyer. Droplets of melted snow glittered like tiny diamonds on the shoulders of one heavy black overcoat. I pulled it off its peg and riffled through the pockets. Leather gloves, cigarette case, restaurant receipts in the outside pockets–and in the inside pocket, something that felt like an unusually heavy cordless shaver.

I pulled it out and flicked it on. Blue electricity arced and crackled across the two prongs on the face of the stun gun. It was a wicked-looking device.

Where should I zap myself? Shoulder? Stomach? Side? I finally decided on my stomach. I sat down on the carpeted floor, flicked it back on, and plunged the gun into my midsection.

The pain was intense, even for someone as accustomed to pain as me. Every muscle in my body jerked spasmodically, uncontrollably. My hands flew up as I convulsed, and the stun gun tumbled away and landed under a chair.

After an interminable two seconds, the muscle contractions passed. I was sweating and dizzy and nauseated. Worse, I was still in Linda's body.

An hour later, I pulled up to the assisted living facility in Linda's blue BMW. It was hard to suppress the full-on panic screaming inside my skull. Was Linda suffering in frigid darkness? I had to put things right.

I signed in at the receptionist's station and was hurrying toward the elevators when a man said, "Jane?"

I stopped, turned, and said "Yes?" before I could think better of it.

A man sitting in a chair by a huge potted fern set aside the newspaper he'd been reading (or hiding behind), stood and smiled at me.

"Right on time," he said cheerfully. He was a white man of about forty, on the handsome side of average, and had graying blond hair and a long, angular face. His eyes were dark hazel. He wore a blazer and khakis and could have blended in almost anywhere.

I'd never laid eyes on him before, I was sure, but his voice was ringing all kinds of bells. "Have we met?"

His smile widened and he extended his hand. "We haven't met in person, no. I'm Brandon Wilks. We've spoken on the phone many times. And I believe you've been enjoying the necklace I sent."

My hand went to my bare neck. I wished I'd brought the stun gun with me. "I…I'm not…"

He stepped closer and spoke more softly. "Not Jane? But you *are* Jane. You just aren't currently inhabiting her body. Don't be afraid; I'm here to help you."

"Do you know what's happening?" I asked.

He nodded. "I do, and I will explain, but I'm rather concerned about your body upstairs. They tend not to remain stable in the absence of consciousness. We should hurry."

He had an air of gentleness and competence, and frankly I was so frightened that I was ready to cling to anyone who had even half a clue, so I took him up to my apartment.

We found my body unconscious where I'd left it in bed, my cell phone dead on my chest. Brandon pulled a stethoscope out of his blazer and listened to my body's heart and lungs.

"Are you a doctor?" I asked.

"I studied to be a physician, yes, but my career has moved in some interesting directions over the years." He pulled the stethoscope off his ears and hung it around his neck. "Your breathing is a bit shallow, but your heart seems fine. For now."

"That's good," I replied. "How can I get back into my body? I'm worried about Linda."

"As well you should be." He leaned down and removed his jade necklace from my body and held it out to me. "Put this on, please."

I gave him a hard side-eye. "Why? What's going on?"

"A bit of quid pro quo, I'm afraid. I need you to use your gift to accomplish something for me before I can help you. Don't worry; it's quite simple, and won't take long."

I bit my lip and stared at the necklace. "I have questions."

"I'm sure you do," he replied. "But we both know you don't have time. Just do as I ask and I'll be on my way. You can even keep the necklace; it's the trigger for your powers, and with it you can sample other lives as you please. Or not; it's up to you."

I met his steady gaze. "Why me?"

"Yours is a family gift; it skips generations. Your mother, alas, she is not gifted by any definition of the word. I tested your sister first, when she came of age, but all the power rests inside you."

"You tested me?"

He smiled. "In our conversations. I could sense the potential in you, and I knew you'd be the one we needed when the stars were right."

I took the necklace from him and dangled it from my fingers, gazing at the strange carvings. "What is it that you need me to do?"

"I need you to help us make the world a better place." He pulled an older model smartphone out of his back pocket and scrolled to a contact entry. "Call this number. Enter the mind of the man who answers. Ask for Jebediah. Do what he asks. You can refuse if anything seems immoral or risky."

"How do I get back here?"

"He'll make sure you return. And then I'll see to it that you get back into your real body safely and Linda's soul is returned to hers."

I paused for a long moment.

"All right." I put on the necklace and took the cell phone from his hand. Pressed the button to dial. Focused on the tone.

"Barker. Talk." The voice was gruff and male. Maybe mid-thirties. Sounded bored and suspicious. I could picture the gray uniform and automatic weapon strapped across his muscular chest.

"Hello," I replied in Rayne's voice. "I know we haven't met, so this is crazy–"

Vertigo, hard and gut-churningly cold like being dropped from a plane through a hurricane into the Atlantic Ocean.

"–but call me, baby." My words, the gruff man's throat, tongue, and mouth. I was staring down at a scarred wooden desk, military surplus from the 1950s. A fluorescent light glared and buzzed overhead. I took a deep breath, inhaling smells of dust, metal, motor oil, and unwashed male bodies.

"Is Jebediah here?" I asked.

"Here," I heard behind me.

I turned, and saw a row of cells with heavy steel doors painted battleship gray. A pair of pale fingers wiggled through a barred window slit.

I approached the cell, Barker's boots ringing heavy and hollow on the damp steel diamond plate floor. Were we on a ship someplace? Barker's memories were a lot harder to access than Linda's had been. It was like trying to grab melting ice cubes with chopsticks.

"Took you long enough," Jebediah muttered.

"Sorry." I paused. "Uh, what do you need me to do?"

"Keys at your belt. Unlock the door."

"Right. Sorry." I shifted my automatic weapon to the side and found the key ring on a retractable cord. The third one I tried turned in the lock, and I pulled the door open. A small, slightly built man with close-cropped hair and a black eye stood there staring at me uncertainly. He wore a gray uniform similar to mine, but the insignia had been ripped off. His shirt was partly open, and I could see that his upper chest was covered in curvilinear tattoos like those on the jade necklace. His feet were bare and bruised.

"What now?" I asked.

"Can I borrow your knife real quick?"

I glanced down at my belt, and on the side opposite my keys I had a sheath for a fixed-blade fighting knife. A KA-BAR, maybe? "Yeah, sure."

I unsheathed the knife and offered it to him handle-first.

"Thanks, brah."

He took the knife and rammed it through the side of my neck.

I stumbled backward, the pain hot and intense, blood spurting from the severed artery, but then my knees gave out and I just kept falling, falling through vertiginous blackness–

–I thrashed awake in my bed at the assisted living facility, coughing, gasping for breath. The pain of being inside my old body was almost worse than getting stabbed through the throat. Linda lay across the foot of the bed, and for a terrible moment I thought she was dead. But then she let out a little moan and stirred as though she were having a bad dream.

"You've done your bit, and so I've done my bit," said Brandon. "And now I must bid you adieu. I regret that I'll no longer be calling you to chat about movies; I'll miss our talks."

"Wait." I was dizzy on top of the pain; my body felt starved for oxygen, and it was hard to think. "That guy…he *killed* me."

"Yes; that's the most effective way of returning to your body in the absence of…other release."

What kind of a man had I unleashed on the ship? What had I just done? I felt sick.

"What's he going to do now?" My voice shook.

"Well, at this moment, I suspect he's preparing to launch a cruise missile from the defense contractor vessel. A little wake-up call for our Master to rouse him from his nap in the Pacific."

I blinked. "What happens when your Master wakes up?"

Brandon smiled enigmatically. "Oh, that's weeks off, I'm sure. A being of his magnitude won't be up and about quickly. In the meantime, enjoy the necklace. If you have any concerns that your actions might inadvertently ruin anyone's life…don't. Trust me, nothing you do from this moment forward can cause any lasting harm."

Executive Functions

Bradley Pendleton smiled at the underling across the table from him. He'd practiced his expression in the mirror a hundred times; he knew it would come across as warm, sincere, comforting.

"I can't promise you anything quite yet, but I agree that your attendance and yearly reviews are the things we look for when promoting worthy employees."

Grateful tears shone in her cow-brown eyes. "Oh, Mr. Pendleton, the senior accounting position would mean the world to me and my family."

Her daughter–he'd forgotten the brat's name–had some type of cancer. It probably wouldn't be terminal if the dowdy accountant could throw enough money at enough doctors. But it was a lingering illness either way; a drain on the company's insurance fund. At the executive team's weekly golf outing, their chief human resources officer had hinted strongly that it would be a gold star on his record if he found a reason to fire her. But she'd filled out FMLA paperwork the week her daughter was diagnosed, so her medical absences couldn't be held against her. And despite his monitoring her every move on her computer and at her desk, she was an exemplary employee. She didn't so much as check the weather on company time.

Authentic reasons to let her go were nonexistent, and she had certain qualities that made him reluctant to manufacture any. Her loyalty was dogged, and her heart as soft as butter. She might not earn him any bonuses, but she couldn't hurt his status.

He let his smile grow warmer. "As I said, I can't promise anything, but I will do everything I can to make this happen."

"Thank you, sir. Thank you *so much.*"

"I'll let you know by next Friday."

After she left his office, Pendleton turned on the monitoring software that let him tap into her computer's webcam. The little light wouldn't come on to alert her. She'd gone straight back to her office, and she was smiling, weeping just a little bit, but getting right to work, ever the busy little bee.

He had no intention of letting her know anything that next Friday. He'd wait until Monday, tell her there was a bit more red tape to cut through, but not to worry! He'd let her know. He'd string her along a few more days until her anxiety was perfectly ripe, and then he'd drop the bombshell that, in fact, she wasn't getting the promotion. Because, after all, there was some other employee with just slightly better review scores, or slightly more seniority. More to the point: there'd be a man whose scores looked better than hers on paper. He wasn't about to let a critical position go to a *female*. Even if he hadn't been enjoying his game with her, it just wasn't good business sense to promote women past a certain level. Everybody knew that.

The accountant would take the news stoically, nod and smile and tell him she understood...and then she'd go back to her desk and weep. And he would watch those big, fat, salty tears rolling down her plain cheeks. He'd want to lick them off her unpowdered face like bitter caviar. But he'd content himself with his voyeurism.

And the best part? She wouldn't quit. She'd put too many years into the company to just up and quit. It was too much risk for a fearful little cow. She'd stick to the job she knew at the company she knew. And so he'd have the chance to dangle hope and snatch it away all over again the following year. And the year after that.

And maybe her daughter would die. Her tears would flow beautifully, then, stain her papers for days and weeks. And she certainly wouldn't quit the company after that–what else would an inconsequential person like her have to hold on to?

It was possible, he mused, that she might kill herself. But he'd identified other crybabies: a ratchety secretary, a dumpy tech writer, a brunette in the mailroom who wasn't pretty enough to fuck, even if fucking her might be the best way to get her to weep. There were almost certainly others. Women were so emotional, and so easy to manipulate. None of them belonged in the cutthroat world of business. But since he had to spend his time on them, he might as well make them useful. A man with his responsibilities needed regular stress relief. It was simply his due.

Suddenly, he was aware of a pungent stink. *The* stink: it smelled like sewer gas and rotting fish and spoiled milk. It came and went, an olfactory phantom. It had plagued him since he joined the company the previous year. A few other managers said they smelled it, too, but none of them could quite identify what it was. He had the janitors double-check the trash and restrooms, and maintenance checked the heating and plumbing systems. Nobody found anything amiss, and in fact none of the lower-level employees reported smelling anything at all.

Pendleton wasn't satisfied. It wasn't just that it smelled bad; it made him feel itchy and queasy, as if he were having an allergic reaction to it. Sometimes, it made his heart race unpleasantly. His skin never got a rash or hives, but he had the terrible feeling that something unpleasant was all over him. His *health* might be at stake here.

And then he had an epiphany: maybe one of the employees on the floor was a connoisseur of terrible foreign foods. The janitors had checked for moldy containers, but not for esculent abominations frozen in microwave boxes. That *had* to be it!

Feeling triumphant, he locked his computer and strode down the hall to tell whoever was microwaving raghead vindaloo or ching-chong glop to knock it off and bring a burger next time.

But nobody was making food in the break room.

The only person there, sitting all alone in an orange molded plastic chair, was a luscious college intern reading a paperback mystery with a black cat on the cover. She was maybe 20 and had the kind of curves you saw on '50s starlets, long legs sheathed in a clingy blue pencil skirt, and thick, glossy blonde hair nearly down to the crack of her ass. He entertained a brief fantasy of twisting her arms behind her, bending her over the break table and reaming her 'til he could see his own face reflected in the puddle of her tears spreading across the bland Formica.

She looked up from her book and met his gaze. Her eyes were the color of his favorite dark chocolates.

"Good afternoon, Mr. Pendleton." She had an upper-crust British accent he found devastatingly sexy.

"Afternoon, Miss..." His gaze fell on the ID badge dangling at her delicious hip, and he couldn't help but raise an eyebrow in surprise when it told him that she was with the IT department. Probably she did something with the phones. "Miss Alewhite. Have we met?"

"I don't believe so."

How had he not seen her before? How were they not having a long lunch in the motel around the corner right that second? Dammit, HR *knew* he wanted to meet all the new interns. Could they have onboarded her when he was vacationing in Tahiti? They must have.

She smiled, her teeth perfectly straight and white. A flawless specimen of femininity, he had to admit. Probably had men showering her with compliments day and night. Time to shake her up a little and show her she wasn't anything special in his world.

"I love your hair," he said. "Is it a wig or a weave?"

She laughed and set her book aside. "Did you just neg me? *Seriously*?"

He frowned, feeling an unaccustomed heat creep into his face. "Miss Alewhite, perhaps they haven't taught you proper business behavior at whatever liberal college your hippie parents sent you to, but that is *not* the kind of tone you should take with a superior in the workplace."

He expected her to turn pale and start stammering an apology, beg him for forgiveness, but she just grinned.

"'Did you know you're beautiful when you're angry?'" She said in a playfully seductive voice. "I bet you've used that line on plenty of women before. Annoying, isn't it? And, in your case, totally untrue."

"Miss Alewhite!" he thundered. Clearly, his action item for the day would be to teach this little cunt her place. Maybe she was the daughter of a duke or some damn thing over the pond, but here? This was his world. *His* rules. She would show him respect, and more.

"Can I let you in on a little secret?" she stage-whispered. "I took a wee peek into your personnel record. Remember that psychology test you took after you interviewed for your position here? You're a *total psychopath*."

He paused, silent, gazing at her warily. Even *he* hadn't seen his psychological results; as far as he knew, only the company owner could access them. Was she lying to him? Was there a game afoot?

She nodded, black eyes wide in mock surprise. "It's the truth. Clinically, you're an awful human being."

He stared down at her, feeling an itchy bead of sweat roll down the small of his back. Was she a corporate mole, a spy? What was going on?

"But it's okay!" she declared. "All the executive staff members are psychopaths. The whole lot of you. If you hadn't been, you'd have never been brought onboard."

Alewhite stood up. She was taller than he expected, taller than *he* was, and he glanced down at her feet to reassure himself that she was wearing high heels. But she sported black canvas sneakers. He hated them. And was surprised that he hadn't noticed her unflattering, unfeminine shoes before that moment.

"I know you'll be quick to brag that it's because you psychopaths are just better suited to the ruthless corporate world." She had the kind of tone schoolteachers used with very young children. "You know, willing to cook your own families to succeed and all that. But you'd be wrong."

She came around the table, leaned in close, and whispered in his ear: "Your brain is fundamentally broken, Mr. Pendleton. You're neurologically insensitive to certain things that normal people can easily perceive. You know how humans on the autistic spectrum have trouble interpreting social cues? You psychopaths have trouble sensing reality. Or rather, the loss of it."

"That's ridiculous!" he replied coldly. "Nothing escapes my notice! I am a *highly* perceptive man."

"Modest, too!" She laughed, and he wanted to punch her teeth right down her throat. But if the company owner had sent her to test him, giving her the violence she deserved would be the end of his career.

"But no," she continued. "You've been fooled. For months and months now. But–what luck!–I can help with that."

She reached out and touched his forehead.

The world he knew tore away like a flimsy canvas stage backdrop.

A huge white claw–a bristled insect leg–hovered over his face, and Pendleton tried to scream and step back, but neither his throat nor his body would obey him. The claw withdrew, and he saw a monstrous ivory-colored arthropod gazing down upon him. The wedge-shaped, suitcase-sized head reminded him strongly of a mantis, as did its clawed forearms, but the mantid thorax merged with a round, bleached spider body. The only spot of color upon it was its big black eyes.

He heard a woman's laugh inside his mind, and then Miss Alewhite's voice: "Surprise! Do have a look around."

It was then that he realized, first, that his throat was sore, aching like he had strep, and second, that he was naked. Worse, he was shambling forward in line with a bunch of other naked people. The back of the man in front of him was filthy, covered in grotesque fungal growths that seeped a pungent ichor. The stink. Or part of it, anyhow.

He looked away from the man's back, and what he saw made his breath catch in his aching throat. They were all in some huge subterranean cavern, and there were hundreds of lines of thousands of filthy naked people, all shuffling forward, eyes glazed. Strange glowing orbs hovering in the air lighted the cavern. The vast room echoed with thudding footfalls and wet noises.

The floor beneath him didn't feel like dirt; it felt soft, and clammy. With effort, he tilted his head down so he could see what he was walking across. More fungus, he realized. His toenails were cracked, split, infected with the same foulness he'd seen on the man's back. His legs and body were covered in broken pustules, each bearing its own cloud of tiny red gnats.

"And this is where it gets interesting," said the Alewhite monster, prompting him to look up again.

The man before him dropped to a crouch in front of something that looked like a gigantic purple sea anemone, although the thing's glistening tentacles had a strangely plantlike look to them. The tentacles reached for the man's face, pulled him forward, and after a few moments of vigorous movement, they spat him back out. Unseeing face dripping with goo, the man stood and shambled to the back of another line.

"Your turn," said Alewhite.

Pendleton's legs suddenly went weak and he fell to his knees. What was happening to him? The tentacles grabbed his head and pulled him down. Something rubbery and slippery forced its way between his lips and tongue, slithered down his throat. It pistoned harshly inside his esophagus, spewing a foul, viscous liquid directly into his stomach. He couldn't breathe, couldn't move.

The tentacles held him fast as the monstrosity filled him. His stomach ached from the pressure, and just when he thought it might burst, the tentacles released him, and he jerked to his feet like a puppet.

"Go on, now," Alewhite said, pacing him.

Pendleton stumbled after the others up a huge mountain, his belly aching terribly, his throat sore, his head pounding. The goo in his stomach was leaking up into his throat, and it tasted like spoiled clam chowder. What kind of terrible place was this?

"Not long now! Keep going."

He crested the hill, and he saw the gigantic, pink, shuddering maw of some impossibly huge creature buried in the fungal earth. It was as wide as a football field and lined with sucking tentacles. People were falling to their knees at the edge of the mouth, vomiting the contents of their stomachs into the hungry chasm.

He caught a whiff of the terrible stench rising from inside the maw–and knew for sure that this was the awful thing he'd been smelling. A horrible nausea took him and he dropped to his knees, body wracked with spasms as he puked up everything the anemone had pumped into him–

Pendleton abruptly found himself back in the break room staring at the beautiful intern with the insect-black eyes. His skin wasn't covered in yellow pustules. He was wearing his fine Armani suit again.

"Oh God." He looked around at the familiar coffee maker, the stainless-steel refrigerator, and the parquet floor, took a deep breath and exhaled. "Thank God."

"Don't be fooled." She wagged a finger at him. "You're still a good little drone in a big hive of fungus. You just mostly can't see it. Because your poor widdle bwain is bwoken."

She made a clownishly sad face at him.

"It *isn't.* It isn't!" he snarled.

"Pop quiz. Who owns the company?"

"Uh...he's...." Pendleton had played golf with the old man a dozen times; why couldn't he remember?

"No? Okay, this should be easy: what's the *name* of this company?"

"It's...it's...." His frustration became a vein-popping monster in his head, but he couldn't think of the name. He'd been working here for over a year, for Christ's sake! But there was nothing. No name. Nothing. He collapsed into one of the orange plastic chairs, feeling profoundly confused.

"See?" She smiled. "You don't know because none of this is real; you're sharing a corporate fantasy with a few hundred other drones. Our dreamweaver didn't even have to spend much time customizing it for you; it's practically straight off the rack. We only had to add the lady with the sick daughter, and you didn't even need her name. How sad is that?"

She shook her head. "But I fixed your cerebrum, just a little. You'll see your true reality every so often. Not most of the time. Maybe once or twice a day. Just enough to remind you where you really are."

"What–what can I do?" he choked.

"Nothing. Well." She paused, looking thoughtful. "You *could* get religion. Pray for your soul and such. But honestly, I don't think you have a soul, and you're already vomiting semen to feed the only god you'll ever meet, so...no. Nothing you can do."

"W-why did you..." he trailed off.

"Show you your reality?" she prompted. "Because my job as your overseer is really quite dull considering the lot of you just stumble around in your little dreams of being masters of the universe. It's just...just *nice* to see one of you scared out of your wits every so often. Makes the day go by faster.

"Unfortunately, now that I've destroyed your illusion, your drone body will fail sooner, maybe much sooner. Madness and misery always affect the flesh. *But!* My unit's productivity numbers are quite good, and they always let us omit a few poor performers from our metrics. You won't matter in the end."

She cocked her head to one side, seeming to listen to something he couldn't hear. "Oh, and now my boss is returning from his dinner. It's time for me to go back to being invisible to you. Ta ta!"

With that, the intern disappeared completely.

For several minutes, Pendleton just stared at the spot she'd occupied.

Then he walked slowly back to his nonexistent office, closed the door, laid his head down on the wide illusory desk, and wept.

The Yellow Death

"Lady..." I whispered.

My sister stood there in the doorway of the Freebirds' clubhouse, the fall wind blowing dead leaves in a dervish around her sandaled feet, ruffling the hem of her dandelion-bright sundress, and suddenly the laughing and roughhousing stopped. All the bikers and their sunburned old ladies just stared at the girl.

The silence probably only lasted twenty seconds, but in my mind it stretched out to an agonizing hour. I didn't know whether to trust my own eyes. She didn't look like the sister I remembered, but she'd only been twelve when I ran away from home. And that was eight years ago. A lot can happen to a girl in nearly a decade. Adolescence, for instance. And also the Apocalypse.

The young woman in the doorway was tall, nearly tall as me, but slender and elegant as any of the ballet dancers we used to admire as they walked home from the theatre. Her dark hair looked impossibly clean and cascaded down past her shoulders. The bikers called me Beauty to mock my scars, but they'd call her that because they hadn't the words for anything better. Any old French poet would spend sleepless nights trying to capture this strange girl's pulchritude in serifed letters. But she had the same cornflower eyes and she gave me that dreamy smile I remembered so well. I didn't wonder how she'd tracked me down. She'd always been the one to locate the missing book behind the couch, our mother's lost earring in the drain, forgotten song lyrics in a notebook in her bag.

"Hey Louise." The years had turned her voice seductive, husky. Pure aural sex. I could practically smell the men's sudden desire, a musky pheromone note cutting through the stink of beer, motor oil, and tobacco. And I could feel their old ladies' anxiety and jealousy build alongside it, like the charge in the air before a lightning strike.

"Found you," she said, and made a languid motion as if she were tweaking my nose.

My brain teetered between joy and terror. Because if that wasn't Lady? We were probably all fucked five ways to Sunday. I craned my neck to try to see past her, see if the prospects on guard duty were still up on the wall or if their guts were scattered across the concertina wire. I saw nothing but the glaring floodlights and darkness beyond.

The problem with vampires is that before they get inside your veins, they crawl inside your mind. You think that you've opened the door to your neighbor or your Aunt Heather, but in reality, you've just let in a pallid, toothy monstrosity that's about to rip your jugular out and drain you like a juice box. If you're lucky. If you're not so lucky, the local hive needs more hunters and it's just there to nip you, grab a quick drink, and flap away, leaving you to your slow, torturous metamorphosis.

I knew what that looked like better than most living people. My fiancé Jack got bitten in the first wave, right before anyone outside the CDC had any inkling there was a problem. He'd carried the trash out to the alley in the dark. Something hiding in the ivy covering the low cinderblock wall attacked him. He never got a good look at it, or even a sense of its size, so we figured it was a rat. We washed the bite with peroxide and got him to the doctor the next day. Antibiotics and rabies shots cleared out what was left in our bank account, but we imagined he'd be fine after that.

He ran a low-grade fever–the doctor's office said the rabies vaccine could cause that–and his mood went straight to hell. Jack was normally pretty hakuna matata about money, even when we were flat broke, but suddenly he wanted to count every miserable cent coming in or going out. It was almost enough to make me call home and beg forgiveness just so we'd have access to the trust fund I'd given up years before. Almost. I accidentally spilled some Tylenol down the drain one day and he made me wait while he counted and re-counted the rest in the bottle so he'd know exactly how many we had to replace. It didn't matter to him that we still had plenty. He was losing his mind right in front of me but at the time I figured he was just cranky.

When his eyes turned yellow from jaundice, it seemed like a side effect of the antibiotics. He refused to go to urgent care, because that would be fifty bucks we couldn't afford. It was only four more days until his next doctor's appointment for another rabies shot anyhow. I was worried, but I let it ride.

That night, he woke me up around four AM when he started going berserk in the living room. Jack was yanking books and movies off the shelves and throwing them around. He'd smashed the big blue sunfish lamp he made in ceramics class and the floor was covered in jagged shards. The bottoms of his feet were in tatters, but somehow he wasn't bleeding. He picked up my special edition Blu-ray of *Sorcerer* and made a motion as if he was going to snap it in two.

I tried to grab it away from him. He slugged me in the mouth and I dropped like a sack of potatoes; I didn't know how to take a punch back then. The sight–or maybe the smell–of the blood from the gash on my lip then sent him into a whole new orbit of madness. He grabbed me by my hair, dragged me screaming to the radiator, gagged me with a dirty handkerchief, and lashed my hands to the pipe with the cord from the busted lamp.

Jack stared down at me for a long time, not saying anything, his expression shifting between rage and confusion. He paced back and forth, asking me who I was and if I'd seen the sign. I couldn't quite reach the rag in my mouth to try to pull it out to talk to him, so I just lay there, waiting. A dog started yapping a few houses down. So then I thought, well, we'd both made a whole lot of noise after he hit me. Surely someone heard him and called the cops.

I felt a surge of hope when I heard a police siren, but it passed us by. And then I realized that what I'd thought was a dog was really a woman barking "Fuck you!" over and over.

Jack abruptly stopped interrogating me and flopped down on the couch. He turned on the TV–the one thing in the room he hadn't tried to wreck–and just started flipping through channels as if nothing happened. The local station was showing a live feed of a female reporter standing near a police car in some other neighborhood. I started trying to work the stiff cords off my wrists, quietly as I could.

"We're here at the site of a hostage situation on Grant Street," the reporter said. "This is the tenth such situation that local police have been called out to in the past three hours. News Ten is sending teams to the other locations. We will update you as we get more information. It's not clear if this is some terrible, violent coincidence or if it represents coordinated terrorist activity. Police are asking that people stay in their homes–"

My boyfriend switched off the TV and stared at me. The madness was wearing a new face, and he seemed to recognize me again.

"They'll kill you," he whispered. His eyes had turned so yellow they looked like they'd been carved from brimstone. "You're not of the body. You're not in His image."

Jack went into the kitchen and came out with a sharp boning knife. "If they don't see the sign, they'll kill you."

I started struggling in earnest then, desperate to get loose, but he dodged my kicking legs and sat on my chest, pinning me to the scarred hardwood floor. With one hand, he shoved my head against the cold pipes of the radiator and with the other he slashed the left side of my face. The pain of the blade razoring through my flesh was bright, intense. The second slash nearly made me vomit. The third made me pass out.

I came to a little while later. Jack was licking the tarry pool of my blood off the dirty floor. When had his tongue gotten so long?

"I saved you." He grinned, pleased, his teeth red with gore. "I'm your savior."

I passed out again.

The next week or so is still pretty hazy; I can't sort out what was a hallucination, reality, or nightmare. I heard voices and screaming. When I was finally fully conscious, my head was baking with fever and the slashes on my face were a throbbing agony. My left eye was swollen shut, and for a while I was scared he'd cut it out.

Jack came in and out of the room, sometimes just staring at me, sometimes pacing and rambling about cosmic signs. The words coming out of his mouth sounded like English, but they just didn't make any sense.

He must have realized my mutilated face was horrifically infected because he started feeding me his antibiotics along with water and occasionally a piece of bread. But he didn't seem to understand the part where I'd needed to go to the bathroom, or the part where the antibiotics would give me diarrhea. I was lying in terrible filth; I could feel my skin blistering and ulcerating under my clothes. I prayed for death.

I was a disgusting wreck, and so was the house. But Jack looked clean and healthy, his hair combed, wearing his good khakis and best button-down shirt. He appeared that way as long as I was looking at him straight on, that is. When I glimpsed him from the corner of my eye...I couldn't quite make out what I was seeing, but the shambling, tattered-looking thing wasn't the Jack I knew.

I finally awoke one morning and my fever had broken. I was weak as hell, but at last I had the focus to kick my shoes and socks off, grasp a fragment of broken lamp between my toes and flip it up toward my hands. After six flips, I realized I wasn't going to catch any shards, and even if I did, my fingers were too numb and clumsy to do anything. So I concentrated on trying to stretch the cords again. After what seemed like fifteen years, at last I slipped free from one of the loops. The others were easy to shake off after that.

I climbed painfully to my feet, back and sides aching, and dropped my ruined jeans and panties. Jack kept his grandfather's shotgun in the back of the coat closet. He'd showed me how to handle it once. I found the weapon in its tan canvas case and the shells under a pile of winter hats on the upper shelf. It took me a couple of tries to get them down, each sending sharp pains through my strained, stiff shoulders. Once I got my hands working well enough to load the old double barrel, I crept through the house with it, dreading what I would find. I remembered the corner glimpses of something terrible and I knew Jack wasn't simply insane. Something much worse had happened. My hands ached and the weapon seemed impossibly heavy in my weak, shaking arms.

Upstairs was empty of any life but a few scuttling cockroaches and spiders. I took a deep breath, held it. My aching guts told me he was still in the house, but he had to be down in the basement. The very last place I wanted to be.

Once I got my hands to quit shaking, I ducked into the bathroom to wipe off the worst of the filth, slipped on a pair of his boxer shorts and some old sneakers and slowly went downstairs. The stench of spoiled meat hit me the moment I pushed open the basement door. I wanted to puke, but there wasn't anything in my stomach.

Three pale, bloodless corpses lay on the concrete basement floor. Two were neighborhood kids; one was the old lady who'd lived next door. Their throats had been torn open, their exposed flesh pale as raw chicken meat. Not a drop wasted. They were still wearing all their clothes. Perversion paled in comparison to murder, but it was nice to know that Jack's madness had its limits.

I hadn't thought of the word "vampire" until then, but with all that evidence spread before me, nothing else made sense. In my mind, I could picture Jack reaching out to them, trying to bring them to the house to protect them like the good guy he was. But once they came inside, he saw me tied to the radiator and realized that if he saved them, he'd have to drain me. Because a guy has to eat, right?

My heart beating so hard I was lightheaded, I stepped over the corpses and opened the utility room door. The creature my boyfriend had become was curled up in the corner by the washer, asleep in a nest of soiled clothes and pages torn from old books. The sight of it should have made me want to run screaming, but that demanded energy I just didn't have. Its hairless skin was a dark yellow, and its body was practically skeletal. I remembered that birds have hollow bones so they can fly. His spindly arms hadn't quite transformed into batlike wings yet. There was a little of Jack left in the thing's distorted face, enough to make me sure it was him, but not enough to make me pause before I blew its head off.

The recoil from the shotgun knocked me flat on my blistered ass. After I got myself up, I found a bottle of Drano on a shelf, and poured the gel all over the creature's still-twitching body. The caustic goop made its flesh sizzle like bacon in a pan. The stink was incredible, and made my eyes water and nose run, but I wanted to be damned sure the thing was dead. I'd have set it on fire, but I knew I was too weak to abandon the house. I shut the utility room door, blocked it with an old trunk, then went upstairs and locked the basement door behind me.

We still had electricity. I found my cell phone in the bedroom but the battery was dead; I plugged it in and tried 911. Got a busy signal. I tried my friends' numbers; they all went to voicemail.

I stared down at the phone, feeling sick again. I left it charging on the middle of the bed and went to get cleaned up and examine my wounds. The bathroom looked about the same as I'd left it; I guessed vampires weren't much for hygiene. I killed the cockroach I found in the tub, flushed it, and took a hot, soapy shower to get the filth off my skin. My crotch, ass, and thighs were covered in a constellation of sores and pustules. Some broke at my touch, and I soaped up again and tried to clean out the wounds as best I could. At least the antibiotics Jack had given me had seemingly prevented the worst infection. After I dried off, I found a tube of diaper rash cream left over from when we'd babysat Jack's infant niece and slathered myself up.

Then it was time to check the real damage. I wiped the steam off the mirror and took a look at my face. The left side was still puffy under a scab the size of a saucer. It itched something fierce, but I didn't want to touch it to risk re-opening anything. I didn't know if Jack had bitten or licked me while I was unconscious. But neither my skin nor my eyes looked yellowed. I hoped for the best.

I got dressed in a pair of loose palazzo pants and a tee shirt and raided the fridge. Half the food was fuzzy with mold but the tortillas and lunchmeat still looked edible, as did a couple of tangelos. You wouldn't think you'd be able to eat knowing you were standing just twelve feet above three dumped murder victims and a dissolving vampire, but you might surprise yourself. Hunger is a powerful drive. I made myself eat and drink slowly so I wouldn't get sick. I knew I couldn't afford to waste food.

My adrenaline finally ebbed after my belly was full, and suddenly I felt as though I was wearing a lead bodysuit. It was all I could do to drag myself upstairs and brush my teeth before I passed out on the bed. I had exactly the kind of nightmares you'd figure I'd have, but I slept for over eighteen hours anyhow.

When I woke, I ate again, washed again, and tried to figure out what I should do next. My eyes and skin still weren't yellow. The TV stations were all static, so either the cable was out or something far worse was going on. I tried my friends' numbers again and left messages.

I almost wet myself with joy when 911 answered. A pleasant-sounding young woman took down my details–I told her my boyfriend had killed some people, but didn't detail the bit about him becoming a vampire because I still cared about whether people thought I was crazy or not. She said she'd dispatch an officer to my house.

Sure enough, fifteen minutes later there was a knock at my front door. I answered it, and a nice-looking, red-haired uniformed policeman stood on the porch.

"I'm Officer Curtis," he said, polite and pleasant as a Boy Scout selling candy bars. "May I come inside?"

"Sure." I turned to set aside my shotgun–

–and got a glimpse of the thing at my door from the corner of my eye.

When the smoke and haze of blood in the air cleared, I realized I'd blown a hole in the screen door and had blasted the vampire's head clean off its spindly yellow shoulders. The rest of the batwinged body that lay sprawled and jerking on the concrete steps was practically a clone of what Jack had turned into.

I shivered. It wasn't even wearing any clothes; nothing about the vampire actually looked like the cop I'd seen. I glanced up at the sky. It was early morning and overcast to boot...but it certainly wasn't dark, either. These things could stand daylight, or at least some of it.

As I got more experience killing vampires, I learned that they went blind in bright light. The sun would never make them burst into flames, but fifteen minutes was enough to give a vampire a blistering burn and after that, the light made their bodies sprout grotesque tumors. Their mutability always made me uneasy about leaving one staked out to die in the noontime glare, lest it turn into some day-stalking monstrosity. Their wiry strength was formidable and they were plenty tough, but they weren't immortals that could only be slain with a stake through the heart or decapitation. A couple of solid body shots with hollow-point bullets would settle any flapper's hash, as would a dozen crushing blows with a Louisville Slugger.

Their biggest weapon was their psychic camouflage. And even after three years, I still had a hard time seeing through their glamour. But I knew full well that a clever vampire could wreak diabolic chaos in a room full of people by making everyone see something different.

So, as my sister Lady stood there in the bikers' clubhouse looking nearly as improbable as the angel Gabriel bearing two large supreme pizzas from Donato's...I was straining my eyeballs to try to glimpse her sidewise. No matter how I gazed upon her, she still looked the same.

Lady finally broke the silence that had fallen on the room.

"Aren't you going to say hello?" She stepped toward me and reached out to touch my cheek.

I flinched away from her, wishing I hadn't left my pistol back in my bunk. I had my KA-BAR strapped to my belt and a throwing dagger hidden in the top of each of my tall boots, but you don't take a knife to a vampire fight if you can help it. She didn't seem to notice my discomfort.

"You've got the sign," she whispered, gazing in awe at my scars.

I reflexively covered my cheek with my hand. "What?"

"The sign." She held up her wrist. Just below her delicate blue veins was an ornate tattoo, a beautiful version of the weird symbol Jack had carved into my flesh. Seeing her ink was like being hit with a taser. Until that moment, I hadn't seriously thought that the marks on my cheek meant anything outside the confines of my boyfriend's fevered mind. Some people had claimed it looked like part of a misshapen Chinese character for fate or death or whatever, and one old man claimed it was a stylized Arabic curse, but I'd figured it was just a living Rorschach blot.

"What does it mean?" My voice shook.

"It's a sign to the minions of the King." She gazed at me earnestly. "It tells them that although you are not of His body, you are not to be touched."

She leaned in close and whispered, "Someone must have loved you very much to mark you so."

I remembered the agony of steel cutting skin and muscle, the torment of lying bound and bleeding in my own filth. That didn't feel like love. If that was supposed to be genuine love, I wanted no part of it.

"This fucking thing is supposed to protect me?" I couldn't keep the anguish out of my voice. It made me feel naked in front of everyone, frail in front of people who already mocked me for my supposed weaknesses, and I hated her a little for it. If my face hadn't been all fucked up, they probably would have called me Brownie Scout instead. "I've had plenty of creeps come after me."

"The King allows his servants to defend themselves and their hives. And once a servant joins the body, some measure of free will remains." Her cool gaze moved across the men and women in the room, all of whom had earned at least one felony conviction apiece before the vampires showed up. "Not all choose to obey the laws."

Bear, the Freebirds' sergeant-at-arms, snorted and slid off his barstool. His booted feet clomped loudly on the wooden floor.

"What's all this yammer about vampires an' laws?" His voice was belligerent and slurred by beer. "Evr'body knows them things is just giant bloodsucking bugs. Mansquitos." He laughed at his own pun.

Lady just watched him warily as he swaggered over.

"Ain't you a pretty little thing, though." He reached out to paw her breast, but I pushed his meaty hand away from her. He scowled at me. "Don't step twixt a dog and his meat, Beauty."

"She's not your meat. She's my sister. You need to step back, please." I held his stare in mine. Everybody else in was silent; if tension was electricity, you could have lit a skyscraper with what was in that room.

I knew it was dangerous to challenge him, but I also knew what the men did to women and girls they saw as pretty enough to be proper bike decorations. And Lady was far more beautiful than any of the strippers, runaways, and drug addicts the Freebirds normally attracted. When the club members found me on the road, exhausted and half-dead after four months of trying to survive on my own, I was deemed too ugly to fuck and therefore probably useless, but the club president took a shine to me anyhow. They assigned me the same scut work they gave the prospects: cleaning toilets, disposing of bodies, cleaning up puke, and degreasing engines. Because I was female, I'd never earn my way to a patch and club colors, but most of the time I thought I'd at least earned their respect, especially considering how good I was at killing vampires. I'd been able to stop rapes and abuse before. So I figured there would be a little staring contest and Bear would back off and get back to his drinking.

But I guess he could see how much Lady meant to me, and he was enough of a sadist to want to hurt me that day. Or maybe his unspeakable grief needed an outlet, and I was a handy target. His old lady had just lost their baby; the stillborn infant would have been his son and the first new child any of us had seen since the horror began. The army had put something in the air and water to try to kill off the vampires, but the only thing it definitely did was fuck up women's hormones and make us all infertile. It seemed a mercy, really; this was no longer a world fit for children. But Mama Bear's pregnancy was a great joy for the men and women of the club, and it seemed nothing short of a miracle while it lasted.

Nobody minded when he cried over the tiny body the night she went into premature labor, but after that, the rest of the club expected him to man up and get over it. We saw death every day. But how can a man get over something like that? So Bear had to swallow down his misery, pretend it wasn't there. I wasn't surprised that it had grown into something terrible there in the shadow of his soul, and I really did feel sorry for the guy, but I wasn't about to let him molest my sister. Not for fun or spite or out of despair or anything else.

"I don't take orders from ugly cunts." Bear spat on my boots.

"It isn't an order, friend, but I'm here to protect family," I said, just loud enough that I was sure the whole room could hear me. "I was there when she was born, and if you or anyone else tries to hurt her, I will stop it by any means necessary."

His gaze turned hard and distant. I can't be sure he was suicidal, but I can't say that he wasn't, either. He never struck me as the smartest guy in the club, but he'd have to be an idiot to ignore what I was capable of.

"Fuck you, gashface." Bear gave me a hard shove and grabbed Lady.

I'd braced myself and he didn't knock me over. What happened next took less than a second. I drew my KA-BAR and swung the knife at him as hard as I could...and I swear to this day I meant to hit him upside his thick head with the flat hammer pommel. I just wanted to knock him out. But he let go of my sister and dropped, and when he lay there sprawled on the floor, I saw I'd sunk my blade into his temple, nearly all the way to the hilt. His staring eyes were empty lights.

"Oh no," whispered Lady.

I heard the click of a Ruger Redhawk being cocked right behind my head.

"Hands up, Beauty."

I raised my arms and slowly turned around. Eric "Gun" Gunnarson, the club president, was pointing the huge revolver right between my eyes.

"I didn't want that to happen," I said, trying to keep my voice steady. "I'm sorry."

"I figured." Gun's expression was hard, and his pistol hand didn't waver.

I looked him right in the eyes, and it was like he didn't recognize me. What I saw in his stare reminded me of Jack the night he carved my face up. I'm sure no bystander would ever guess that just two weeks before, Gun kissed me on my forehead and confessed that he loved me. Just like they never would have guessed that he'd wept alongside Bear over the body of his tiny nephew.

He pressed the revolver up under my chin and moved in close.

"I get that she's your sister." Gun whispered in my ear, too quietly for anyone but maybe Lady to hear. "But Bear was my brother and a club officer. If you were *anyone* else, I'd have killed both of you by now. Fact is, you're too damned useful to kill. So that means you get to live this time. But there's a price to pay."

He called two guys over to haul Bear out to the dead shed where his son still lay wrapped in his baby blanket, waiting for the weekly cremation out in the field.

"Clear off that pool table and put my chair over there," he ordered. "Rentboy! Rentboy, get your skinny ass over here!"

A young, model-handsome prospect ducked out from behind the bar, hurried over, and stood at attention in front of Bear. I could see the hard-on in his Levi's; it was impressive even to men raised on a steady diet of hardcore porn. He looked completely terrified. That's why he was a joke to all the guys: fear made him pop massive wood, every time, unless he was close to passing out from booze. On one of my many nights of insomnia, I found him drinking at the bar by himself. He started weeping and told me his aunt did something awful to him when he was little. But that was as much as I ever knew; I didn't press for more details, and I kept it to myself. He probably wouldn't talk about it even to a sympathetic counselor–boys don't get raped by women, right? They just get lucky–and so there was no way in hell he'd confide in any of the Freebirds. He pretended like it was a fun thing, a party trick, and so scaring him into an erection was an unending source of hilarity around the club.

"We need us a show, Rentboy!" Gun pointed at the cleared-off pool table. "Take the lovely lady over there and show us what you can do."

Rentboy's eyes bugged out of his head and he stammered, "But...but I don't think she wants to."

"I don't care what she wants." Gun was impassive, immoveable.

"Please, sir, don't make me." Rentboy looked like he might start crying.

At that, Gun turned his revolver on Rentboy, and in the back of my mind I knew I could grab the weapon, but I was still in the center of attention in a room full of armed men. I'd die, and so would my sister. I had to wait for a better opportunity, and pray that one actually came along.

"Do you want to get patched, son?" Gun demanded harshly. "Or do you want to get carried out to the shed?"

"Please don't do this," I whispered. I'd spent enough time around Gun to know he was capable of awful things, but until that day I'd seen him commit his crimes only out of need. I couldn't think of him as a monster. Not yet. But I knew the pressure we were all living under was burning away his decent parts bit by bit. Maybe monstrosity would be all that was left of us, whether we ever got bitten by vampires or not.

He turned the revolver back on me. "Did you say something, you ugly whore?"

His question was loud and clear. No respect offered me in front of the club. No admission of the feelings he'd declared to me in private, not even a simple nod to all the blood and sweat I'd poured into the club's common good. I didn't even rate the consideration the other females got because I wasn't anyone's old lady.

Sure, Gun could have stepped up and told everyone Bear got what he had coming to him. Gun could tell everyone that I was *his* lady, had been for over a year, and he could have made me the new sergeant-at-arms, because I'd be a fuck of a lot more competent at the job than his brother had ever been.

Gun could have done all that. And monkeys could have come flying out of my ass, too.

"Did you say something, whore?" he asked again.

I shook my head, my mouth clamped shut, rage firing through every synapse in my body. The train had left the station, and there was no easy way of stopping it now. Gun was acting how he thought a boss should, and what he was doing made sense by a certain sociopathic logic.

Problem: a strange, beautiful woman shows up, and you know your men are going to fight over her because they don't see her as anything more than a trophy to be won.

Solution: tarnish her shine and break her, then hand her off to a lieutenant like a toy you're tired of.

Problem: the woman you love just killed your brother in defense of said beautiful stranger and challenged the club's power structure.

Solution: humiliate her in front of the club and break her, too. A boss has to make personal sacrifices sometimes. Besides, you can always find another gun hand and another woman to declare your secret passion to.

"Good," Gun replied. "Keep your whore mouth shut until it's time for you to open it."

He waved the Redhawk toward the pool table. "Get over there and kneel in front of my chair."

At least I knew where I stood, right? My whole body shook with the anger I couldn't express, but I did what I was told.

He settled himself in the worn leather recliner, unzipped his fly, and pulled his cock out. Rapped me on top of my head with the barrel of the revolver like I was a misbehaving dog. "Do what you're good at."

Goddamn it, I thought. *Goddamn him and this whole place all to hell.*

Meanwhile, Rentboy hadn't taken a single step toward my sister. He stood there, his eyes closed as if through sheer force of will he could make himself teleport to someplace far away.

"Boy, what did I tell you?" Gun barked.

"Yessir!" Rentboy hurried over to Lady and took her by the hand.

"No." Lady tried to pull away, but the kid held her fast.

"It'll be okay," I heard him plead, his voice low. "There's no choice–let's just do it and it'll be over soon."

"It's over when I say it's over," Gun replied loudly, lord of all he surveyed. "Someone bring me a TV table and a beer."

Two prospects hurried to obey him. He rapped me on the top of my head again, harder. "And what did I tell you?"

So I started doing the thing I'd done a hundred times before, always in the dark in Gun's room, always under the illusion that I was doing it for a man who cared about me. A man who wasn't a complete and utter fucking bastard. I focused on Gun's hardening tool, tried to block out the sound of my sister's and Rentboy's misery on the pool table behind me.

I chanced a glance around; almost nobody was looking at me. A few horrified or titillated gazes were aimed at the table; most everyone else I could see was staring at the floor, unfocused, sending their minds someplace else.

You guys could stop this, I thought to them all, wishing I were a vampire so I could project the idea into their heads. But they should have gotten that idea all on their own.

Someone stop this.

Nobody did anything but watch.

After that, I let my fastest hand trail down to the cuff of my boot where a dagger rested, and kept track of the Redhawk out of the corner of my eye. I prayed to every god I could remember for some kind of a chance.

I heard my sister choke, then the sound of her vomiting. Puke splattered on the floor behind me. Gun's cock went soft.

"Goddamn it!" He slammed the Redhawk down on the wooden TV table in frustration.

I remember what happened next in quick strobe flashes. I drew the dagger and rammed it up through his balls and into his bladder. Then the Redhawk was in my hand and I was blasting away at all the people who'd just stood and watched my betrayal and my sister's violation. Something inside my head disconnected for a few seconds, and when I came back to myself, I had another pistol in my hand–a svelte little .38 semiautomatic–and my naked sister was standing between me and Rentboy, her hands up, pleading. Thin vomit dripped down her chin and her face was very white. He was curled up in a ball under the pool table, sobbing and wailing like the world had come to an end.

"Louise, Louise, stop, please stop," Lady begged. "You did it. They're all gone. Just stop. The boy didn't want to."

Dazed, I looked around. I'd murdered everyone in the clubhouse. Patched members, officers, old ladies, prospects...everyone. Faces and chests were blown apart. I'd slit a prospect's throat with my other knife, and try as I might, I couldn't bring up even a hazy memory of doing so. But my blood-covered hands and shirt told the tale. I couldn't find any wounds on myself except for a couple of scrapes and a bloody nose.

"Are there any other biker guys?" Lady asked. Her voice and expression were supernaturally calm. I wondered if this was what PTSD looked like on her.

I counted, realized we were seven short, and remembered that the vice president had taken his favorites to search for food in a nearby abandoned town. They'd be back at dawn. His old lady lay among the bodies; I'd put a round through her pretty left eye.

"Yeah. We better get the hell out of here."

❖

While Lady put herself back together, I washed the blood off at the bar sink and then quickly gathered supplies–weapons, ammo, food, a medical pack, and jerry cans of gasoline, plus my rucksack of clothes and what little personal stuff I'd kept–and got my battered Yamaha V Star ready. Lady had arrived on her own bike, a shiny Honda NC700X. Meanwhile, Rentboy wouldn't stop crying and didn't want to come with us, and frankly I didn't want him along anyhow.

"Are you okay?" I asked her as we walked out of the clubhouse to load the bikes.

"I'm fine." Her face was a pale mask.

For the first time, I noticed she was wearing an antique gold signet ring and was twisting it round and round her index finger.

I knew all about trauma, but I sucked at knowing what to say to help people through it. I guess if I had any talent for it, I'd have majored in counseling instead of English. "If you need to talk–"

"I don't. Honest." She flashed me a quick, unconvincing smile. "What's done is done, and once we've left this awful place, I can put it all behind me."

"Okay," I replied gently. "Where do you want to go?"

"Our father wants you to come home," she replied. "He wants our family back together."

I stopped in my tracks. My first thought was *No fucking way*. The second was, *That old bastard's still alive?*

"Seriously? This is for real?" I asked her aloud.

"Of course," she said. "Father wants you home."

"He didn't exactly beg me to come back after I left," I said. "In fact, when I called Mom to let her know I wasn't dead in a ditch, she said he'd disowned me."

Lady shrugged. "I know he wasn't very nice to you back then. I was there for most of it, remember? I know how hard he was to live with."

I let out a short, bitter laugh. "But he liked *you*. You were his little princess. I was just a tomboy who never liked what he liked and never did as he ordered."

"I promise you, he's had a change of heart. The world is different, and so is he."

I thought back on all his narcissistic rages and Napoleonic mood swings, and my stomach twisted in dread. But I also remembered him hugging me and telling me he was proud of me, once. Maybe that could happen again. "Really?"

She nodded, smiling brightly, and drew an X over her chest. "Cross my heart."

We hit the road and put three hundred miles between ourselves and the massacre before we stopped to rest at an abandoned gas station along I-10. I did two searches of the property to check for vampires before we set up camp in the part that used to be a convenience store. The shelves still held stale candy bars and boxes of crackers under a thick layer of grime blown in from the road through the broken glass doors.

"Did you know our family's royalty?" she asked as I set up my camp stove to warm some water for tea. She was fiddling with her gold ring.

I laughed. "All you need to be royalty in this country is money, and Father always had plenty of that."

Our father got his money the old-fashioned way: he inherited it. And despite his talent for waste and alienating other people, he did have a certain knack for playing the stock market, and he started out life with enough capital to keep the cash flowing in.

"No, I mean we're *actual* royalty," Lady insisted. "Father showed me the documents. We're the most direct descendants of Duke Louis de Calvados Castaigne. You're even named after him. Alfonso the Third promised he would rule over New Spain once it was reclaimed in the name of the King."

She pulled off her ring and showed it to me. "See? Our father inherited this. It bears the sign of the King."

I paused, not sure how to respond. "But that whole reclaiming thing never happened, did it?"

"Look around," she said. "Who rules the land now?"

I shivered.

After a sleepless night in which I thought way too much about Gun and Bear and the stillborn baby, we rode on for my parents' house in Mill Valley. The morning sky was a flat, gray-yellow expanse, and the air smelled of sulfur. Xinantecatl was blowing ash down in Mexico. The new eruptions of the long-dormant volcano started a few months before the first vampire attacks were recorded, and so some people claimed that the mountain had released the ancient, predatory race from hibernation deep in the rocks. I didn't know if the tale was true or not, but the coincidence was compelling. People told all kinds of stories about the vampires. Some folks claimed NASA brought them back from Mars. Ultimately, their natural history didn't matter. Staying alive did.

The highways were holding up pretty well considering they hadn't had any maintenance in two years. Everything seemed deserted, even the parts of Los Angeles we traveled past. I'd braced myself to have to flee from roving paramilitary or urban gangs, but the city was a ghostly expanse of silent concrete, decaying buildings and weed-eaten blacktop. San Francisco was nearly as desolate, although I glimpsed a few figures hurrying to duck into buildings or behind vehicles when we approached.

It occurred to me that I might have single-handedly wiped out a double-digit portion of the remaining human population in Arizona, and I didn't feel very good about that.

We got to the house shortly before sunset. The roads leading up to it were choked with vines and ferns, but everything inside the tall iron gate was pretty much as I remembered it. The rolling expanse of lawn was weed-free and freshly mowed. I could even see the lights of the dining room chandelier.

"I've kept the place up," Lady said as she punched in her security code. The gate creaked open. "I and a couple of the servants, anyhow."

Servants. That used to be a normal thing for me: living in a house with a butler, a couple of maids and a gardener. Some of the people I related my story to shook their heads and told me that I was crazy for walking away from so much money and privilege and choosing to live in a world where spilled Tylenol mattered, but I was miserable in Mill Valley. I could remember happiness in my life: it was with Jack, before something bit him in the dark.

She saw me gazing at the chandelier. "The solar panels cost six figures, but they were an excellent investment; we were off the grid well before the King awoke his servants."

"That's good," I said absently. My sister's talk of the King was starting to get on my nerves. She'd always been a little strange, but now I was starting to wonder if she was delusional. Still, her eyes were clear of jaundice, and the house looked fine. I knew to stay on my guard–I was *always* on my guard–but I was pretty curious about what my family had been up to since I'd been gone.

We rode up the long driveway and parked our bikes in the circle around the bubbling marble fountain; Father had it imported from somewhere in France.

Lady eyed my gun belt and the machete I wore in a leather sheath strapped across my back. "You don't need those in the house."

"I'd feel naked without them."

She shrugged, smiled dreamily, and knocked on the front door. Our old butler Mr. Yates answered and escorted us inside. He didn't look much different than he did back when I still lived there. The inside of the house was bigger than I remembered, and all the marble and mahogany and brass fixtures were burnished to glossy shines.

"This way, gentle ladies," Yates said. "The rest of the family is gathered in the parlor."

We followed him back, and he pushed open the double doors. My father sat in his favorite easy chair. My mother stood behind him, and my Aunt Hilda and her grown children Constance and Archer sat on the sofa nearby, drinking tea from bone china cups.

My heart soared, and I forgot my old hatred of my father. The whole family had survived? It was nothing short of a miracle.

"Welcome home, Louise," my father said.

But then Yates moved off to the left...and I caught a glimpse of him from the corner of my eye.

Instinct took over before I had a chance to think. I drew my machete and swung at the elderly butler. My blade met its mark and the vampire scrambled back, shrieking and hissing, clutching its severed wing.

"No!" shrieked Lady, cowering away from me.

At that point I'd glimpsed the rest of the family side-wise, and what was still human in me wept while I drew the .38 and started pumping hollow-points into everything that moved.

A huge vampire flapped toward me, its wings yellow tatters, the gunshot wound in its leg dripping ichor like amber sap.

"Explain yourself!" it boomed in my father's regal voice.

I danced aside like a matador, met it with the machete, and took its head raggedly off.

And when it died, the house around me changed. The light sconces glowed not with electricity but guttering oil lamps made from old cans; I recognized the smell of burning human fat. The brass was green with corrosion, the windows shattered. The fine couches were torn and stained with blood from a hundred victims. What I had taken for plush clean carpet was a matted pile scattered with human remains, and in the dimness beyond, I saw the gleaming eyes of dozens of vampires huddled against the walls.

And I realized I could hear them whispering, *The princess is dead...long live the Queen...the Queen...the Queen.*

Lady was on her knees, weeping. She still looked human enough, but her yellow dress was ragged, her hair thin and tangled, her eyes dull and uninteresting. The only thing upon her that retained its previous luster was the golden signet ring.

I pointed at her with my ichor-stained machete. "Why? Why did you do this?"

"You were the first-born," she sobbed bitterly. "I couldn't be Queen while you lived. I couldn't."

I almost asked "Queen of what?" but I saw the clustered vampires and could hear their whispers all over the house. They feared me. More than that, they respected me. I had a power I'd never asked for and surely didn't want. But it might come in handy anyhow.

I stared down at her. "And you brought me here...to die? So you could be queen?"

She nodded. "Yes. I only ever wanted to serve the King and now I can't."

"But you saw what I did at the clubhouse." I shook my head, still not able to wrap my mind around what she'd tried to do. "You saw what I'm capable of. You could have made me leave my weapons outside but you didn't."

"They were just people." Her tone was supremely dismissive; she was her father's little princess, all right. "I didn't think you could hurt the family."

"Why do they need a human queen?"

"To lead them to new prey."

I almost said, "I'll never do that," but I suddenly realized my will had nothing to do with it. I could hear their whispers because my brain was connected to the hive-mind now. The vampires could see through my eyes, hear through my ears. The moment I found survivors, friendly or not, the hive would know exactly where they were.

And if I closed my eyes, I could feel the King watching me from someplace far away, a land lit by dark stars, a world the ancients called Carcosa.

"What happens when they run out of prey?" I asked, already fearing the answer.

She shrugged. "The servants will starve. And the world will be silent but for the wind in the trees and the waves crashing upon the empty shores, just as the King wishes it to be."

Neither of us said anything for a long time.

"I can't ever trust you again," I finally told her. "I take betrayal very badly."

"I know." She sniffled, wiped her eyes, pulled off the ring and set it on the stained carpet. "That's yours now. I just ask that you make it qui–"

I brought the machete down on the back of her neck before she could finish her sentence. Her head rolled away into darkness. The vampires chittered and gazed at me, waiting. I was useful to them, and so I could live. For now. For a price.

If I'd been a better person, I would have reloaded my pistol, put it to my head and ended things right then and there. Done my bit to save humanity. But...I couldn't do it. It wasn't just that I'd been raised to think of suicide as a sin. I had struggled so long to stay alive, and I'd once sworn to myself I wouldn't die in my father's house.

I rescued the ring from being drowned in the spreading pool of my sister's blood and slipped it onto my finger. It felt as though it had been made just for me.

Two days later, I was back at the Freebirds' clubhouse. I found Rentboy all alone, dragging bodies out of the shed to pile them in the field. It was cremation day. His pretty face and bare chest were covered in bruises.

"They beat the hell out of me when they got back," he said, only looking at me from the corner of his eye. "But they let me live. And then they left. Said they couldn't stay here no more and I couldn't come with them."

He heaved a dead woman onto the pile and turned to face me. Then just stood there, squinting, puzzled. "Beauty? Is...is that really you? You look... different. Where'd your scars go?"

I twisted the ring on my finger. "I'm a bona fide queen, did you know that?"

Rentboy was staring at me, mesmerized by my new glamour. What was that I saw in his eyes? Was it fear? Was it hatred? No. It was utter adoration. It should have made me feel uncomfortable, but I took at as my due.

I held out my hand bearing the ring, and he fell to his knees and kissed it.

"Do you pledge allegiance to your queen?"

"Yes, ma'am."

"Do you swear your life to me?"

"Yes, I do."

"Good." I made him get up. "Pack up the supplies. We're going into the desert where nobody lives, and we're never coming back."

Santa Muerte

Co-written with Daniel R. Robichaud

"It'll be an easy score." Halulu's grin was infectious as influenza. It almost convinced Kai that the proposal was nothing riskier or more legally questionable than selling ice-cold lemonade on a baking hot summer afternoon. Almost. But rent and tuition were due, his trust fund was gone, and how else were any of them going to come up with the cash?

The Hawaiian pointed at Kai's roommate Patrick: "You hold the case. Then, when I tell you, make the exchange."

Then he looked at his other roommate Mikey. "You keep your gun out, just so nobody gets any ideas. Don't stick it in your pants and blow your dick off."

Kai asked, "What about me?"

Halulu's gaze rested on him, sharp and heavy as a bowie knife. Then he clapped him on the shoulder. "Kai, you have the most important part of all. You stay outside and keep the engine running."

"That doesn't sound important," Mikey scoffed. "I mean, I'm the one with the gat, right?" He pointed a finger like a pistol, hand cocked ninety degrees like a total gangsta. "Cough up the cash bitches!" His finger-gun dropped. "Hell of a lot more impressive than sitting on your ass."

"Ignore the hater." Halulu's tone was butter-smooth. "You are our escape clause, Kai. Remember: There's no *us* without *you*."

"You sure this deal is hitch-free?" Kai asked.

"Hell yeah," Halulu said. "I know these guys. What can possibly go wrong?"

⊠

Two hours later, Kai's beat-to-hell Pontiac sat idling across the street from the hand-off site. On the radio, fading Gorillaz beats eased the tension in Kai's head before station identification. College radio was the best; they played the uncensored shit.

Kai did not like looking at the place Halulu had led them to. It was just another cramped, dingy Karl Road tract house, but some intangible quality cast it in a sinister light. While the other homes seemed sleepily inert, this one had a jittery, predatory vibe.

Kai patted the breast pocket of his bowling shirt. The feel of the spliff reassured him. He considered lighting up. Maybe a drag would kick the shake from his hands and heart. After three seconds weighing, he muttered, "No way, man." It could wait until they were done and gone. Knowing it was there was enough. For now.

A man's gravelly voice emerged from the radio, talking about things "Everybody Knows," when the night's action veered in an unexpected direction.

First, came the roar of an approaching engine. With a rubber-ripping tire screech, a Cadillac rounded the corner–a Series 61 model, a touring luxury car that must've been cherry off the line but had aged about as well as Charles Bukowski.

It accelerated down the street, headlights laying the street bare. Tire rubber ground wind-tossed garbage into mash without pause. The car slammed to a halt just two houses down from Kai's Pontiac. The windshield reflected the moon, making the bone sliver crescent a lopsided grin. The passenger door swung open with a screech, and then a bundle tumbled out. Shoved or kicked. As soon as it hit pavement, the car's engine growled anew and the car leapt away. When the Caddy rolled past, Kai caught sight of a sallow-eyed man in a porkpie hat. He grinned at Kai, and his capped teeth gleamed like rusty razors.

The bundle lay still for three seconds and then sat up. It was a girl with a round face and slender throat. Wearing goth-finery: black crinoline, black and white checkerboard pattern leggings and plenty of leather, buckles and lacing on her top and boots. She was a pale little thing, made all the more ghostly by the moonlight. He found himself wanting to run his fingers down the graceful curve of her bare neck, feel the texture of her crinkled skirts.

She pushed herself up to sit, but collapsed again.

She needs help. Halulu's "Stay in the car" order echoed in Kai's thoughts, but his Samaritan impulse shoved it away. The night's chill slapped him with fresh shivers when he got out of the car.

The dumped girl was tiny, maybe two inches over five feet. He couldn't see any blood. Makeup and night hid the finer details of the girl's features, but Kai suspected she was around his own age. Maybe nineteen? Dark hair, and dark smudges around her eyes lent her the creepy presence of a Japanese ghost. He wanted to reach for her, but feared his touch might shatter her.

"Hey, you okay?" he asked. "You live around here?"

She blinked, focused on him, and emitted a torrent of inebriated giggles along with breath that smelled like whisky. Drunk girls. He sighed; they could be so fucking annoying. And yet she was no less alluring to him than before.

"Can I get you to a porch or something?" he asked.

She offered him dreamy-pleased eyes and a Cheshire cat grin.

"Look," he said, stooping down to offer a hand. "Do you–?"

A firecracker pop stopped his words. He looked back toward the house as the front door jerked open. Halulu and company spilled onto the porch. No briefcase, no satchel. They were running for the car. Patrick still had Halulu's 9mm, but it could have been a crooked baton for all the good it did him. Shadows approached the yawning doorway: gangbangers with pistols and sawed-off shotguns.

"Sweet Jesus," Kai whimpered. Before he could race back to the car, the girl caught his hand and pulled him down for a deep kiss. This was clearly *not* the time, and yet he could not stop her or himself. And the kiss...he could feel something flowing away from him, into her. Heat. *Something*.

She broke off the kiss and waved toward the house as though warding off gnats. At her gesture came a new commotion–a noise like a dozen stones ground to gravel under a bulldozer's treads. But no gunshots.

"My name is Alice." The girl licked her lips. "I didn't think you'd mind if I borrowed a little of your essence. To help your guys."

From the car came Patrick's surprised "The *fuck?*" and Halulu's "Kai! Get your ass over here!"

No gangsters stood on the porch. The front door hung broken and crooked from a single twisted hinge. What had she done? He couldn't just leave her there. Kai scooped Alice up and hurried back to his Pontiac.

They assembled in the living room so King Halulu could hold court. He took the Barcalounger and everyone else sat on the floor. "They have all the money, the meth, and what've I got? A bunch of pantywaists who can't do their fucking jobs. And a fucking *witch*."

"Meth?" Kai asked, feeling sick. "I thought it was weed."

"Who the fuck wants to buy weed?" Halulu asked. "I got this from Detroit. Now we owe them big, big coin we don't have." Then, he directed a pointed glare at Mikey. "And what the hell you doing? Capping Cruz puts us in deep shit, man."

"The gun just went off, okay? I didn't even have my finger on the trigger." The 9mm in question lay on the floor before him, barrel pointing toward a wall.

"Guns don't fucking go off on their own," Halulu said. "You were fucking around."

"What happened?" Kai asked.

"We tried to make the deal." Patrick's face was sheet-pale. "They gave us shit, and the Lone Ranger there showed his piece."

"I just wanted to scare them," Mikey said. "The gun went...it went off. And that big guy–"

"Cruz," Halulu said. "His name was Cruz."

"He dropped, and they were set to cap us. We ran, and they got to the door, but then, they just flew backward. Like God herself swatted them out of the way." He indicated Alice with a tilt of the chin.

"Hey biscuit," Halulu said. "Look at me. Now, tell me. How did you do that?"

"My name is *Alice*, not biscuit. And I did a magic spell." She enunciated each syllable for extra bitchslap.

"I'm not playing with you."

She scowled. "Haven't you ever heard witches are subtle and quick to anger?"

"Ain't nothing subtle about you." Halulu eyes roamed her disheveled loveliness. Then he caught something in Kai's expression he didn't like. "What up, Kai?"

"Dude, don't be such an ass to her," Kai said.

"I'll be however I want." Halulu studied his palms, then slowly curled his fingers into fists. "Witchy-tits there should be doing *something*, since this is all her fault."

"All her what?" Kai asked.

"You heard me."

Alice's eyes narrowed to slits. "What did you call me?"

"Bitch, please. *You* show up and things go bad. Kai forgets his fucking place. And...the gun goes off all mysterious? Sounds like voodoo bullshit to me, and you're the only one here supposedly does voodoo *bullshit*."

"Clap your hole, Halulu," Mikey said, finally looking up from the pistol on the floor. He tugged at his Buckeyes football shirt as though it was suffocating him. "I...misspoke around a witch once. You don't want one thinking you're a dick. You really, really don't."

Alice turned to Kai and took his hand. "Take me somewhere we can talk. Your room?"

"We're not done here, biscuit," Halulu growled at her.

"Let her go," Mikey urged. "When they want to go, just let them."

After a heavy exhalation, King Halulu dismissed Alice and Kai with a courtly backhand. "You motherfuckers got some explaining to do later."

Alice paid little mind to the cluttered floor, the spliff stubs and ashes heaped in the ashtray, the hookah collection and the smatter of CDs and comics and dirty clothes. He cleared off the bed, while she performed the complex task of taking off her knee-high Doc Martens, and then they sat across from each other, legs crossed and knees touching. She took his hands, laid them palms up on her thighs, and tickled his love lines with her nails.

He gently pulled his hands away. "What's the story with the guy who dumped you on the street?"

"That was Daddy Dedman. Auntie always said I should never ride with Loas, but I never listen." She chuckled grimly. "I wouldn't fuck him, so he dumped me. Not even *he* can take what I don't want to give."

"What...what kind of witch are you?" he asked.

"Auntie says we're an esoteric offshoot of the OTO. The Ordo Templi Orientis? It's all a riff on Crowley's stuff. 'Do what thou wilt' with a splash of Eastern mysticism and whatevs. I call us Passion Weavers because that's how it all works in my head. It's all about energy redirection."

"What kind of energy? Like flinging fireballs?"

"Well, maybe. But that's totally not my forte. See, when I do this?" She ran her nails up his arms. Across his shirt, across his nipples and then higher. She leaned in until their lips met, and then another kiss triggered sensation overload in Kai's head and heart.

My God, he thought, *she's so hot.*

"When I do that," she said, "it makes energy. A little bit of ecstatic charge." She giggled. "And if I can get enough of it, I can weave an enchantment or a manifestation."

"You kiss people to make magic?"

"I have to find passion to weave," she said. "Drinking or smoking. Turning on. Kissing and full on *doing it.* Even singing and dancing can make a little bit. And I can borrow it from other people, too."

"How would you return something like that?"

"Well...maybe *borrow* is the wrong word. Does that answer your question?"

Kai had to think about what his original question had been–not easy to do, when she was drawing fiery impressions along his arms–but then he nodded.

"Why are you dealing with this Halulu person?"

"He's sort of new around here. He needed a room, and we needed money. Still need it. Halulu paid for the attic space, and he had some cash, not a lot. But he had connections, right? We could score weed, or...."

"Or harder stuff," she said.

Kai nodded. "Well, my trust fund had been what kept us in this house. I mean we all chip in, but I've had to cover expenses a bunch of times. Jobs suck, you know?"

"I know."

"And well, my eldest brother wanted me to come back to Boston. He's been in charge since Father got sick. We argued, and he had Father's lawyers cut me off. Cold. We were worse than broke. And then Halulu came up with his plan, and…" Kai shrugged, embarrassed. "It seemed like a good idea at the time."

Alice teased him with her nails. "Halulu is a jerk, but your brother sounds like a royal ass," she said.

"He is." Kai exhaled slowly. "And now we're in a real mess, a man's dead, and I don't know what to do."

Alice went silent for a moment, then smiled. "I have an idea. Make love to me."

"What?" His heart beat faster. "But we just met–"

"Trust me." She leaned in, and gave him a melting kiss.

He poured every ounce of energy into her. Muscles twisted along his calves, his sides, his belly. Still he drove into her. Her moans sounded sweeter than any angel's song. When she spoke his name, it was the only motive he needed to drive harder, faster, now. *Yes,* he thought, *yes, yes, yes.*

She shivered and moaned through two orgasms before it was all too much. "I'm going to come," Kai said, pulling back. Her nails hooked him, held him inside two heartbeats too long. His dick twitched and spat, and his vision went white with pleasure.

When he beheld her after that moment, she possessed an unearthly beauty. Then, an ugly realization flowed into him: he hadn't worn a condom.

"My God," he whispered, "I'm so sorry."

"Shh," she said. "You didn't do anything I didn't want."

"I came in–"

"Shh," she said. "I'm weaving."

Then, she planted both palms on his chest. Like a human defibrillator, she shoved, and kicked Kai right out of his body.

First thought: *The fuck?*

Second thought: *Who is that?*

Third thought: *That's...that's me!*

Fourth thought: *It can't be.*

Yet there he was, hanging in space, over and behind himself. Kai watched his naked body slump sideways onto the bed. *Holy shit,* he thought, *I died fucking.* The idea was suddenly not as cool as it had once seemed. Then, Kai saw his chest rise and fall. Shallow breathing. Sleeping?

Kai tried to moan, but there was no sound. No air. No solidity. No substance.

Shit oh shit oh shit, he thought. *Worst. Dream. Ever.*

"It's no dream." Alice glanced up, away from his body and into the ghostly thing he had become. "And you're not dead. Calm down. Panic screws everything up."

What did you do to me? Damn it. He couldn't speak. He could open his spirit mouth and try to scream, but to what effect? Yet somehow she understood his words.

"I am giving you a chance to fix the foul-up I've been blamed for," she said. "You can go to the house, you can lay claim to things, and you can return. You don't have much time so don't dawdle. Understand?"

No, he thought. But strangely enough, the panic was flowing away. Alice's steady voice was a source of stability, of calm. It was a voice he could trust. A voice he *had* to trust, but more it was a voice he *wanted* to trust. She had fucked him into this predicament, and she alone could fix him.

What do I do? he asked.

"Remember the place with as much detail as possible, build it in your mind and you will go there. Enter the house, find what your guys lost, and mark it."

How?

"Pass your hand through it. When you're done, come back here the same way you left. You'll come back no matter what. Time is burning." She reached into her lap, brushed her fingers across her belly and shivered.

He thought about Karl Road. The neighborhood. That creepy house.

Then, his room turned and whirled. Visible space coalesced to a bright circle surrounded by impenetrable darkness, and that point slid toward him. Washed over and through him. Soaked him in inky oblivion. This emptiness had presence. It clung and then burned away like film caught in a projector gate. In that place beyond the receding darkness, he saw a nighttime street. A neighborhood. The tract house where a man named Cruz died.

Then, he was there. Wind whistled around and through him. A sprinkling of dark glitter on the asphalt marked the spot where he found Alice. Twenty feet away he saw drips of transmission fluid from his Pontiac.

He willed himself to move toward the lawn, and it happened. He willed himself closer to the scary house, the scene of Mikey's crime. The now-closed door loomed before him. It was cracked and splintered, as if it had been smashed by a SWAT team battering ram. Duct tape held it together.

He wondered what was inside the house. The next thing he knew, he was in a living room. Battered red velour couches, amateur artwork in gilded frames on the walls. Blood spattered the grimy carpet. Two doorways led deeper, one toward bedrooms, the other to a kitchen and beyond to a room where a television blared a soccer game.

Kai followed the blood trail through the quiet hallway into the second bedroom. A man lay on a green tarp on the bed, his arms crossed and a black bandanna over his face. The gunshot wound in his side stained his white tee shirt with blood. At the bedside knelt another guy, dressed in the same clothes, wearing a similar bandanna. He had broad shoulders and a neck lumpy with muscle. His hands were wide, and his fingers were thick as shotgun shells.

Overlooking everything, a three-foot tall, blackened bronze statue stood on a round table at the foot of the corpse's bed. It was a feminized reaper, dressed in flowing robes that bulged over her chest, eye sockets filled with twinkling red costume jewelry. Three dozen folded dollar bills were taped to the statue's base and robes.

Kai had heard of this in his anthropology class. She was Santa Muerte. Saint Death. Central Americans worshipped her despite the Vatican's disapproval. Her rictus was too much to behold. He looked down and away as quickly as possible.

On the floor below the statue's table sat two cases. One of them was Halulu's. Still closed, still locked, still holding the meth. The other case stood open, showing plenty of green packets bound in white tape. Benjamins.

This was more cash than Kai had ever seen in one place. It stirred him, seeing all that paperbound power. His gaze once again moved up to meet the saint's terrifying face. Did this statue have any real power? Would Santa Muerte stop him from taking back the offerings to her?

The weeping gangster turned, his tear-streaked face contorted with an apoplectic rage.

"The fuck you doing here?" The guy's mouth didn't move. No breath escaped his lungs.

Are you astral, too?

"Astral? I'm fucking *dead,* pendejo. I'm mourning myself, before they come for me."

Who's coming for you?

"Whoever takes the dead to Hell. I know that's where I'm going. There's no Heaven for me. Not after all the things I've done."

Cruz's eyes slit. "You're with those other guys. The puta who shot me. The king puta who put him up to it."

Wait. What?

"I called him a fat ass Samoan," Cruz said. "He had your boy draw down on me. So, maybe I invited that bullet."

I thought it was an accident.

"Accident? That little bitch had his nine in hand. He…he…" Cruz's shade slumped. "His finger wasn't nowhere near the trigger, was it? Something else happened. Chance? Ghosts?" Terror dawned in the young man's spectral face and eyes. "How many more of you are there?"

There's only me. Even as Kai thought this, he sensed something moving behind him. It was a cold sensation, like the surprising first autumn breeze that heralded the end of another summer.

"You are so wrong," Cruz said. His attention focused on the space beyond Kai. On the door and the hallway and on the dark things filling that place. "Nino, is that you? Jesus, man, I'm so sorry, but I needed blooding. You know I had to...oh God, who's with you?"

Suddenly, the gangster turned away. "No, Nino. Don't let her come in here." In a much quieter voice, Cruz said, "I'm so sorry, mamasita. I didn't mean to do it. The gasoline, it spilled. The matches were already going, and…"

Something weighty shifted in the space behind Kai. A stink like paint thinner pinched Kai's eyes shut. From the ensuing darkness, something spoke. A dozen voices, familiar but not quite right, whispered, "Turn around, Kai. We've come for you. See our faces."

No fucking thanks. He floated forward, and brushed his hand across both cases. In death's costume jewelry eyes flickered twin candle flame reflections and something else. At once, a dark mass. Like a storm cloud. But in it, moving shapes, nearly human. If he stared, he might discern them. Or might he grant them identities?

"You can't run, Kai," that droning choir said. "Not from us. Not forever. We will catch you up, sooner or later. Best it be now."

Kai squeezed his eyes shut and thought about his room, about his bed, about his body and Alice poised near it. Sweet, lovely, lonely Alice. No bending of light.

Cruz pleaded. "No, mamasita! Please don't! I'm sorry, sorry, sorry!" The last syllable rose into a shriek, before the sound of wet fabric torn and then lusty lapping.

None of it was real. It was all illusion. What could affect a being without a body? Spirits?

"Face me like a man, son."

Dad?

Impossible. His father wasn't dead. He was alive. He was...he was stuck inside a steel life support tube. Because of the hate-spawned cankers and cancers and a plethora of drug side effects, the old man's body had been shutting down one system at a time for years. Kai couldn't bring himself to go see him.

"Enough running, Kai. Face what you've done, and reap what you've sown."

Father called him Kevin, not Kai.

Leave me alone, Dad! Leave me alone the way you left Mom alone! The way you drove her to...to...to do what she did! Drove her to the bottle and to the razors and to the pills and then out the door.

"I've forgiven him, Kevin." The voice had changed, now. Or a different voice had come to the fore. A woman's empathic tones. "But you? I can't forgive you, Kevin. Not for what you said. For the way you sat next to the tub and told me those terrible things when I was bleeding from the cuts in my wrists. I needed help, Kevin, and you sat there crying and useless to me. It was so disappointing."

Kai turned now. *Mom?*

She was there. And Dad. And Sharon Zulkowski, who he had really liked when he was nine and she was ten and coaxed her into a game of doctor–*we were playing, and you were cool with it; you told me so!* But he had always known she wasn't cool with it. Not at all. And there was Kane Hogan, whose left eyeball Kai had cut with a carelessly thrown rock on Woodrow Elementary School's playground–*accident! It was an accident!* Others stepped forward when those he identified stepped back. Kai knew them all. Everyone he had ever hurt. Everyone he had ever made cry. Every person he had ever betrayed. Everyone he had stood by and let suffer, knowingly and unknowingly. They swarmed together, dark and terrible and creeping forward slow and relentless, a hellish oil puddle.

"We hate you, Kai. We've always hated you, and we always will. You deserve this, our hatred. You know you do."

God help him, he did. In his mind's most remote place, the Siberia where the truth that is too terrible to acknowledge is held behind locked doors, he knew. He deserved whatever they were going to do to him. He–

He pleaded with them all, a catalog of denials, which culminated in his holy trinity. *Don't, Dad. Don't, Mom. Please don't. I didn't mean to hurt any of you. I didn't mean it. Didn't mean any of it. I'm so sorry! So sorry!*

Space shimmered. Went indistinct. Collapsed into a point. Sped toward him.

This time, it did not pass around him like water. It slapped and pulled him like a riptide. Knocked him backwards, through the table and its terrible statue.

And the cold darkness surrounded him. Cinched in noose tight. A crushing womb. Kai tried to shriek. It squeezed him into a ball. Then tighter. Smashed his spirit into its components.

As it threatened to crush him further, squeezing him to nothingness, a pinprick appeared in the womb. Through it, light. He squirted through the hole, extruded.

Into his own body.

Someone held him tight, singing nonsense in whispers. The music was damned familiar. The lullaby theme, he finally realized, from *Pan's Labyrinth*. Kai's head leaned against a bosom.

Song turned into comforting words. "It's okay, Kai. You're back. You're safe."

"Alice?"

"That's my name," she said.

"Alice, I saw my mom."

"Shhh. It's okay. You're home."

"I saw my fucking mom!"

"No you didn't," she said. Her tone was firm and final.

"I–"

"You didn't see anyone you knew," she said. "And now you're back, so it doesn't matter what you saw."

But it did. Of course it did.

"What just happened to me?" he demanded. "Tell me something, anything."

"Call it tulpa, if you like," she said. "Call it yearning. Call it a spirit vulture. Call it a feeder on the soul's darkest guilt. Call it an opportunistic scavenger. They're different attempts to constrain an uncontainable entity. It was real, but what it showed you wasn't."

Her mouth found his. Taste. He realized he had been without real taste sense during his out of body experience. The feel of her reminded him that what he had taken as touch-sense was pure perception and imagination. She felt more real than anything he had encountered.

Her hair carried weight and scent and strands. Her mouth moved in a way that he could not articulate but could wholly appreciate. Her taste was heady. He wept, and their kiss broke, and she held him for a while longer.

In time, his sobbing subsided. His body relaxed. It was then he realized there were two cases on the floor. And a table with a Santa Muerte statue atop it, her costume jewelry eyes gleaming with mirth and deadly promises.

Success had come hand-in-hand with a profound emptiness.

He stood up. Pulled on his pants. Carried the drug case downstairs. Halulu still held court in the living room. Without looking up, the king said, "We need a plan for dealing with the guys in Detroit."

Kai dumped the case on Halulu's lap, and the Hawaiian's words–"Is this my case? No way!"–quickly trailed into confused syllables.

"This is over," Kai said. "I want you out of here before morning."

"How did you get this?" Halulu looked up. Whatever he saw in Kai's face made him flinch. "I'll be gone, man. Gone."

Mikey still stared at the pistol on the floor. "I shot him."

"It wasn't your fault," Kai said. Mikey looked up, wanting to believe. "Halulu, take that gun with you when you go. Make it disappear."

"I will."

Kai trudged back to his room.

The act of walking was downright therapeutic. Nothing quite connected a body to life the way that walking did. It quickened the heart. Kai drew deeper breaths. Being out of his body had removed so much of his sense of what was right and real. He wondered if he'd ever get it back.

Alice had draped the comforter over the statue. "She unnerves me."

"I can't do that again." Kai's voice shook. "Be out of my body."

Alice nodded. "I'm sorry I sprung that on you. It seemed like the only idea."

"It was a shitty thing to do."

"I'm sorry." She winced, looking sad and small. "You want me to leave like Halulu?"

He held out his hand, and she took it. He led her to the bed and sat her down.

"I really like you," he said. "We haven't known each other long, but it feels...like we should stick together. At least for a little while longer. And see what happens."

Her face brightened. "You mean that?"

He considered this for almost a second and then nodded.

They kissed, and then they loved again. Afterward, she brushed her blue painted fingernails across his temples before she asked, "Don't you wonder how this all happened? I mean, what started hours, days, or weeks ago that built to this moment?"

"Actually, no," he finally said. "I don't wonder that at all. Wanna go to the 'Dube and get some burgers?"

She pushed his shoulder and laughed. It was a pretty sound, her laughter. Kai couldn't help himself; he joined her.

Dark of the Moon

The sound and stink of the casino assaulted Velocity's senses. Drunken gamblers brayed and shrieked with laughter while the gaming machines blasted their cacophony of ringing, clanging, shouting and wheedling everywhere. Colorful lights flashed nearly as bright as stun grenades. The air was thick with the stench of sweat, nicotine vapors, and a hundred varieties of Cleaver body spray, each more obnoxious than the last. If she could bottle the pong of the place, she'd sell it under the name "Mal Choix de Vie." A terrible translation of terrible life choices. But people would still buy it because it sounded French and fancy.

Felician and his stupid meetup sites. This place had to be teeming with electronic eyes and ears, scammers and gangsters of every stripe. At least there hadn't been a weapon check at the front door. She could keep her twin .45s strapped beneath her black leather jacket where they belonged, just in case anybody tried anything funny. Her backup credit hung in a shielded pouch on a chain around her neck, nestled snugly between the girls. Her primary credit was tied to the forged electronic ID she used when dealing with Felician; he'd been a good fixer in the five years she'd been taking jobs through him, but she knew full well that any situation could turn bad in a moment, and she'd have to dump her current identity and run.

She had a real, precious-as-gold ID to fall back on–her parents were wealthy enough to buy her citizenship when she was a baby. Almost nobody who was born poor in the States was granted citizenship these days. But since her bona fide ID was tied to her actual medical records, she needed to go to great lengths to protect it. As far as the authorities knew, Velocity had nothing to do with Kitty Wong, a perpetual college student whose treatments and enhancements all stemmed from her love of extreme sports.

Shouldering her way through the crowd, Velocity intended to head straight down the neutral green carpet that led through the acres-huge casino floor to the shops and restaurants in the back. Felician wanted to meet up at a place called the Jurassic, a buffet that advertised vat-grown dinosaur meat. How anybody would know a fake brontosaurus roast from a fake pork roast she had no idea, but for 60 bucks a pop, the place had *better* serve some epic grub. At least booze was included. Doc Sawbrains had told her to steer clear of any heavy drinking until her grey matter healed up a bit more from the neural interface malware that had nearly turned her brains to a brûléed flan, but a girl had to get her money's worth somehow, right?–

Suddenly, she was no longer in the loud casino, but was standing naked on a beach. Green waves teeming with dark serpentine forms surged and foamed, crashing at her feet. Salt and the stink of rotting kelp lay heavy on the chilly wind. The serpents writhed free of the waves, spilling onto the wet sand in shiny coils as though the ocean had been eviscerated, and slithered toward her while she remained frozen, rooted to the spot–

–Velocity found herself back in the casino and felt a wash of relief that, according to her smartwatch, she'd hallucinated for less than a second. But her relief faded just as quickly: she'd stumble-stepped off the green strip, and was now standing on the garish casino carpet. Already the machines around her had lit up, and were pulling themselves free of their floor sockets to greet the fresh meat.

"Welcome, Player!" A penny slot sidled up to her, spinning its holographic dials seductively. "Ten dollars gets you a hundred chances!"

"Don't listen to that junker," replied a chrome-and-neon Wheel of Fortune machine. "His payouts are terrible! Try me!"

"No, try me!" squeaked a machine with a Japanese pop soundtrack and dancing cherries.

"You'll try me first," growled a sleek black poker machine. "Unless you just can't handle the best!"

Dammit. The wheedling machines had her completely surrounded. The casino's programmers knew exactly how long the average new gambler had to play to get hooked, and this bunch was set to hound her into playing until she'd crossed the threshold. And she had neither the time nor interest in this.

Velocity entertained a brief fantasy of pulling out her twin pistols and blasting them all into sizzling glass-and-plastic shrapnel, but each one of the machines was probably worth more than the job Felician had for her. Satisfying though shooting them might be, she could neither afford to pay off the casino nor afford to blow her professional reputation as an operative of supreme chill.

"C'mon, darlin', don't be coy." The poker machine slid up close to her, positioning its controls right under her hands. It stank of Cleaver–the exact fragrance was probably called Throwdown or Anarchy or something–which was probably olfactory residue from a gambler who'd recently abandoned it, but for all she knew the machine had scent jets to attract ostentatious losers. "Just thirty bucks to play Texas Hold 'Em, and you could win up to 50K!"

Velocity grabbed the top rim of the poker machine and flipped up and over the coaxing machine, landing softly on the carpet behind it. She smoothly stepped back to the safety of the green strip and strode toward the buffet as the thwarted machines emitted electronic groans and synthesized trombone *womp-womps* behind her. Hardly anybody had noticed her escape. Good.

Still, her brief fugue to the scene on the beach left her a little rattled. She'd need to increase the brain candy Doc Sawbrains had prescribed, that was for sure. The hallucinations and dreams had all started after she'd gotten slammed with the malware while she was trying to hack into the LalinLabs servers to steal intel for a rival corporation. Doc said that was pretty normal, considering the hit her brain had taken, but...it all seemed so weirdly *real.* Realer than her regular life, even. It was the same scene over and over–the beach, the ocean, and the serpents–but each time there was just a little bit more.

It all felt as though it should *mean* something. It felt like prophecy, not just misfiring brain cells. She knew that there was more to the world than her senses could convey to her brain, and that knowledge made her uneasy. She liked gunning and driving; she did not like prophecy, not even as a concept. Beneath all the mechanical complexities of weapons and vehicles was the solid, controllable predictability of Newtonian physics. Prophecy meant her life was subject to an unpredictable spiritual world she had absolutely no control over. And that felt more like drowning than her dreams.

❖

Velocity found Felician sitting in an alcove in the back of the buffet's dining hall with a guy she didn't recognize. She spotted them before they noticed her, so she hung back behind the fronds of a potted cycad tree, taking in the scene and feeling acutely annoyed that her fixer hadn't come alone like he said he would. Their plates were piled high with brontosaurus prime rib and garlicky algae mash. A discreet surveillance jammer sat beside Felician's sweaty mimosa goblet, projecting a white noise screen and hologram blurs over their mouths to foil lip readers.

Was the stranger her client? She didn't like clients knowing her face and voice; that's why Felician got his cut. *He* was supposed to be the face of all the deals, and he was supposed to deal with the heat they brought. He got paid so she could remain anonymous.

But the mystery man didn't look like a corporate type. He wore a street-anonymous dark tee shirt and jeans, but he had an electric blue topknot and a whole lot of facial piercings. And the lack of telltale scars behind his ears from his studs getting tacked into his skull meant he didn't get in many fistfights. And *that* meant that he was either a crummy fighter (and maybe a total poser)...or he was good enough with his tongue or another weapon of choice that he didn't need to brawl. His face reminded her of a half-dozen movie stars. He looked to be in his mid-20s, which probably meant he was in his 40s or even a bit older, a seasoned pro. His gracefully sinewy forearms bore only one visible tattoo–a two-headed coral snake coiled atop his left wrist–but she did see a couple of healing blade scars, the kind you inevitably got going in for the kill. Yes, this guy liked to play with knives. Not a brawler, but a fighter for sure.

And that realization made her feel annoyed all over again. Felician *knew* she worked alone. She didn't want to have to worry about some dumb bolt screwing up the job, nor did she want to have to chase down a dumber jack who decided to run off with the loot. She'd been on awful crews her first few years, and she was *done* with that nonsense. Her requirement for solo jobs *only* was her hardest rule. Why had Felician ignored it and invited another operative to their business discussion?

She fixed a neutral smile on her face, stepped out from behind the cycad, and cleared her throat. Felician glanced up and beamed at her.

"Ah, Velocity, my love!" He raised his drink in greeting. "So glad you could join us!"

She extended her hand to the mystery man. "Hi there. I'm Velocity. And you?"

He gave her a bright grin and replied, "Hi, I'm Borealis."

His voice was deep and smooth as Belgian chocolate, and he had a knee-weakening New Orleans accent. She ran hot and cold with sexy Southern boys. Sometimes they were easy on the eyes and no good at all in the sheets, but the ones who were good were *oh my* so very good...

She struggled to keep her expression steady. The last damn thing she needed was this kind of distraction right now. Was Felician trying to get her killed?

"Have a seat, Velocity." Felician scratched his short dark beard in a gesture that she'd long ago learned was a sign of nervousness. "We can all have a nice friendly chat."

She slid into the booth next to the fixer and gave him an expectant look.

"So you're probably both wondering why the other is here," Felician said. "Well. You two have so many things in common."

"One being that we both prefer to work alone?" Borealis said, his eyebrow arching up ever so slightly.

Another beard-scratch. "Yes, that's one thing. But! Both of you ran afoul of that particularly nasty neural malware that LalinLabs deployed to protect its interests last year. I got a taste of that one myself recently; quite nasty. My neurotherapy bills have been astronomical."

He grimaced and took a sip of his mimosa. "Personally, I would love a chance to count coup against that particular corporation. I believe you two would as well, yes?"

Velocity and Borealis glanced at each other and shrugged.

"Because you're both still recovering from that unpleasantness," Felician said, "you also both need to stay in meatspace, so this won't involve cyberspace. Under usual circumstances, this job would be easy for either of you to accomplish as a solo mission. However, your ongoing recoveries would make a team effort more prudent. So I would ask that you set aside your solitary preferences, just this once."

"What about the payment?" Velocity asked. "Half of my usual fee isn't going to keep me in coffee and ammo."

"There's plenty to go around." Felician texted her a number with enough zeroes after it that she was suddenly imagining taking that trip to Tahiti she'd always dreamed of. And she could stay at a real beachside resort, not a flop by the wharf. And afterward, she could get that skeletal enhancement she'd had her eye on; never again would she have to worry about busting a bone if she had to take a dive out a fourth-floor window.

She glanced over at Borealis, and she could see by the gleam in his pretty silver eyes that he was daydreaming about well-funded funtimes, too.

In hushed, calm tones, Felician laid out the plan. Their client wanted them to break into the mansion of a LalinLabs executive named Morgenstern Moon and steal a metal storage box he kept hidden in his panic room. Velocity and Borealis would deliver the box unopened to a specific drop site, whereupon their mysterious client would upload the money into Felician's account. Within 24 hours, Felician would share out the funds.

"I have blueprints for the house, and Moon and his guards will be away at a charity fundraiser the night of the heist. It'll be a quick, tidy job, and I'm sure you'll both sleep better knowing you royally reamed the suit who signed off on the malware program that burned us all."

Velocity glanced at Borealis. It looked like he was still doing math in his pretty head, and liking the sum he was coming up with.

She put her hands on the table. "I still need to know who I'm working with before I can agree to this. No offense."

Borealis nodded. "None taken. I feel the same way."

Felician smiled. "I've uploaded your respective resumes–with sensitive details redacted, of course!–to your dropboxes. Get some food, take a look! Take your time. I have every sincere belief that you'll both get on like a house on fire."

So Velocity cued up the file on her smartwatch and slowly scrolled through it as she walked through the buffet line. Her initial impression that he was a blades expert was correct. Borealis had a background in covert ops. He'd worked for a popular private police force early in his career, but had gotten fired and nearly killed after he refused to exterminate a bunch of street children whose panhandling had been deemed a nuisance. Velocity knew that kind of moral code was laughably old-fashioned, but if she was honest with herself, she didn't want to kill kids, either, not even when the money was too good to pass up. Softie or not, Borealis had been on dozens of successful heists and covert ops missions since his dishonorable discharge. Client recommendations praised his quiet, low-key efficiency.

He certainly seemed like the kind of guy she could do a job with. The bigger question was whether his file was accurate or not. They *could* be playing her. That was *always* a risk. But why would Felician try to trick her into working a job with him? Who would benefit from that? She laid out the known facts, and no matter how she sliced them with Occam's Razor, she came to the same conclusion: this was a straightforward job. Felician's nervousness was probably due to worry that he'd lose his cut on a sweet gig because she and Borealis would refuse to work with each other out of paranoia or stubbornness or both. If her jobs were typical, it would also be more money than he'd seen in months.

She got back to the booth with her plate filled with fried archaeopteryx eggs and stegosaurus sausage, a tall mimosa in her other hand, and said, "I'm in."

"Me, too," said Borealis, and they bumped fists.

"Out*standing*." Felician gave them both a wide, relieved smile. "Let's go over the details...."

Three nights later, Velocity picked up Borealis and his gear bag outside a downtown coffee shop. She drove a nondescript, aging Toyota she'd picked up after the brunch; she'd done just enough work on it to make sure the engine, tires, and brakes were all solid and would stand up to a fast getaway over rough ground. But they were going to dump it after the job no matter how it went, so it had been a Duct Tape Special for sure.

Borealis wore dark jeans, boots, and a long-sleeved, deep red shirt that nicely contrasted with his hair under the fluorescents, but would look black in low natural light. She could see the faint outlines of body armor beneath it. So far, he looked and acted like a real pro.

Felician, for your sake I better not regret this, she thought.

"You got the plasma cutter?" he asked.

"I got everything on your list," she replied. "It's all in the trunk."

"Mind if I put on some music for the drive?"

"The speakers are trash, but go ahead."

He cued up an old album by Ivan and the Suckmunkies.

"Wow, I haven't heard this in forever," she said.

He seemed surprised she'd heard it at all. "What do you think of Bässgrindeur?"

"I love those guys! But really, Basterd Rat did his best work with the Broken Nose Trio...."

They continued bonding over obscure bands as she drove them out of the city into the woods. The road to the executive's valley compound wound through hills and trees so tall she could barely see the darkening sky. Shortly after sunset, they crested a rise above the valley and saw a huge glowing dome that looked like the Moon itself had fallen to earth and embedded itself in the valley floor. Her knowledge of lunar terrain was minimal–it was hard to see it very clearly through all the air pollution–but she saw craters etched in the surface, and thought she recognized Mare Imbrium and the other dry seas of the rocky satellite.

"Well, that's an amazing replica," Borealis said. "*Way* better than I was expecting."

"The blueprints say it's ten stories tall at the apex, but the panic room is directly below the first-floor master suite." Velocity pulled the car off the road and killed the headlights. "We're about a mile away. Can you sprint that if we need to bug out in a hurry?"

He nodded. "I run every day."

"Good. Felician's intel says that the best way to get there is to just cut through on the southwest side."

"Below the replica of the Grimaldi crater, yeah. I see exactly where it is."

"Okay, let's roll."

They gathered their gear and headed down through the trees to Moon's palace. At ten kilos, the plasma cutter was the heaviest piece of equipment they had to carry, but if it performed as expected, it would make short work of the exterior wall. And in a pinch, it would make short work of any armored guards they encountered. Most of his security detail was supposed to be with him at the charity event, but there were always at least one or two guards left behind.

"You getting a body count with the infrared scanner?" she whispered as she deployed four tiny laser replicator drones to make an undetectable hole through the security grid. She could just barely see the network of red lasers against the bright backdrop of Moon Palace. Still, the dome wasn't as blinding as she'd expected; up close, its luminance seemed much gentler.

"Nobody outside, at least not on this side," he replied. "The walls are too thick to detect anyone inside. Think we should try to hack into the house automation to check?"

She sighed; she *could*, but then she'd be useless with vertigo. "I'm still too burned for that. You?"

"Same."

"Slash and grab," she said. "Let's get in, get out, and get back. If anybody discovers us, well, it's their damn unlucky day."

They ran through the laser gap to the wall. Borealis hefted the cutter and fired it up; a wicked two-foot blade of red-white light emerged from the tip. He plunged it into the glowing surface of the dome, and it sank straight through, cutting the sparking LED matrix like it was cake frosting. In seconds, he'd cut a doorway, and she kicked it into the building. It landed with a crash that made the cat burglar in her cringe.

She froze at the smoking opening. The room inside was dark and silent, but through her enhanced eyes she could see it clearly enough: a richly appointed bedroom with a satin-covered bed big enough to sleep at least seven people. The padded headboard was taller than she was, and she saw recessed D-rings affixed to the posts. Clearly, Moon enjoyed having a few friends over for parties.

"Let's do this." She jumped over the fallen wall to the plush carpet beyond.

Suddenly, the bathroom door swung open.

Velocity's hands were on her guns and she fired before the bald man in the purple silk bathrobe and bunny slippers could utter anything more than an indignant "What the–" He fell where he stood, a bullet in his heart and another in his brain.

"Fuck me," Borealis muttered. "That's Morgenstern Moon!"

"Oh, crap." She blinked, wondering what accidentally assassinating the master of the palace would do to the terms of their payment. "We better find the box in the panic room before–"

Four guards in full battle gear kicked down the hallway door. Huge, probably cyborg enhanced, but she couldn't make out their race or sex under all that armor. Felicity plugged the first two in the neck where the Kevlar was weakest, and she heard the wet *pop!* of their bodies and skulls getting pulped inside their carapaces. The other two fell back, but laid down fire she and Borealis had to dance sideways to dodge. More guards bellowed in the hallway: reinforcements were coming fast.

"Get the box!" she shouted. "I'll deal with these guys."

Borealis set to cutting open the floor behind the cover of the huge bed while she ducked and dodged and plugged the massive guards one by one. This was a dance she'd done on more jobs than she could remember; her legs moved and her eyes aimed and her hands fired seemingly all of their own accord. Time seemed to stretch like taffy, every smoking shell taking an eon to hit the fancy carpet. She was faster than any armored guard. Tonight, she would be faster than bullets, faster than death. The highly trained, loyal men and women in the hallway dropped one by one, minds literally blown.

It took her a moment to realize that Borealis was yelling, "Got it!" and sprinting for the hole in the wall. She killed the second-to-final guard and backed out, guns still blazing, and they both sprinted for the road.

After they'd dumped the Toyota at the waterfront and sprinted a half block to the Nissan that Velocity had parked as a second getaway vehicle in case things went south, she took a moment to examine the lockbox that cost Morgenstern Moon his life. It was just a battered metal storage case airbrushed with decorative stars. Sturdy, certainly, but it screamed "band gear" more than it did "corporate espionage." Borealis had scanned it for bugs and trackers while she drove back to the city, and hadn't found anything. Still, they couldn't be 100% sure something in the case wasn't sending somebody a signal unless they got inside it, and the terms of the deal were that they were not to open it no matter what.

"So, you think it's bearer bonds, patent secrets, or just a mic once owned by his favorite rock star?" she asked.

Borealis shook his head, frowning. "I care more that Felician isn't answering on any of his channels. And he or someone else appears to have shut off his accounts. All my messages are bouncing. We need to figure out what's going on, and why."

Velocity pursed her lips. Felician disappearing could mean he'd been targeted by whoever had fed him bad intel. Or it could mean the client was murderously pissed. Or it could mean that the gig had gone mostly according to Felician's plan, except that she and Borealis were supposed to be bleeding out on Moon's fancy carpet, and now their fixer was dodging them. Or it could mean something else had happened that had nothing to do with Moon. "Well, if he had to go to ground, I think I know where he'll be."

"Are we still taking the case to the drop point tomorrow?"

She nodded. "That's still the plan. No sense in getting multiple bounties on our heads in the space of two days without good reason. But we better find Felician first. We know we're in some serious guano here, but he might actually be able to tell us how deep it is and which sewer gull dealt it."

Felician's downtown office was stripped bare. He'd cleared out–or *been* cleared out–in a hurry. The lack of bloodstains or telltale solvent odor made Velocity reasonably certain that he hadn't been murdered and dragged away. So she took Borealis on a tour of the bars and dives that Felician thought she didn't know about.

They found him sitting in the back of a biker bar called Buster's. He was at a narrow high table, morosely nursing a gin-and-tonic and pulling at his beard.

Velocity pretended to scratch her collarbone and let her hand drop inside her jacket to the grip of her lefthand pistol. "Felician. What the fuck happened?"

With a start, he looked up, his face paling. "Velocity. Borealis. I–"

From the corner of her eye, she saw the stun grenade sailing toward them, and she barely had time to grab Borealis and dive into an unoccupied booth before it went off. When she popped back up, she saw a whole corporate security goon platoon swarming through the front door. Fortunately, the biker regulars reacted with extreme prejudice to the invasion and were raising a violent ruckus, efficiently blocking the squad's progress through the bar. At least a half-dozen fistfights broke out, and the place soon filled with the din of smashing glass and fracturing furniture.

She turned back to Felician's table. The fixer had taken the full blast of the stun grenade and was sprawled unconscious on the floor, bleeding slightly from his nose and ears.

"We gotta get to the safe house," she told Borealis. "Grab Felician. I'll cover us."

He nodded. "You're the boss."

A few armored corporate sedans tried to chase them down, but Velocity managed to lose them all in a suburb with hilly, twisty streets and plenty of handy alleys and confusing cul-de-sacs. They ditched the Nissan and switched to an old Honda she'd left parked in uptown.

An hour later, they were carrying Felician and the case up the steps to the #3 safe house, an abandoned regeneration clinic. Fading red logos of the bankrupt company that originally built it decorated the gray concrete walls.

Once they were securely locked in, they put Felician in a dusty, high-backed office chair and checked his pupils and pulse.

"Looks like he'll be okay," Borealis said. "But who knows when he'll regain consciousness."

Velocity pulled a pair of chrome handcuffs out of her rucksack.

Borealis cocked an eyebrow at her.

"Those professional, or recreational?"

"They're whatever I need them to be, sweetie." She snapped the short chain at him and then set to binding Felician's hands behind the chair.

"I get the feeling he knows how to wriggle out of tight spots," Borealis remarked. "Better use some rope, too."

After they got Felician as securely bound as they could without impeding his breathing, they went upstairs to the lounge.

"Want something to drink?" she asked.

"Sure, what's here?"

"Um." She got up and checked the fridge. "Looks like you can have anything you want as long as it's bottled water or cherry-beet IcyAde."

"I'll take water, thanks."

She found a couple of coffee mugs in the cabinet, poured their drinks, and took them back to the sofa.

"Well, this whole evening has been a royal trash fire," she said, "but you were good back there."

He gave her a slow, sexy grin. "High praise, indeed."

She felt herself redden in an unfamiliar blush. "Well, I mean...I was never much for group projects, even back in school. But working with you...yeah, it was good."

His grin widened, and his silver eyes sparkled. She had to resist the urge to just lean in and kiss him.

"I can't say I've enjoyed the complications, but I *have* enjoyed the company." He raised his mug in a toast. "To solid partnerships, and better gigs in the future."

"From your lips to Fate's ears." She clinked her mug against his.

"Fuuuck!" Shrieking at the top of his lungs, Felician charged up the stairs, still loosely bound in the ropes. The handcuffs dangled half-open from one wrist.

Velocity pulled her gun, at first thinking that he'd gone mad and was charging at them, but he just kept barreling up the stairs.

"What the hell is going on?" Borealis asked.

They both got up to look down the stairs–and saw dark grey water rising fast in the stairwell. It was already higher than the front door. The salty, rotten-kelp smell of the ocean slid up her nostrils. The temperature in the room was dropping, but the water looked like it was boiling...

No. Not boiling. She stumbled back, wondering if she was going to faint. The water was roiling because it was teeming with serpents. The same dark, coiling monstrosities she'd been seeing in her prophetic hallucinations.

"Fuck me," Borealis moaned, staring at the rising water in horror. "Not freakin' *snakes.*"

"But...your tattoo. Don't you like snakes?"

"Hell, no. I got this because of the goddamn dreams. I thought...I thought it might help."

Her heart beat faster. "What dreams?"

"I'm standing on a cold beach, and all these serpents come out of the water..."

"I know that dream. I've had it myself."

He looked startled. "Really?"

"Yeah."

The water rose faster and faster, and more and more snakes seemed to be coming with it. Just looking into the serpent-infested waves made her sick with vertigo.

"This *can't* be real," Borealis whispered.

It couldn't, but every cell in her body was telling her that it most certainly was.

"Felician had the right idea; let's get some altitude," she said. "This can't possible get much higher, can it?"

A huge wave of seawater and snakes abruptly washed onto the landing, and they ran upstairs. The sea surged up behind them, faster and faster. Soon, breathless, they slammed open the door to the roof. Felician was standing there untying the last couple of Velocity's knots.

She drew her pistols and put Felician in her sights. "Talk. What the hell is going on?"

He raised his hands in an appeasing gesture. "I don't know, I swear! I got to my office and somebody had cleared it out, and then my accounts all got shut down–"

"Oh, hell," Borealis said.

Velocity glanced behind her. The sea was surging up over the threshold onto the roof and snakes were flopping over with it, writhing and hissing. One coiled up and lunged at Borealis' booted feet. He drew a throwing stiletto and neatly impaled the serpent's head. But a dozen more, a hundred more, a *thousand* more were wriggling onto the roof behind it.

Velocity fired at the front edge of the wave, blasting the snakes to red mist... but she knew she didn't have enough ammo. Not *nearly* enough. She wouldn't have had enough if she'd been so loaded down with bullets she couldn't stand up.

"We could go over the side of the building," Borealis said as they backed away from the snakes and waves.

"I used less than five meters of rope on Felician," she replied. "All the rest is still in my bag downstairs."

"We could just climb down, though?" Felician sounded hysterical; clearly he wasn't a snake fan, either. "It wouldn't be that hard, we'd just have to...oh, fuuuck me."

Felician was staring horrified over the edge of the building. Velocity followed his gaze. The serpent sea wasn't just in their building; it was *everywhere.* Rising waves and poisonous snakes as far as the eye could see down all the streets and alleys, everything grey and surreal in the early morning light.

A vertiginous nausea took her, and she wobbled backward. This was her nightmare made flesh. And there was no escape from it...except for the bullets in her pistols.

Velocity closed her eyes. *No.* This literally *could not be happening* despite what all her senses and instincts were telling her. She was missing something. What was really going on?

Open your eyes and really see, she told herself.

She took a deep breath to gather her focus and turned in a slow circle, taking in the scene around her. Ignoring the snakes and the water and Felician and Borealis. Her eye caught the slightest wavering of air beside the ancient HVAC unit. It could have been a mirage of hot air, but it wasn't quite in the right place.

Whatever it was, it didn't belong, and Velocity fired at it. The explosive round found its mark, and she heard a woman's gasp of pain a moment before all the snakes and the water utterly disappeared.

"What!" Borealis spun in a circle.

Velocity's eyes and brain were finally making sense of what she was looking at: someone sprawled dead beneath a chameleon cloak. A bare hand and a foot in a fashionable moccasin poked out from beneath the mimetic fabric, giving the illusion of random, bloodless severed limbs lying on the roof.

She strode forward and pulled the cloak off. Beneath it was an odd-looking blonde girl wearing the trendy hippie throwback stuff popular with rich kids in the area. Her belly had an enormous hole from the explosive round, and there was another, smaller bullet hole in the neural projector unit lying beside her body. The slug had gone through the projector first without detonating.

Velocity kicked the dead projector away and stomped on it twice for good measure. Neural projectors were cutting edge, highly controlled, and very expensive; with a strong enough unit, a person could make an entire crowd hallucinate and riot. Getting the shielding right was tricky, so the user ran the risk of hallucinating just as badly as the targets. Guns were a hell of a lot safer. And this girl wasn't wearing any shielding at all as far as Velocity could tell.

"Either of you know her?" Velocity asked.

"Crap, that's your client." Felician scratched his beard. "Well. Hm...this might complicate us getting paid."

Velocity was gobsmacked. "Who is she?"

"I'm pretty sure that's Astrid Moon," Borealis replied. "Morgenstern Moon's daughter. I've seen pictures of her on the news feeds."

"His daughter?" Velocity said. "But why would she do all this? If she wanted us dead, why not call in an air strike?"

"You both have real citizen ID, am I right?" Felician asked. "Yeah, I know, you have the forgeries, but you two also have real ones?"

Velocity and Borealis looked at each other and reluctantly nodded.

"So, technically, killing you could be murder," Felician said. "Killing citizens has to be investigated. If I stood to inherit a whole lot of money from a father I didn't like so much, and I didn't want an investigation, tricking a couple of robbers into killing him and then tricking them into killing each other with the murder weapons would be pretty tidy, wouldn't it? I mean, aside from the blood all over everything."

"Wow..." Velocity stared down at the body and realized she and Borealis had both started having the dreams and hallucinations about the serpent sea after they'd been infected with the neural malware from the LalinLabs job. And Felician said he'd been hit with it, too. Their brains had been deliberately primed for the hallucination Astrid attacked them with. She didn't need shielding because the neural projector was stimulating only what she'd already planted. This double-cross had been set up *months* ago. "That's pretty hard to prove."

"Let's open up that box and see what's inside," Borealis said.

They picked the locks and gingerly lifted the lid. In addition to $750,000 in crisp bank bundles, there was a copy of Morgenstern Moon's last will and testament.

"An old-fashioned paper will?" Velocity mused. "*That's* a surprise."

"Some people are paranoid enough to want dead tree backups," Felician said.

"I get the feeling he had good reasons to worry." Borealis picked up the document and began to read it. "Whoopsie. Astrid *wasn't* going to inherit a whole bunch of money. Looks like dear ol' Dad was leaving everything to his housekeeper. And his cats."

"*That's* why she wanted the box," Felician said. "She was going to hack his will and needed to make sure this copy disappeared."

"Well, either way, looks like his housekeeper's going to make out like a bandit, and we got our sweet payday." Velocity patted the stacks of bills. "I say we go drop Miss Moon here in the medical waste disposal unit in the basement, and then let's get some breakfast."

Borealis grinned at her. "I like the way you think."

She grinned back. "Thanks."

"You want to do this partners thing again sometime?"

"Sure. Sometime. But I think I'll go to Tahiti for a couple of weeks first. Shake off the rest of the burn in my head while I work on my tan."

"An excellent plan," Felician said. "I think I'll go on vacation myself. Excuse me while I rearrange some meetings."

The fixer stepped a few feet away and started tapping at his smartwatch.

Borealis' eyes twinkled. "Sun, sand, drinks, and great scenery...sounds like some hard suffering."

"The hardest," she said.

"Want some company?"

She paused, then smiled again. "Yeah. I think I do."

Fraeternal

Billy grins at me over his coffee. "You're holding out on me, Sis."

"I'm not." I fish the teabag out of my cup and set it on the saucer. This roadside diner isn't fancy enough to have anything but Lipton, but that's okay. The nurses make the tea too strong and bitter, and bottled teas taste weird to me. Especially after all the psychoactive meds we've been taking. We got doses of our daily experimental regime just two hours ago, and the drugs have a ridiculous laundry list of possible side effects we haven't felt yet, but you never know. I'm not sure either of us should be away from the research facility.

"We're going straight back after this, right?" Any minute, I expect Agent Mainward and a bunch of armed guards to come swarming through the door to retrieve us. "I don't want us to get in trouble."

He laughs and dumps another packet of sugar into his coffee. "Worrywart. We're fine."

His tone tells me that he didn't merely scam Mainward into giving us day passes but wove an entire justification around the situation to convince him that we needed day passes for solid therapeutic reasons. We *needed* to get out for a while to clear our heads. Or, more likely, to clear *my* head. He probably told them that he needed time away in a more comfortable environment to talk his poor anxiety-ridden, developmentally-challenged twin sister into getting with the program.

People take one look at me and Billy and a whole lot of them think I'm retarded. Yeah, I know: "retarded" is a terrible, awful word and I shouldn't use it. But most everybody else thinks the word. Even the nurses. Sometimes *especially* the nurses, who should know better. The word is slithering through their brains like parasitic worms, and I can see it on their faces when they're plastering on fake smiles and pretending to take me seriously.

Situation is, I'm not slow; Turner syndrome almost never causes mental disability. I could join Mensa if I were into that kind of thing. But, lucky me, I have all the most obvious symptoms of missing a sex chromosome. And for some people, nurses included, that looks enough like Down syndrome that they make snap judgements about my mind's capacity. I'm short, chubby, thick-necked and have droopy eyes while Billy is tall, slim, athletic. He's handsome in a familiar way: he probably reminds you of a character on a TV show you like. He looks smart and capable, and I do not. And, yeah, he's a man, and I'm not, and that makes more of a difference than most people want to admit.

The other piece is that he's a legitimate genius who learned calculus when he was 8, whereas I struggled with it in high school like most other reasonably bright kids. So, yeah, I look slow by comparison. It's annoying going through life being judged as less by people who can't think half as well as you can. Sometimes that offers a tactical advantage, but being underestimated every second of your life is mostly a burning itch you can't salve.

I don't resent Billy for any of this. He is my brother and I love him.

In an ideal world, Billy and I would have been identical twin boys. But early on in my embryonic development, a key cell decided, *hey, we don't really need this stupid Y chromosome* and dumped it like old coffee grounds. And that cell lived long, and prospered, and I was born a girl with only one X chromosome in 90% of my cells. Because I'm a genetic mosaic, I do have a few chromosomally complete cells here and there. Mostly in my heart, apparently, because the doctors say I missed all the valve malformations that Turner patients tend to get.

But, because we should have been identical, Billy got us into the Janus Project. There was another fraternal set in the early experiments, but they had nervous breakdowns and had to drop out. That's been happening a lot lately. Shit has been getting real, and some of the other twins aren't coping well.

"You *are* holding out on me, though," Billy says. "I've seen your alpha wave patterns after the visualization exercises. They're the same as mine. You should be having the visions same as me. But you say you aren't. I think you are."

I don't meet his eyes. He's not wrong. So I might as well come clean. "If I open myself up to the visions, sooner or later I'm going to see my own death. And I really don't want to."

Billy sighs. "*Lindy.* C'mon. This is ground-breaking work. I can't advance unless you do. Don't hold me back."

His attempt to send me on a guilt trip makes me want to throw my tea in his face. But I don't. Again, he's not wrong: the experiments are set up to rely on the kind of shared memories and shared mental traits that twins have. Each twin in a set must alternatingly function as the experimental driver and the experimental observer. There's more to it, all stemming from a complicated branch of quantum neurophysics that I'm embarrassed to say I don't understand. Billy understands it, which is why he worked so hard to talk us into the experiments.

I lay my hands on the table and lean forward to whisper. "I don't see how you can be so sanguine about all this. Once I see my death, it's a *fixed point.* I have observed it and can't change it. What good is that kind of knowledge if I can't do anything about it? How is that anything but a terrible burden?"

Billy is still looking at me as if I'm being stupid, as if we're at the water park and I'm a kid holding up the line at the water slide because I'm afraid to climb the ladder. "That's not how this is going to work."

"How can you say that? Dr. Klingler straight-up told us that it's physics. The future is the inevitable product of the past, and once we observe the future, it *cannot* be changed."

"Dr. Klingler doesn't understand the science as well as he thinks he does."

I'm so frustrated that my stomach is starting to churn, so I glare down at my tea. "How can you say that? He writes physics textbooks, for God's sake. He was very clear: we can't change our observed future any more than we can change our past."

"Well, he's correct on that last point."

I look up, startled. Billy is smiling enigmatically. He reaches out and takes a very firm grip on my left wrist as if we're about to try another joint visualization exercise.

"We can't change the future any more than we can change the past," he says, "but we can't change it any *less*, either."

My brother drops his voice so low that I can only just barely hear him. "This isn't about turning ourselves into useful Cassandras for the military. This is about becoming time travelers. The difference between what we're doing and what visionaries like H.G. Wells predicted is that we don't need a special vessel–we just need our own bodies. We're limited only by our own timelines, but I assure you that our expiration dates are not fixed by first impressions unless we're too afraid to be masters of our own destiny."

I feel a chill and an electric rise in my core, as if Billy is channeling energy into me. I can feel the door inside me opening, and this time I don't try to shove it closed.

"Do you remember when we were both kids in late 1997?" he asks. "Apple stock was just about the lowest it had ever been, but just a few months later they'd release their G3 line and stock would bump, and a couple years later they'd unveil the first iPods. And then their stock would rocket and never come back down. Can you imagine what our lifestyle would be like if I'd talked Dad into investing his savings in Apple stock back in '97? Or, hell, Amazon? Or both?"

Billy has always been good at talking our parents into things, and in 1997 we were 8 and they were both in awe of his rapid-onset genius. His golden boy status would get a bit tarnished when he was a teenager who got busted for writing a worm that siphoned money out of a local corporation's mainframe systems–Billy used every bit of his charm to talk his way into probation and community service for *that* one–but when he was a little kid, Dad would have done nearly anything Billy laid out a solid plan for.

So I can absolutely picture him approaching Dad after school with statistical predictions and company histories all done up in colorful PowerPoint slides on his laptop while I played with Legos in the corner by the hearth.

"This seems like a great opportunity," Dad mused.

"We need to act soon," Billy replied earnestly. "These stocks won't be cheap for long. Other people will figure this out."

I feel dizzy as if I've been turned upside-down, and I have to close my eyes to still my vertigo and keep myself from vomiting.

When I open them again, we're not in the diner. We're in an upscale restaurant, the kind that specializes in molecular gastronomy. The walls are painted black, and the ceiling is exquisite graffiti by artist Hiroyasu Tsuri. Billy's sipping a smartini–gin and vermouth with suspended bubbles of neuro-enhancing herbs–and I'm drinking a very pleasant Tieguanyin Oolong that cost more than most people make in a day.

"We'd be very comfortable," I say.

"But is comfort enough?" Billy asks. "Ultimately, what is the point of living well if you're still going to die?"

"Invent immortality?" I ask. If anyone is smart enough to do it, Billy is.

But he shakes his head. "I was born 50 years too early for that. Next century, sure, people with our kind of money will escape death. We can make it to 120, but no further, and we'll still get old."

He's right. I can see myself sitting in a theatre listening to a talk on longevity research, wistfully rubbing age-spotted hands. "The information is there…"

"But the implementation is just out of reach. Too many pieces, and I can never get my hands on them all in time."

"You could freeze yourself," I offer. "Get thawed out when the technology is in place."

"Cryonics are no good; there's always irreversible tissue damage."

"Then I guess you'll have to take out an old-fashioned genetic insurance policy and have kids like everybody else." I can't have kids, probably, because of the effects of my genetic abnormality. I sip my expensive tea.

"What do you know about our great-great-grandfather?" he asks.

I refill my cup from the dainty pot. "I'm not sure I even know his name."

"I'm *very* sure I don't know his name," he replies. "And that highlights the problem with descendants: even if you were the best parent who ever lived, you'll probably be forgotten fifty years after you die. Unless you did something that put you in the history books, and then kids don't matter anyway."

"So the point is to be…historical?"

"The point is to be *remembered*. The point is to have *mattered*. At a *species* level."

"That's a tall order."

"Maybe not as tall as you think. Consider religions, and all the influence they've exerted on history. The Abrahamic religions in particular–Christianity, Islam, and Judaism–have ruled the history of the Western world for the past two thousand years. And what do Abraham, Muhammed, and Jesus all have in common besides geography, sandals, and Y chromosomes?"

The chromosome comment feels like a dig, but if I remark on it, he'll just accuse me of being oversensitive. "They were individual men with loyal followers?"

"True, but what else?"

"They were prophets?"

"And what's a prophet?" he asks.

I know it's a largely rhetorical question, but I answer anyhow. "A person, nearly always a man, who communicates with the Divine to bring new knowledge and wisdom to humanity."

"And often that knowledge comes in the form of predictions of the future, does it not?"

I nod. "It does."

"So how difficult do you think it would be for a young boy, a boy with extraordinary powers of persuasion and calculation and a real ability to see the future, to form his own cult? A cult that then grows to become a perfectly respectable and flourishing religion?"

Modesty was never my brother's strong suit, but again, he's not wrong. And I can absolutely picture him staying up late at night to watch televangelists, practicing their speech patterns and stage moves in a mirror, then convincing our dad's Pentecostal sister Sally to take us to a tent revival. The hayseed preacher lets 9-year-old Billy have the mic, and Billy spins a sermon that gets the entire crowd on their feet hollering Hallelujahs. By the time he's 15, he has his own church, and at 20, he's got his own cable TV show and is on a first-name basis with televangelists like Creflo Dollar and Joyce Meyer.

I feel intensely dizzy again, and must close my eyes and swallow down the nausea.

"It would take some work," I say once I find my voice again. "A lot more work than playing the stock market."

Now we're sitting in the private parlor of his $30 million megachurch sharing a pot of Earl Grey. He's half-listening to me while he looks over his latest audience ratings reports.

"But I suspect you'd get a very loyal followership," I add.

"Oh, very loyal, indeed." He smooths the front of his white dress shirt and adjusts his white satin tie. "And I'm confident that what I've started will continue long after my death."

He sounds profoundly discontented, and disappears into his statistics again.

"But?" I prompt.

"But as a prophet, I'm not effecting the kind of change I want to see in the world," he says. "I'll need to keep working on audience expansion and make the jump to national politics in another eight or nine years. That way, I'll be ready for 2028."

"What happens in 2028?"

"I'll be old enough to run for President."

I'm genuinely startled at the notion. "You'll only be 38…that's very young for President."

"And Donald Trump is very old. And at best an average politician. But his election demonstrates the power of cultivating a television audience. And proves that a demagogue can skip warm-up positions in government. Think I can improve on his model?"

Oh, yes. I can see his campaign unfold in a blur of white suits and American flags. The cheering, chanting crowds, the handshakes, the photo ops. The dizziness hits me like a punch in the stomach, and it takes all my will not to vomit all over the expensive white carpet. I close my eyes and pray, and finally the room stops spinning.

"But you're no demagogue," I gasp as I open my eyes.

"True, but I played one on TV." He winks at me. He's older, grey at his temples, but he's still wearing a white suit.

I look around, disoriented. We're seated across from each other on red-striped sofas in the reception area of the Oval Office in the White House. Between us is a bone china tea set; I recognize the smell of Orange Pekoe.

"Can I let you in on a little secret, Lindy?"

"Absolutely, Will." After I say it, I remember that in this improved version of his life, he decided he preferred that name right around the time he founded his first church. Will fit his ambitions better and kept him from sounding like a Billy Graham wannabe.

He leans forward, and I lean toward him so that he's whispering into my ear over the tea set.

"I don't believe in God," he says. "And I think religion is a rotting fungus infecting humanity. It's irrational and has inhibited progress in almost every meaningful human endeavor."

I blink. "But you've–"

"–been using it as a means to my ends. Nothing more or less. And now that the ends are in my grasp, I'm going to gradually drop my pretense and turn up the heat. Slowly, so that the croaking chorus of Christiamphibians who voted me in don't realize they're going to be boiled if they stay in their pot."

Will was always a bit cynical and arrogant, but apparently those traits are his alpha and omega now. "What do you intend to do?"

"The fundamentalist religions have got to go," he says. "Fortunately, I can start with Islam and orthodox Judaism before I move to eliminate the strains infecting stubbornly religious whites."

Someone knocks on the door.

"Come in," Will says.

A man in an Army colonel's uniform enters with his hat in his hands. "Mr. President, the drones are ready for deployment. But there are a lot of women and children in the targeted mosques, sir. Are you sure–"

"Yes, I'm quite sure," Will says. "We must eliminate the terrorist threat at any cost. Initiate the strikes."

The colonel looks profoundly troubled, but he nods. "Yes, sir. I'll pass along the order."

The door shuts with a click.

"Jesus Christ," I say. "You're deliberately killing innocent people?"

"I'm eliminating survivors who would be moved to activism and revenge. I'm eliminating people infected with fundamentalism who would pass it on to others. I'm bringing death to people who would have eventually died anyhow. I'm helping humanity throw off the chains of superstition so it can reach its potential."

I cannot believe what he's saying. Is this my brother? It looks like him, but does not sound like him. Apparently, those decades of preaching television religion broke his moral compass.

"Do you have any idea how many people you're going to kill?"

"According to my calculations, between one and three billion, give or take. But the ideal limit on human population to ensure sustainability is no more than two billion. So even after I'm done, we'll have to figure out how to achieve another 50% reduction in population. Regrettably, any military action is fairly damaging to the environment, and we'll have to seek remediation for those effects as well."

I rub my eyes. My head is spinning, but the room won't change. "You're going to take credit for the calculated deaths of billions of people?"

"When it's all over, of course. I'm making a difficult but necessary decision. When I'm done, the Earth will be ruled by rational minds, and I will be remembered as the architect of a bright new world."

I pause for a long time and we drink tea in silence. My hands are shaking, and I try to still them. This version of my brother would probably have me shot dead if I showed even a quarter of the dismay I'm feeling. No, I can see that future: he *will* shoot me dead. He needs to believe I'm still on his side, or at least a neutral observer. My mind is cranking as hard as it ever has, trying to grasp infinite probabilities and causes and effects as I attempt to find a solution for this nightmare.

"Do you remember when we were kids?" I finally ask. "I mean, little kids, before anyone figured out you were a genius."

"Like when we were four or five?" he replies.

"Yes. When we were four. Do you remember when we went to Oxbow Lake for a picnic? And Mom and Dad fell asleep on the picnic blanket but you and I wanted to go look at tadpoles?"

I can picture it very clearly in my mind. Billy and I walked down to the shore where tadpoles and minnows flitted in a few feet of water. It was a beautiful day with a soft breeze and cloudless blue sky. The only sound was the water lapping at the muddy shore and the buzz of dragonflies zooming through the air.

"Look, look, little fishies!" Billy leaned down to point at the silvery flitters.

And I gave him a hard shove, and he tumbled forward into the water. He hadn't had any swimming lessons yet. His thrashing carried him farther from shore into deeper water. I stood transfixed, watching him rise and sink, rise and sink. And sink.

When he'd been down for ten Mississippi, I gave into my panic and ran shrieking back to my parents. My father woke, realized what had happened, and dove in to save Billy, who'd gone without oxygen for nearly two minutes. He performed CPR while Mom drove us to the Ranger's station to call for help. The ambulance arrived and took him to a regional hospital. I remember sitting in different waiting rooms with a coloring book, feeling sick to my stomach.

Billy was in a coma for nearly a week, and when he came out of it, he wasn't the same. Not nearly the same. Suddenly, I was the smart one, the lucky one. And Billy was my brother, rather than me his sister, and because I could never admit to the terrible thing I'd done, I swore I'd always be there to take good care of him.

"Don't 'member." With shaky hands, Billy sets down his sippy cup of iced Lipton tea and slumps back in his wheelchair. He puts his hands over his ears; the diner is filling up with the lunchtime crowd and I can tell that all the noise is bothering him.

"I know." I lean across the booth table to wipe a bit of jelly off his chin with my napkin. He can't recall anything about the day he nearly drowned. It's better this way. "But you still like fishies, right? You still want to go to the aquarium at the zoo?"

He brightens and smiles crookedly. "We see purposes?"

That's how he pronounces "porpoises." He's not so good with words, but he's still a charmer, and he's got the nursing staff at his care facility all wrapped around his little finger. I take him out someplace every Sunday and most Wednesdays if I can manage it. My workplace offers a flex schedule, and I take advantage of it for Billy's sake.

"You betcha!" I tell him. "Porpoises, and manatees, and penguins, too!"

"Lindy?"

Ada, one of the aides who works Billy's floor, has paused by our table. This diner is just down the street from the care facility, and staff frequently come in here for coffee or a quick bite between shifts.

I smile at her. "Hey, good to see you. Working this evening?"

"I'll be on until midnight." She turns her attention to Billy and speaks just a little louder. "I can't miss a chance to hang out with my favorite mister!"

She pats his shoulder and he grins up at her, resting his head against her hand. He's adorable.

"It's a real joy seeing you come in so often to take him places," she says. "Most folks, they put someone in a nursing home, they don't visit much, you know?"

I nod. "He's my brother, and I want to do right by him. I wish I could keep him at home, but he needs more help than I can give."

"Billy's a real light in the place. I know he makes a difference in my life, and you make a difference in his, and that's great to see."

A hard knot rises in my throat. "Thank you."

"Oh, and we're showing *Finding Nemo* in the rec room at 7pm. He loves that movie, and he'd be sad to find out he missed it."

"I'll be sure to get him back in time."

We exchange a bit more small talk, and then she goes to a table she's sharing with some other aides. I pay our bill, brush the crumbs off Billy's Superman tee shirt, and wheel him out onto the sidewalk. The stop for the bus that will take us to the zoo is just a couple of blocks away.

"Miss Jameson?" a man calls.

I turn and see a smiling white guy in his mid-30s walking toward me. He's wearing a dark suit that practically screams government agent. Something about his face is familiar, but I can't place it.

"Yes?" I ask.

"My name is Robert Mainward, and I'm working with a special research group called the Janus Project." He shows me an official-looking government ID. "We're looking for twin volunteers, and I have reason to believe that participating in our program would be very beneficial for your brother. And you."

I shake my head. "Thank you, but I'm not interested."

"I am absolutely sure that we could offer your brother a chance at a fully productive life," Mainward says. "Wouldn't you want that?"

"Of course I would."

He pulls a business card from his inside breast pocket. "Please call me later when you're not busy. I promise you won't regret it."

I take the card, utter a hurried *Thanks, goodbye* and push Billy to our bus stop. I pause at a nearby trashcan and stare at Mainward's contact information. As I toss the white cardboard rectangle inside, it occurs to me that I have no idea how I'm going to die.

Some regrets I can live with.

"Purposes?" Billy asks.

"Yes, we'll be seeing them soon."

A Noble Endeavor

The linen room door slammed open, and Mariette nearly dropped the towel she was folding. She tried to be very still and didn't turn around. The stump of her left knee ached inside the leather cup of her peg leg.

"You!" The plantation foreman Zeke sounded annoyed and worried. "Girl! Go on up to Doc Bronson's lab."

Her heart beat faster and her vision seemed to go dark at the edges. She focused on folding the towel just so. Told herself that it was only the sharp odor of the lye soap that was making tears rise in her eyes. There were four other girls working shoulder to shoulder with her–the Master had seven legitimate children and it took nearly that many slaves to handle all their laundry–so he could have meant any of them. Couldn't he? But deep down she knew that since she was the only girl in the room who still had all her fingers, he had to be calling her out. Dr. Bronson only wanted helpers with good hands.

Oh, Lord, please don't let him mean me, she prayed. *Ain't it enough I lost my leg? I got to lose my mind and my life, too?*

"Girl!" Zeke's huge, calloused hand landed on her shoulder and spun her around. The tip of her peg skidded on the polished floor and she nearly fell.

He glowered down at her, his gray eyes bloodshot from sun and smoke and rum. "You deaf, girl?"

"No sir," she stammered. The other girls were staring at her; she could practically feel their relief like the ocean breeze upon her sweating skin. "I'm sorry. I didn't 'spect you meant me?"

"I do mean you. Get on up to the lab."

"He need fresh linens?" *Please, Lord, let it be that he just needs sheets or a towel or a clean chamber pot.*

"I reckon he probably does, but that damn fool Bo touched something he shouldn't and now what little brains he had are drippin' out his ears."

She froze again. Dr. Bronson's laboratory had only been up on the hill for a year but already six boys had gone in as assistants and been carried out weeks later, stone dead or babbling with madness. Rumor was that Dr. Bronson's research back in London had killed so many working-class apprentices that eventually the boys' grieving parents revolted and burned the laboratory to the ground. Dr. Bronson escaped across the Atlantic with his life and lab books and sought refuge at his cousin's Barbados sugar plantation.

Nobody quite knew what was going on inside the laboratory, nor would Mr. Turner speak of the arrangement he'd made with the scientist. Some folks whispered that Dr. Bronson had promised Mr. Turner tremendous riches if his research succeeded. They said that surely Dr. Bronson was trying to create a Philosopher's stone to turn lead into gold. Others said that Mr. Turner was desperate to save his eldest son Johnny from the dissolution and vicious rages he'd flown into ever since the young man returned from a stint in the British navy. If the doctor had promised a cure, then perhaps he was driving his slave assistants mad on purpose to test remedies for Johnny. But if not...Mariette shuddered.

The foreman cuffed her on the side of her head, making her ear ring painfully. "Quit yer dawdlin' and get up there! If I catch you lollygaggin' I'll take you to Johnny. You want that?"

For a moment, Mariette thought she might faint, but she forced herself to say, "No sir."

Her mind fogged with terror, she moved like one of the clockwork men of Boston as she loaded a set of towels and a fresh set of sheets into a basket and marched out of the linen room. Whatever horrors awaited her in the laboratory, they would be far better than being a plaything for Johnny Turner.

He was the reason she'd lost her leg. After Johnny returned from the navy, his father made him foreman over the family's sugar cane plantation, reasoning that with his military experience his eldest would maintain good order and keep the slaves productive. Mr. Turner didn't mind if his boys satisfied their male urges on female slaves or entertained themselves by thinking up ever-more-gruesome ways of tormenting recaptured runaways. He was fond of saying, "A scared slave is a hard worker. Make them fear you more than they fear God and you'll always have a bountiful crop."

But Mr. Turner was first and foremost a businessman; as much as he figured slaves needed harsh discipline and that his sons needed to blow off a little steam now and then, he'd sunk good money into his slaves and didn't want to see his property damaged without reason. Johnny started carrying a boarding axe he'd kept from his navy days and anytime a slave displeased him, he'd lop off one of their fingers, starting with the pinkie. Some slaves healed up well enough but others got infections and lost hands, arms, even their lives. And the doctoring got expensive. It was Mariette's own crippling that finally made Mr. Turner lock Johnny in his rooms and bring Zeke down from South Carolina to work as his new foreman.

When Mariette was ten, a slave named Tom ran away and was recaptured when he tried to stow away on a ship bound for London. The slave catchers brought him back beaten half to death, but that wasn't good enough for Johnny. He made the slaves build a gibbet in the yard and hung Tom from it by his arms. Then Johnny made the slaves pile dry brush beneath him and light it. He made all the slaves stand in a circle around the gibbet and watch as Tom screamed and slowly burned to death.

Mariette stayed rooted to the spot, but when the flesh started peeling off Tom's feet, she closed her eyes. Johnny noticed her averted gaze and flew into a rage.

"You watch as long as I tell you to watch!" He pulled his cane from his belt and stabbed the blade through her bare foot into the red dirt.

She remembered the sudden mind-breaking pain, and then everything going black. The days after that were hazy in her memory. She remembered lying on her mother's cot in their tiny coral hut, her mother trying to get her to drink some bitter medicinal draught. Then there was the horror of waking up to find herself strapped to a board, a leather strip in her mouth to keep her from biting off her own tongue or breaking her teeth, and the physician from Bridgetown heating his bone saw in the fire while telling her mother, "Hold her down. This won't take but a minute."

When she finally awoke from the fever, her leg was gone from a few inches below her knee and she was so weak that all she could do was polish silverware in the manor. Her weakness lasted close to a year; Mr. Turner seemed regretful and had his own family physician check on her to make sure her wound healed as well as possible. Mariette was light-skinned enough to be a presentable house slave, but the frowns that Mrs. Turner cast in her direction made her begin to suspect that the man who put her in her mother might have been Mr. Turner himself. Even though Johnny was seldom allowed outside, the mere mention of his name caused an unparalleled terror amongst the slaves throughout the whole parish.

I'll survive this, Mariette vowed to herself as she marched up the hill to the laboratory. She could hear the chug of the steam-powered generator behind the building. It ran day and night and reminded her of a cabless locomotive with no track or cars. Heat from the engine made the air above the laboratory shimmer like a mirage. Her peg leg was sticking in the muddy road and pulling it free over and over hurt her knee and hip and made the leather straps around her thigh chafe. *I don't know how I'll survive, but I will.*

"Come in!" Dr. Bronson called in response to her knock. "The door's not locked."

Mariette went inside. Her breath fogged in the frigid air. How could it possibly be so cold inside when it was so hot outdoors? She shivered in her thin cotton shift.

The layout of the laboratory seemed similar to the first floor of the plantation manor–Mr. Turner had hired the same architect for both. But whereas the Turners had made their entry hall into a light, airy parlor with comfortable seats, Dr. Bronson had blocked off all the windows with heavy oak bookshelves whose boards bowed under the weight of leather-bound tomes and wooden shipping boxes filled with manuscripts and correspondence. The only chair in the room sat behind a candle-lit writing desk piled with more books and papers. Deprived of sunlight and only dimly illuminated by the desk candles and gaslamps guttering in sconces, the room seemed as oppressive as a mortuary. The strange chemical stink in the air added to her goose-fleshed feeling that she'd stepped into a house of death.

"Hm." A tall, thin man of about fifty stepped from a shadow and approached her, leaning heavily on a silver-filigreed cane. He looked her up and down, disappointment clear on his gaunt, clean-shaven face. "I told the foreman to send me a boy."

Mariette set the linen basket down, mind racing to pick the words least likely to anger the scientist. "I reckon Zeke couldn't find any to send. All the men are needed for the cane harvest."

"Hm." His eyes fell on her peg. "Did you lose your leg in the fields? I'm told that a cane knife can cut a grown man nearly in two."

She shook her head. "I disobeyed Master Johnny."

"Ah. Of course. Well, I hope you intend to be more obedient here, because you'll be handling lethal substances and a failure to follow my instructions will have dire consequences."

"Yes, sir."

"I'll have you know that I do not approve of this peculiar institution of African slavery," he remarked. "The Empire should have abolished it when I was just a lad. But alas, the House of Commons rejected the Slavery Abolition Act and no one has resurrected it. I expect that it has not seemed an urgent matter ever since Charles da Vinci began producing his wondrous clockwork automatons."

Dr. Bronson sighed wistfully. "The best plantations have already replaced their black chattel with gleaming brass servants. I keep telling my dear cousin that he should modernize his operation and replace the lot of you, but he insists that he needs your wits as well as your backs. I have my doubts as to what kind of wits are necessary to cut cane, but I do concede that the mechanical men are rather dear, and of course cannot produce more of their kind. One cannot deny the fertility of negro women."

He grimaced. "In the meantime, whites are forced to share their civilization with Africans, which inevitably leads to...miscegenation."

The simultaneously leering and disdainful look he gave her made her flush with anger, and she could not stay silent. "I was born here in Barbados. So was my mama, and *her* mama. We're Bajan. I don't know anything about Africa."

Fortunately, Dr. Bronson seemed to take her words as a statement of ignorance rather than a rebuttal to his declarations.

"I have visited that Dark Continent on several occasions, and it is a wonder." He smiled down at her. "So much gold, ivory, and diamonds! The wildlife and landscape...amazing. Truly Africa is wasted on Africans. The best thing for the place will be for European nations to colonize the whole continent and take charge of its natural resources."

"What about the Africans who live there?" She struggled to keep her tone neutral.

"Indeed! I do have a plan I intend to propose when the time is right; I admit that my reputation has become somewhat tarnished, but I fully expect that the success of my endeavors here will result in considerable acclaim. My ship shall rise on a very high tide indeed, and royals from all countries should rightly seek my advice on intellectual matters.

"But I digress. Aside from the problem of Africans, England and Europe face the problem of the underclass. Mostly people of corrupted Irish, Gyptian, and Spanish blood, you know. Those in poverty breed disease, commit crimes and foster wretchedness. Some of my colleagues think we should let the poor starve. Natural selection! But tenderhearted women and religious sorts are forever running soup kitchens and charities and the human corruption keeps spreading.

"What I propose is that we offer a low-cost, nutritionally-sound potted food to the English and European poor. The food would be spiced with silphium and asafoetida to induce infertility in the women who eat it. Thus, the poor will stay healthy enough to serve as useful workers or soldiers, but they'll stop breeding like confounded rabbits. The poor shall only exist as needed to turn the wheels of commerce. Civilization will prosper like never before!"

Mariette blinked. "That seems like a well-turned plan, sir. But what has it got to do with Africans?"

"Ah! I thought that bit was implied. Africans will serve as the meat component of the canned food. I have extensively plotted the logistics, and they're entirely economical. By the time our canneries run out of Negroes, I expect the underclass breeding problem will have been splendidly remedied."

Mariette's heart pounded and her vision was starting to go edge-dark again. In her mind, she carefully removed her peg leg and with both hands drove it straight through Bronson's loathsome chest, mud and all.

Instead, she took a deep breath, bent and picked up the linen basket, keeping her head down for fear that her eyes might show her rage. She knew she needed a few moments alone to calm herself down. Because if she was not very, very calm, she would die in this house, and Bronson would move on to the next hapless girl.

She'd spent her whole life hearing people, even other slaves, say that the world would be a better place without Negroes in it. It was common sport for the plantation owners to gather at a fish fry or around a card table to complain bitterly about the blacks who were responsible for their livelihoods. If she'd had a penny for every well-heeled planter who'd declared his slaves were lazy, worthless good-for-nothings who should be fed to the hogs simply because they needed to rest once in a while, she'd have been able to buy her own freedom.

Bronson's vile sentiments were common as scuttle crabs, but normally they were just the idle spouts of spoiled old men. The scientist clearly had ambitions and a twisted moral conviction driving him. Might his monstrous plans reach the ears of equally monstrous people who could make them real?

If there was any chance he might succeed, he had to be stopped. Even if it meant she died under Johnny's hatchet. In her mind, she saw herself creeping up to the laboratory house, blocking the doors shut with timber, and dousing it with lamp oil. It was easy and terrible to imagine Bronson screaming as he burned inside with all his notes.

But perhaps there was a better way that didn't end in fire? She wouldn't know until she found out what he was trying to do. Mr. Turner had surely not brought Bronson here to refine his plans to turn Africans into potted meat. The laboratory work must have something to do with curing Johnny's madness...or anyhow the doctor had convinced Mr. Turner that it did.

"Would you like me to change your bedclothes, sir?"

"Be quick about it. I'll need you in the lab shortly."

Mariette followed Bronson into a short hallway that was even colder than the foyer study, and she could more clearly hear the chug of the steam engine along with the electrical hum of some other kind of apparatus. Twin gaslights brightly illuminated the hall, which only had room for a narrow table along one wall and a rail of wooden coat hooks along the other. A couple of long, padded canvas coats and brass goggles hung from the rack.

"Remove anything you might have in your pockets and leave it on the table." Bronson frowned at her peg leg. "Is that secured with iron or steel nails?"

She shook her head. "It has bronze buckles and such, but the rest is leather and wood."

"Any iron or steel at all?"

"No sir."

"Good. Do you know letters and numbers?"

"Only a little." Mariette's heart beat fast at the lie. Unlike most of the slaves on the plantation, she had learned to read quite well, but her instincts were telling her that she should keep her knowledge close to her bosom. Bronson needed to underestimate her.

As a house slave, Mariette was expected to follow simple directions and recipes and to take messages from visitors. And so she'd been taught to read and write along with Mr. Turner's youngest children. Her lessons ended once she knew practical words like "fish" and "sugar" and "cup."

But while Mariette was still recovering from her amputation, Mr. Turner's mother Helen–possibly her own grandmother, she now realized–started to go blind. Helen loved penny dreadfuls shipped in from England and read them by the boxload until her vision began to fail. None of Mr. Turner's legitimate children had the time for (or interest in) reading to their granny. And so the elder Mrs. Turner enlisted Mariette to read her stories and London newspapers aloud to her. It was hard, at first, but the old lady was eager enough for entertainment and company that she patiently gave Mariette the proper pronunciations once she spelled out unfamiliar words.

"You best not let on to anyone how well you can read," Mrs. Turner said one day when Mariette brought in her afternoon tea. "Folks don't trust slaves with too-sharp minds. Can't say I blame them, but I reckon you're one of the good ones, so it can be our little secret."

The old lady's words were a cozy lambswool shawl draped over a cane knife: *Displease me, and I'll destroy you.*

But Mariette was adept at keeping her perhaps-grandmother happy. The girl's starving mind absorbed the informal tutoring, and soon she was sneaking into the library at night and reading more difficult books, puzzling them out by candlelight with the aid of the huge cloth-bound copy of Johnson's *Dictionary* that roosted on the bottom shelf. During the day, she took great care to dust the library thoroughly so that no one would see the tracks of books being pulled from shelves.

She read the entire works of Shakespeare, and but kept returning to his play *The Tempest.* It was mostly because of the magic-filled story, which she could easily picture happening there on Barbados. But it was also because of Caliban and Miranda. She hated him for trying to rape her, but at the same time she thought that he was right to resent her father Prospero, who pretended he'd done Caliban a favor by enslaving him. And Miranda had no freedom at all, even though she got her handsome prince. The play's happy ending didn't fully satisfy her mind, and she felt compelled to re-read it, as if the words would rearrange themselves and some other ending might emerge.

If there had been any books on Africa, she'd have surely read and re-read them, too, but the subject was of no interest to the Turners.

"I can read some recipes and such," she told Bronson. The other house slaves knew she could read that much, and admitting it meant he'd be less likely to catch her lie.

"Hm," He seemed disappointed. "I suppose I am the victim of wishful thinking, as ever. The African mind is not suited to higher thought processes, but I do miss having helpers who can read things for themselves."

This time, the peg leg she wielded in her mind went straight through his eye and out the back of his skull.

Instead, she said, "I will do my best despite my mental deficiencies, sir."

At that, his eyes narrowed a bit and his eyebrows went up, but she kept her face carefully neutral and his moment of suspicion that she was being sarcastic apparently passed. He took one of the padded canvas coats and one set of the brass goggles from the rack and handed them to her.

"Put these on. There are gloves in the pockets of the coat; put them on, too. Button it up to your neck; you'll want the protection from the cold."

She did as he asked. The gloves she found were made of a thinner waxed canvas and had leather palms and fingertips like Mrs. Turner's gardening gloves.

Everything was several sizes too big for her, but she was able to cinch the strap on the goggles down over her head scarf so that the heavy leaded glass lenses stayed in place over her eyes.

Bronson reached for the bronze knob of the door leading into what had to be the main laboratory and paused, giving her a sharp look. "You are about to embark on a most noble endeavor. It's entirely possible–and, if you fail to obey me, highly likely–that you shall lose your life in this room. But know that you are doing it for the greater good of mankind."

Despite the disdain he seemed to have for her, there was a showman's gleam in his eye. He craved an audience, Mariette realized. And if she were careful in her questions, she could use his eagerness to good advantage.

"What will we be doing, sir? Is it something to help Johnny Turner?"

"He will be helped, yes, but my research will do far more."

Bronson opened the door into the laboratory. There was a strange burnt smell like the air after lightning struck a tree. The first thing Mariette saw was a pair of huge round glass tanks conjoined by a glass box with leather-covered portholes. Each of the round tanks was seamed with riveted brass strips and had enormous gleaming coils of copper wire at the top and bottom.

In the tank to her left, a strange, pulsing mass floated mid-air between the coils. It writhed bonelessly like a living thing. One moment it seemed black as tar, the next red as the setting sun, the next white as the moon. Even though it gave off no strong light, looking directly at it made her eyes ache, and she felt the exposed skin on her face grow warm as if she were standing beneath the noonday sun despite the cold of the room.

"What is that?" Mariette squinted away from the tanks and finally noticed the wall of brass instrument panels and racks of wooden tongs and blown glass bubbles. Thick rubber-coated cables ran from the copper coils to sockets in the base of the panels.

"Achronic aether," Bronson replied proudly. His breath fogged away from him as if he were not a man but a dragon exhaling smoke. "Others have postulated its existence; I am the first to distill it and contain it. And soon, I shall be the only man able to control it."

"W-what does it do?" Her teeth were starting to chatter, whether from fear or physical chill she couldn't tell.

"At the moment, it strips heat from air, life from flesh, and sanity from minds," he replied. "But once it is properly tamed, it shall make me master of both time and space."

She stared at the blob again despite her discomfort, and she felt the hairs rise on the back of her neck beneath her stiff canvas collar. "How?"

"You're beholding a fundamental solvent of the universe. We think of time and distances as fixed, linear. Trinidad is 60 leagues away; even if you took to the skies in a dirigible, you still have to travel the distance. Christmas is seven months away, and the faithful must suffer through every day between now and then. But with a stabilized crystal of achronic aether, a man of intelligence can escape the mundane bonds of time and distance and go when and where he wishes."

Mariette paused, thinking of Scrooge and his glimpse of the future in Charles Dickens' *A Christmas Carol.* "He could go where and when...and change his fate?"

"Of course!" Bronson's laugh was equal parts delight and scorn. "There's no profit in merely being an observer! The possessor of the crystal could go to the future to discover wonders not yet invented...or go into the past and change his own starting fortunes entirely. The possibilities are limitless! But, as per my agreement with your owner, my first proof-of-concept will be to go back in time to convince Johnny Turner to stay here in Barbados instead of joining the British Navy."

Her stomach buzzed as if she, too, had been hooked up to the electrical current from the great steam engine laboring outside. The achronic aether pulsed emerald inside its magnetic glass cage. No science could prove it, but she was certain it was eyelessly observing her.

"How many assistants have you had, sir?"

"Oh, seventy or eighty...I've rather lost count." He paused. "Ours is a world of hundreds of millions of people. One might believe that an individual can have no possible consequence in the swarming sea of humanity, but history has proved otherwise over and over. Imagine that the great Leonardo da Vinci had left no heirs...would the world now have clockwork men and flying machines? He mattered; and soon, I shall matter even more."

Day after day, Mariette took the painful hike up the hill to the laboratory, where she did exactly what Bronson told her to do. It was an endless, nerve-wracking repetition of getting a pair of wooden tongs and a round flask, using the glove box to coax a bit of the aether from the first chamber into the glass, and then quickly transferring the aether-laden flask into the second chamber. Once she'd gotten it into that second chamber, she had to hold it perfectly still as Bronson worked his control panel to increase the magnetic fields to try to crush the aether into a crystalline configuration.

If the magnetic field ever failed, the aether would eat through the side of the glass and then through the tongs, and then the substance would behave as if she had dropped it. And if she ever dropped it, one of two immediately fatal things were likely to occur. The aether might explode into a fine black mist that would latch onto the nearest source of heat and moisture: her. And it would freeze her entire body solid before it dissipated back into the cracks of the universe. The second thing was that the aether might stay intact, but would ring like the very bell of doom, vibrating at a frequency guaranteed to drive most people insane if they were close by, and perhaps turn their brains to soup if they were quite near. Bronson had designed the room so that his seat at the instrument panel was a safe distance away.

Mariette did not drop the glass. Every day, she silently prayed to the Christian God and the forbidden Obeah spirits alike that Bronson would keep the magnetic field working. And when he wasn't looking, she strained her eyes to glimpse his notes and try to figure out what he intended to do once he had his crystal. But she gained no useful clues from his scribbles and equations.

At the end of each session, Mariette's shoulders, hands, leg and eyes ached, and her face was as dark as if she'd worked the entire time in the fields. She fell into an exhausted slumber and dreamed of strange worlds far beyond the Earth. She got Sunday afternoons off, as did all of Mr. Turner's slaves after they'd attended church and dutifully listened to the white preacher's sermons, but she found it harder and harder to make small talk with the others. Just as each day she and Bronson drew minutely closer to getting the aether to conform, each day she felt as though her mind was being forced open and taken away into a dimension of probability and causality. Even the Crop Over celebration, which she'd looked forward to every year since she was a small child, couldn't bring her drifting mind back to shore.

But one day in November, Mariette was grimly clutching the tongs as she tried to keep the flask-bound aether steady in the second chamber. Bronson was trying the 316th new magnetic bombardment pattern he'd designed since Zeke ordered her to the laboratory; she had counted them all. Suddenly the aether crackled like hot molasses candy dropping into ice water. In a blink it had collapsed into a perfect, iridescent tetragon that rang like a silver bell.

And in that moment, she nearly dropped it in surprise and wonder, but she held fast at the last minute.

"Sir, sir, come quick!" Mariette had no faith that the aether would be stable and hold its shape for more than a few seconds.

She heard the clatter of Bronson knocking over the tongs rack in his haste to join her.

"Bring it forth!" he demanded.

"But it–"

"Bring it forth!"

Mariette took a deep breath and pulled the flask out of the chamber through the glove box porthole. Once released from the magnetic field, the bean-sized crystal clinked to the bottom of the glass. For one terrible moment, she was certain it was about to explode or eat through the flask, but it glittered perfect and still. Stable.

"Hold it up to the light!" Bronson wore the ecstatic expression of an atheist who had finally found God.

She carried the flask over to a nearby lamp so that Bronson could examine it more closely. Her mind churned. She'd spent so much time in the laboratory that she wanted very badly to see if the crystal worked as Bronson predicted...but she could not forget the terrible fates he wished on people like her. And he'd never revealed how he intended to use the crystal. Even his notes had shed no light on that part of his plan. Should she wait and see? Should she fling the crystal against the wall to destroy it and probably herself and Bronson, too?

To her profound surprise, Bronson snatched the flask out of the tongs with his bare hands.

Bronson's eyes grew wide with wonder, as if he saw something miraculous in the far distance. "It's..."

But then his body jerked as if he'd been struck and his eyes went dull, unresponsive. His knees buckled and the flask slipped from his lifeless fingers.

Mariette lunged forward to catch the flask in her gloved hands before it could shatter on the hard wooden floor.

The moment the glass-clad crystal settled in the palm of her gloved hand, the laboratory seemed to fall away and she felt as though she were floating in the vast, cold darkness amongst the stars.

"I have been summoned." The voice was all around her. "What do you wish? Choose."

"Who are you?" she whispered, terrified.

"Ylem."

Suddenly, the vast wave of all the possibilities in the entire universe crashed down around her. She could go to any time, any world, any dimension, anywhere. The capacity of her mind expanded as fast as light, but it could not keep up with the infinity of possibility in the universe.

"Choose," Ylem demanded. "I have been summoned, and you must choose."

The impossibility of choice in the face of infinity threatened to burn her mind down like a blade of grass caught in a supernova.

But nonetheless, she chose: "I don't want to be a slave. I don't want to have been a slave. I don't want *any* human being to have suffered as we have."

"You have chosen. Now, make it so."

The lines of history and probability and causality opened before her mind like a vast treasure map, and she raced backward through the ages, an Angel of Death for some, a guardian ghost to others. To kill, she had to but brush her spectral hand through a ribcage to stop a heart. To save a dying infant, she had to but picture healthy lungs or a full belly and it was so. But the more greed and evil she erased, the more there seemed to be. Slavery was intertwined with war and conquest so deeply that it was impossible to separate the two. And the wars seemed to go back forever and ever.

After what seemed like an aeon of saving and slaying, she found herself upon a sun-bleached veldt. A family of dark, slender, slightly-built apes clung to each other, keening softly as a gang of tall, burly apes from a different tribe surrounded them, hooting in victory and brandishing sharpened sticks.

She saw into the minds of the big apes. They would slay all the small males and roast them over the fire they had recently learned to capture from lightning strikes. But they might leave some of the small females alive as breeding slaves. These big apes delighted in killing and taking territory, reveled in the misery of the others they drove before them.

And she saw the minds of the small ones. They, too, had learned to use fire to harden clay for pots and beads and to boil the grains they foraged. The small ones delighted in making love and singing and crafting and only killed when they could find no plants or grubs to eat.

Mariette made her choice.

"It is accomplished," Ylem said when she stopped the heart of the last big ape.

For a moment, Mariette found herself back in the lab, staring down at the crystal in the flask in her gloved hands as Bronson lay dead at her feet.

And then the crystal evaporated and the laboratory melted away.

Mariette–no, her name was Kmbana of the Green–stood on the deck of a ship floating above the clouds, staring down into empty hands. Hands that were brown and quite narrow and which bore short red fur. Completely familiar and yet utterly alien.

"Are you all right?" trilled her sister Nmbena in a language so far from English that she could not compare the two, but she knew it just as well.

Kmbana looked up at her sister's earnest amber eyes and excitable whiskers and made herself smile. "Yes. I'm fine. Just daydreaming."

Her mind now held two completely different memories: her life as the slave Mariette, and her new life as Kmbana, and her brain reeled trying to reconcile it all.

"Do you like the new leg?" her sister asked.

"Oh yes," Kmbana replied reflexively as she suddenly remembered that here, in this new now, she'd lost her leg falling over the edge of an airship when she was just a child. "It's lovely."

And it *was* lovely, she realized. It was a gorgeous work of wood and brass made to match her flesh leg, and inside it had clever tiny motors and clockworks to allow her to move the metal foot like a real one.

"It's amazing," Kmbana added.

"Do you think you would like to take a walk along the seashore? The shipmothers are talking about stopping at the island below us."

Her sister pointed over the railing at a teardrop-shaped island, and Kmbana gave a start when she recognized it from the shape she'd once seen on maps: Barbados! She breathed in the smells of rich soil and seaweed. But here it was the tip of a nameless archipelago. She tried to make out the rise where the plantation would have been, but it was all forest.

She wanted to laugh with joy at the wonders of this peaceful new world, but she also wanted to weep for the good she'd inadvertently erased along with the bad. She and her sister and the other millions of souls upon the planet were people, certainly, but none human as she understood humanity. There had never been a British Navy, nor a Johnny Turner to be twisted by it. But there also had never been a Dickens, nor a da Vinci, nor a Shakespeare. There had been others just as brilliant–the Great Mothers they learned about in school–and people had accomplished great works of art and invention in the absence of war. But they were not the same.

It made her profoundly sad to know that she would never read *The Tempest* again.

Apparently her expression clouded, because her sister added, "I think we might be the first to visit this island. We might get to name things we find! Wouldn't you like that?"

Kmbana smiled. "Indeed I would."

Blossoms Blackened Like Dead Stars

I wait with the rest of the Special Space Operations recruits outside the *Apocalypse Treader*'s training auditorium. Soon, we'll be called in to listen to Lieutenant Colonel Patel's orders. We haven't been assigned to our units, yet, and I can't help but notice that there's a whole lot more than a battalion's worth of uniforms milling around in the warehouse-like foyer. The brass must be expecting some serious attrition during this next step of our training. My legs and shoulders constantly ache from our daily runs and workouts down in the high-gravity hold, and my guts still aren't used to the variable gravity on the rest of the ship's levels. After fifty or so sit-ups, I've been feeling like I've been run through with a damn punji stick.

The only upside to my ongoing physical exhaustion is that most nights I can sleep. Most nights the nightmare doesn't come. But last night was not most nights.

So, I'm taking the opportunity to sit down for a while. Consequently, I'm getting side-eye from some recruits. A lot of the others–young guys, mostly, but some of the rougher ladies, too–are standing ramrod-straight and scowling, or they're swaggering around, laughing too loud. Trying to look hard. Like warriors. For whom? The monsters we're here to fight won't give a damn about how tough anybody acts.

A big blond guy drops onto the plastic bench beside me. "Hey."

Of all the people on this ship I wanted sitting next to me, this guy is the very last one. I spotted him the first day aboard the *Treader*: a mountain of Kentucky meat covered in cheesy heavy metal tattoos and badly erased White Power symbols. At some point in his youth, he thought it was a great idea to get a swastika on his neck, right over his jugular, and whoever lasered it off did a terrible job. He covered it with an American flag, but if the light hits it at an angle, you can see the raised scar of the swastika plain as a supernova.

"Joe Jorgensen." He smiles real big and holds his hand out to me for a shake, like he's a used car salesman about to ask me if I'd like a tour of the lot. "You're Beatrice Muñoz, right?"

I know I'm supposed to be professional with the other recruits. I *know,* right? Brothers and sisters in arms and all that. But this backwoods Nazi bastard thinks he can just sashay on up and plop his beefy ass down and expect me to greet him like an old friend? Nah. I'm in too damn much pain for that nonsense.

So I fix him in a basilisk stare that should turn him and all his illegitimate sprogs back in Dogpatch to crumbling pillars of salt, and I growl, "This. Seat. Is. Taken."

His smile falters just a micron. "It's the ink, am I right?"

I keep staring, trying to kill him with my mind. He isn't the first I've tried it on, but I figure with enough practice, someday it might work. I picture his skull exploding, his brains spattering across the glossy void-gray wall behind us.

No luck. His head doesn't burst, so I have to reply. "Could be."

He holds up his hands in an appeasing gesture, and I see the faint outline of a coiled Gadsden flag snake on his palm. That "Don't Tread On Me" thing. It looks more like a pile of shit.

"I can explain," he says.

"Can you." I try to make my voice flat and cold as the wall, so he will just take the hint already and walk on.

But he doesn't budge, so I continue–dropping my voice low, so it can't be overheard, but speaking very clearly, so he can't misunderstand me. "Speaking as one of the more colorful women in this room: I am not here to absolve you of your past actions or inactions. That is not my role, *motherfucker.*"

He doesn't so much as blink at my anger. "I'm not here to ask for absolution."

"Why are you here, then?"

"To pre-emptively clear up any misunderstanding that may be causing undue stress or that may prevent optimal teamwork in the future. I am only asking you to hear me out."

The intelligence and polite calm I hear in his voice does not fit with what I know about men who get the sort of ink he's wearing. And I've met plenty like him. Some of them hooted racial slurs and filth at me and my little sisters from the safety of their jacked-up trucks while we walked home from school. Another beat my uncle Max with a tire iron at a gas station. And yet another put a bullet between my cousin Hernando's eyes at a traffic light. I still want to cave Joe's teeth in with my sidearm, but I'm also just a little curious.

"Okay. What's your story?"

He quickly touches the swastika scar on his neck, the Aryan fist on his left forearm, and the Totenkopf symbol on his right. It's a bit like watching a Catholic priest cross himself.

"I am a man of violence, and I own that," he says in his soft drawl. "My father was a man of hate, and he led me down that path when I was a boy. These tattoos come from that time, but I cannot deny my own history. I was not a man in any sense when I got this ink, and I am trying to make amends for the harm I caused. Making amends means restoring justice and doing the right thing. Part of the amends I need to make here is to assure you that I have dedicated my violent self to the protection of the whole human race. And I promise you here and now that I will lay down my life to save yours."

I blink. My biggest talent, aside from getting stubborn seeds to grow in a lab, is knowing when people are bullshitting me. He's utterly sincere. But I'm not done being skeptical. "You gonna give that speech to everybody here?"

"Yes, ma'am, if it seems like I ought to. But I figured I'd start with you, seeing as you've been giving me glares sharp enough to shave my chin for two weeks straight now."

I snort, amused. "So what changed your mind about people like me?"

He pales and his expression turns grim. "San Angelo."

I'd never heard of that riverside city out in the big empty part of Texas until the spawn of Azathoth chose it as a primary invasion site. Fewer than ten thousand people from that town of 120,000 technically survived. I say technically because many of them are still in comas or catatonic. Other survivors, the ones who initially seemed to have escaped relatively unscathed, killed themselves in the following year, unable to live with what they'd witnessed.

Simply meeting the blister-eyed gaze of a spawn twists your brains. Most of the time, that means depression, mania, anxiety, full-on psychotic breaks. It's the ones who escaped catatonia but not utter madness who gave us the name of Azathoth. Victims who had no connection to each other would babble or scream the name, ranting about a vast, powerful god beyond our galaxy.

Sometimes, when the spawn twist a mind that's already deformed, it makes it into something more. Not something *healthy*, mind you. But keener. More perceptive. More connected to the dark matter of the cosmos. I wonder if that's what happened to Joe. He doesn't seem dumb, antisocial, or self-destructive enough to stain himself the way he has, and I'm starting to think that he isn't. Not *anymore,* anyhow.

I know I'm not the same woman; she'd never set foot on this warship. She'd have seen this place as a vulgar, ugly, necessary evil she wanted no part of. The spawn left a stain in me far darker than any of my tattoos.

"My family moved there from Corbin, Kentucky when I was sixteen," he says. "Me and my pa and my brothers found work in the oil fields. Good money. Paid for most of my ink. Got connected to the Aryan Circle and spent my nights cooking drugs and hurting people. I should be dead ten times over by now."

He shakes his head and picks at his blurry Totenkopf as if he can simply peel it up. I wonder why he didn't cover it or laser it, but I'm guessing he wants the reminder. It's marginally subtler than a neck swastika, at least.

"How many of your family died when the ships came?"

"All of them." He's staring at the ugly snake on his palm as if it's about to start speaking to him. "You ever see a spawn?"

"Yes. I was at the International Lunar Research Station."

I feel a spark of panic as unwanted memories crowd the edges of my consciousness like flies around a drop of nectar. I can't let myself remember the details, I know I won't be able to keep my shit together if I remember the details... and I breathe deeply.

Instead, I visualize a tall, concrete garden wall rising in my mind, and the synopsis of my disaster is engraved there in stark block letters. A memorial for other lives, not mine. I can simply look at it and repeat the stony text if anybody asks what happened and I won't feel a thing. There were far fewer of us to die: 2,000 on the base and ten of us survived. After the habitat's dome shattered, I spent three days hiding from spawn with nothing but freezing moon craters and my space suit for cover. Just two other people made it out the way I did, and both are in long-term mental care facilities.

Joe doesn't ask for any details; either he already knows what happened on the moon, or he can guess. Instead, he just says, "I sure am sorry to hear that."

He looks at my forearm and points to my watercolor tattoo. It's a twisting ladder of DNA, the rungs wound with blossoms: soft pink oleander, white devil's weed, blue moonflowers, flaming milkweed, and purple belladonna. "Were you a scientist?"

"I meant to be. I was a junior in college, and I won an international fellowship to go up there to study the effects of low gravity on alkaloid production in plants. After the NASA team rescued us, I didn't know who the hell I was. Now, I'm trying to be a soldier."

He gets real quiet for a moment, still staring down at the ugly snake. "You get nightmares?"

I feel a spike of panic as my mind almost turns to examine the horror lurking in my neurons, but I breathe deeply, and the calm garden wall rises with one word chiseled on its smooth concrete.

"Yes." I let the word float out into space. It doesn't mean anything. I am not remembering anything.

Joe nods. He doesn't pry further. And from the look on his face, I don't have to ask if he has terrible dreams, too.

"We can't let them get to Earth again," he finally says.

"No. We cannot."

He and I bump fists.

The doors to the auditorium open, and the COs bark at everyone to take their seats inside.

Joe and I file in with the others and drop into narrow theatre seats on the 22nd row. I stare up at the ceiling, marveling at the construction. Most of the ship is made of a new ceramic matrix composite they dubbed tarakium: tougher and lighter than titanium, it blocks ionizing radiation twice as efficiently as lead, and it welds nearly seamlessly. It's not a good conductor of electricity, but if you apply low voltages to it, it glows like an LED. Any part of any surface can become a light source–or a video monitor. I can see the vague reflections of the audience in between the light spots on the ceiling. If

I stare at it long enough, I think I can see the shapes of the poisonous flowers I left to die on the moon.

Many of the others are staring, too. This ship was only possible because American, Indian, and Chinese scientists salvaged the invaders' downed spacecraft and replicated their technology. Fear being the motivator that it is, our politicians stopped squabbling and threw the whole U.S. economic engine behind development. American tech jumped three hundred years in the space of eight. Nobody grew up with this, so nobody's jaded to it yet.

Lieutenant Colonel Mercedes Patel steps onto the stage and takes her place behind the podium. She scans the crowd of us once, slowly, and begins to speak.

"There was...debate, even up to just a few moments ago, about how much I ought to tell you all about what happens next," she says, looking grave. "My own personal code of conduct calls for absolute transparency in all matters unless national security dictates otherwise. Mine is a traditional view. This, as you know, is no traditional war; the *Apocalypse Treader* and our other warships are scheduled to join with ships from China, India, and the European Union for the next offensive. This is World War III, but every soldier fights to save humanity."

I wonder if that's true. Certainly, every spawn we kill out here–that's the big plan: track down their nests or hives or whatever you want to call them and nuke them to oblivion–is a spawn that can't go to Earth and wreak horrors. But that's not why everyone signed on. Some don't care about the big sweaty mess of humanity but want to save their own families. Some don't give a damn about anyone, but the paycheck's appealing. Others have better ways to make money, but they're itching for the kind of epic fight that goes down in the history books.

And a few once stared into the eyes of a spawn, and the stain on their brain is telling them they've got to do it again.

"Unfortunately, traditional means of combat have proved inadequate against our inhuman foes," Patel says. "We have had to adopt...experimental tactics. And while I can't offer as much transparency as I'd prefer, you all need a better idea of what's in store for you."

Patel pauses again, touching her earpiece, and she nods curtly to someone offstage. "You have all volunteered to lay down your lives to protect America and the rest of the Earth, and we are all thankful for your offer of sacrifice. In most any other conflict, even a highly dangerous one, our soldiers have found comfort in the knowledge that if they do their jobs well and survive, they can return to their homes and families. They know that they will be inevitably changed by war, but if things go well, they can lay down their arms and live out their lives in peace. That...cannot happen here."

I sit up straighter in my seat. A murmur ripples through the crowd. I don't know how I feel about this, mostly because I don't actually have any kind of plan for what to do when this is all over.

Patel holds up her hands. "Please, note that I am not saying that this will be a suicide mission. It is highly dangerous, yes; even those of you who've only seen the spawn on television know that much. We hope for victory. We hope that our soldiers will survive. But we very recently determined that those who proceed with the next phase of training cannot return to Earth. This is due to the possibility of infecting our ecosphere with dangerous biological contaminants. Those who serve here must stay in outer space."

I can tell that many of the recruits are shocked by this news, but I'm not. Obviously, none of us has the security clearance to know what the brass is planning, but I already figured that we'd be throwing bouquets of biological weapons. The spawn don't get the courtesy of the Geneva Protocol. Which means that we don't, either.

"It's possible that we may find a solution that enables a return to Earth down the road," she says, "but for now, this is our reality. And you all deserve time to consider the ramifications of that for you and your families before you've passed the point of no return. You have forty-eight hours to decide. Those who opt out will be reassigned to first-response positions on Earth with no loss of rank, though of course you will lose special combat pay. We have fertility specialists available to extract sperm or ova from those of you who want to continue but wish to send a genetic legacy back to your families."

A genetic legacy. I always figured my boy-crazy little sisters would gladly fall on that grenade for me. Marriage and babies have never much appealed to me, and any interesting genes I have are surely scattered in my siblings, too. I glance at Joe, thinking about his annihilated family in Texas, and I wonder if he's got anybody dirtside who would want to make a bunch of test-tube Joe Juniors. But asking seems cruel, so I don't.

About a quarter of the recruits disappear over the next two days; there's a steady stream of men and women with their duffle bags heading for the transport deck. I'm assigned to bunk with three younger women who recently emigrated from Eastern Europe. They're already besties, and they chat amongst themselves in Belarusian, of which I know not a single word. Part of me realizes that this is a prime opportunity to make new allies and learn a new language. But my heart isn't in it–I still flinch when I remember what happened to Natalya, Yi, and Erin, my roommates on the moon–so I politely smile and wave but otherwise keep to myself. They don't seem to care, and that's fine with me.

On the third day, we take our sedatives, and the ship takes its first nerve-wrenching, equilibrium-mushing hyperspace jump to someplace well away from Earth. One out of every ten of the recruits can't handle the jump; I've got a searing headache, and Joe's turned an impressive shade of green, but we're both still standing. My Belarusian roommates make it, too. The ones who can't get to their feet and just lie there puking on the deck are washouts; I don't know if they'll be condemned to stay in space or not.

The fourth day is more medical tests and a battery of neurologic and psychologic exams. Part of it involves answering uncomfortable personal questions while I'm wedged inside an MRI scanner that's making a terrible grinding buzz; I think this will be the worst, but I'm wrong.

Something worse comes after they give me an injection they say is just a sedative, just something to relax me for the next psych interview, and I blink and find myself waking up in my bunk twelve hours later.

I don't like time going missing in my head; that's why I've never been a drinker. I check myself all over twice, but I can't find any new incisions or punctures, and nothing's sore that wasn't before. I don't think I've been assaulted, but I can't be sure. Nobody acts like anything happened; my roommates tell me I was sleeping in my bunk for the last five hours. So whatever I did or said during the other lost hours or whatever was done to me, the brass is okay with it. Or they're trying to gaslight me into *thinking* things are fine when they're anything but. Or I got hypnotized and implanted with some black ops shit. Or this is all a test to see how I cope with paranoia. Or, or, or...

Joe is missing time, too, but unlike me, he doesn't seem to be wracked with anxiety about it. He thinks that it was some kind truth serum and that the memory loss was just a side effect. His hypothesis seems plausible, but I'm still profoundly uneasy.

The next few weeks are grueling combat training sessions in high-gravity and zero-gee. In some ways, this is worse than basic training. We go hard for three days straight and then get a day off for rest and classroom battle tactics study. Apparently, someone's new kinesiology research says that's most efficient. I'm twenty-eight years old, but at the end of our training days, I feel ninety; I envy the eighteen-year-olds who have the bounce to go off to the canteen and arcade afterward to play. I barely have the juice left to brush my teeth and drop into my bunk, and I'm fast asleep.

I wake with a jerk, and when I see the room I'm in, I want to start screaming and just never stop.

I'm lying on my bunk in the International Lunar Research Station.

I'm. On. The. God. Forsaken. *Moon.*

No.

I can't be. This room got blasted to hell eight years ago. Tech has gotten scary but not time machine scary. That shit wouldn't stay secret. I'd have heard whispers. This must be a trick. A test.

Okay, I tell myself. *You were a scientist, once. Observe and analyze, and don't lose your goddamn head.*

I take a deep breath, visualize the garden wall as a solid, death-proof edifice against my back. Roll off the bunk onto my feet. The gravity certainly feels like the moon's, but they could recreate that easily. I'm wearing a brand-new ILRS jumpsuit: white velcroed polyester with antistatic grey booties, but my underwear is what I was wearing when I went to sleep onboard the *Treader*. The smartwatch strapped to my wrist is old, cracked, and I'm pretty sure it's the one I had on when I was rescued. It went missing in the hospital. I click it on and am surprised it still works. It shows the date and time of the morning the spawn attacked, and I have to breathe deeply to stave off my panic.

I look around. The bunks, the banks of LEDs in the ceiling, the wall panels and doors...it all matches my memories. The air is stale, familiar. Yi's teddy bear is on her pillow, and Erin's bunk is scattered with her socks and Stanford tees. There's my old desk, looking just the way I left it with my old tablet and Lego figures...or does it? Can I trust a memory that's nearly a decade old? Can I trust *any* of my memories after the psych sessions I can't remember?

"Hello," I call out. The inside walls of the dormitory module aren't thick. We could all hear conversations in rooms three doors down. Keeping a low voice was important, and privacy was difficult. "Is anyone here?"

No answer. I hold my breath, listening. The hum of the lights. The exhalation of the air system. Above it all, the faint mosquito whine of a ship's idling stardrive. And if I hear that, this isn't the moon, and this is definitely a trick, and I'm so furious I want to grind the trickster's faces into broken glass. Or is the faint whine just a figment of my imagination because I'd rather be *anywhere* but here?

Regardless, I cannot hear another soul.

Taped on the wall behind my desk is an old photo of my father, Dr. Giacomo Rappaccini Muñoz, kneeling proudly in his overalls between bushes lush with his blue rose cultivar "Mexican Moonlight." He was fifty when he married my mother, and I was only ten when he died of a heart attack. My sisters were just one and two, and they don't really remember him at all. My clearest memories are of helping him in his greenhouse on the weekends and during my summers off from school. While I helped tend his glorious, peacock-blue roses, he lectured admiringly on the poisons and medicines people harvest from flowers. I wanted to become a scientist partly to honor his memory.

I stare at the picture. Is it really the one I left behind that day, the one I thought was destroyed and gone forever? I decide that its authenticity doesn't matter; I pull it from the wall and tuck it into the breast pocket of my jumpsuit.

I look at the door to the hallway. It's the only way in and out of the dorm room. A hundred yards down the hallway, it connects to Greenhouse #4. At the time, it seemed terribly convenient to be housed so close to my work area. But if this re-creation is based on my memories–or my nightmares–I know what's in the greenhouse.

And there is no point whatsoever in delaying.

I step to the door, and it slides open, catching just a little on the edge of the thin blue nylon rug as it retracts into its slot. Just like I expected it to. The round hallway beyond it lit brightly for morning. It, too, looks just the way I remember...except that it is completely empty. Yi and Erin should be by the door to the cafeteria, laughing about a movie. A couple of Russian researchers should be whispering over their coffee as they head back to their dorm room. I reel for a moment and have to steady myself against the molded white plastic wall panel.

For a split second, I'm seeing a double image of my memory overlaid on this alternate reality. Ghosts. They fade. I am alone.

The door to the cafeteria is closed. Locked. The room beyond is dark. I give it an experimental kick, and it doesn't budge. I consider trying harder to break into this forbidden space. The chair in my dorm room is sturdy enough to smash the window beside the door. But I wonder what will happen. Maybe I will be gassed and find myself waking up in the dorm bed again, the clocks reset, my father's photo taped again to the wall. Maybe this has already happened, but I just don't remember.

My thoughts turn outward. Where is Joe? Is he eating reconstituted eggs in the mess hall and wondering where I am? Or is he standing in the empty streets of a dead Texas town? We don't know the details of each other's bad dreams; that's far too much intimacy for a warship.

I walk on, past more locked doors and dark rooms, until I reach my greenhouse. It's lit up like high noon, and I find all the flowers I'd been coaxing from seeds in full bloom: soft pink oleander, white devil's weed, blue moonflowers, flaming milkweed, and purple belladonna. Rows upon rows of gorgeous, genetically modified flowers. The heady fragrance in the air would have been hard to fake. I touch the nearest oleander branch to confirm it's real. It's the experimental phenotype, engineered to reduce its heart-destroying glycosides while boosting compounds predicted to improve immune function. Did they save my seeds, somehow? But I reconsider: I wasn't the only one with the seeds. My notes were careful and complete. I thought they were destroyed–misdirected bombs intended for the spawn destroyed the cloud server sites back on Earth with all our backups–but anyone who found them could have replicated the whole experiment from the start.

I move slowly through the raised rows of plants. It looks like they're all the experimental phenotypes I worked with. The moonflower (a potent *Datura*) has been tweaked to increase brain stimulation and might someday help people with ADHD or Alzheimer's. The devil's weed (derived from a fascinatingly complex *Asclepias* species) is an improved painkiller. The belladonna (or deadly nightshade, an odd cultivar of an already rare *Atropa* species), a better antispasmodic. The devil's weed and belladonna will still probably make people hallucinate; there's a lot of other chemicals in these plants, and nobody knows quite what they do. Which is why I was studying them.

In my dreams, the flowers are here, but there's always something wrong with them: stems twisted, leaves curled as if with fungus, blossoms blackened like dead stars. These look nearly perfect but for the usual greenhouse flaws, like a few withered leaves here and there. I'm afraid, awed, and envious; someone else got to do the work I wanted to do.

A plastic bucket clatters to the floor near the wash sink. The sound makes me jump even though I was expecting it sooner or later.

There, on the floor. A creeping, bubbling mass of protoplasm, shivering as it emits a terrible buzz that bores straight into my brain. I can't describe the color of the thing; it seems to change shade as it bubbles, but none of its vile hues would be seen on a living Earth creature. The spawn oozes the rest of itself through the grate of the floor-level register, and it's rising, rising, taking a shape, like a huge necrotic cancer cell. The horror of it is more than the sum of its parts; its very existence is an insult to the idea of a loving, sane, just God.

The buzzing. The buzzing. I think it's going to break my skull in half.

In my memories, this is where I bolted and ran back the way I came.

In my nightmares, I stay rooted to the spot as the thing devours me with acidic slime.

Today, I grab a claw-headed cultivator from the shelf beneath the nearest plant table, and I start slashing the abomination with as much force as I can muster. The steel prongs rip boiling gashes in the spawn's gelatinous flesh, and the stench of disease and rot steams forth. It flinches, but I'm not seriously hurting it. If it has internal organs, they're too deep for the prongs. There's an awful noise, and it takes me a moment to realize it's me; I'm screaming obscenities at the top of my lungs.

I spot a big plastic bag of quicklime under a table. That might do it.

I drive the cultivator as deep into the spawn as I can and lunge to grab the bag. Rip it open and fling twenty pounds of gritty, corrosive calcium oxide onto the wounded spawn. It emits a shrill fluting screech as the quicklime eats into its gelatinous form, burning it. The heat of the chemical reaction is startling, and I step back. The spawn is thrashing as it melts like a slug under salt. I cough and retreat further as the corrosive powder hanging in the air burns my nose, and I swipe at a burning itch on my wrist that I figure is a spot of lime–

But I feel my flesh bubbling beneath my fingers, and my heart nearly stops.

I look down to confirm disaster. It's not a chemical burn. Sometime in the fight, the spawn stung me with a pseudopod. Its cells are invading my flesh. It'll go into my bloodstream, my internal organs, my brain. It'll make me into its clone, and my bones and muscles will melt into foul, murderous jelly. My memory briefly flashes on Yi screaming and melting inside her spacesuit. If I'm lucky, the transformation might take an hour; if I'm not and my immune system puts up a good fight, I'll be in agony for days. And then I'll be a monster.

I will die before I let that happen.

I stumble among the rows, plucking blooms from every species, shoving them into my mouth, chewing up their nectary bitterness and swallowing them down. Even with the genetic modifications, I'm eating enough toxins to kill a dozen people. This should be quick, unless I start vomiting before an immediately lethal dose enters my bloodstream.

I keep devouring flowers until my knees buckle, and I collapse onto the tiled floor. My vision blooms with color. I've never taken a hallucinogen before, and the swirling fancies are a pleasant distraction from the sharp ache in my distended stomach and the cramping in my infected arm.

Death surely waits. Not long now. Not long now....

I awaken slowly. The bright lights make my eyes ache. It takes me a moment to realize that I'm lying on my back on the greenhouse floor. The same spot where I collapsed. How long ago? I lift my smartwatch to my blurry eyes; if it and my memory of the time are correct, I've been here for twelve hours. And I'm not dead. But my hands and arms *look* dead: my flesh has turned a streaked, greenish blue as if from extreme hypoxia. Or poisoning. But I'm breathing, and my heart is still beating, though it feels different than before. Muffled. My chest feels full and strangely congested. I don't know what that means, but I'm not in pain. My lungs feel itchy and clogged, but I'm getting air. In fact, it feels like I've got far more lung capacity than before, as if sometime in the night I traded organs with an opera singer. I check the sting site on my wrist, and my flesh bears a purple scar like a healing burn.

I'm absolutely stunned to be alive. Has my body cleared the spawn's infection? What about the poison? I certainly look very, very poisoned...but I mostly feel fine. I don't believe in miracles. There must be science behind all this, but it's beyond my knowledge.

I get to my feet and survey the greenhouse. My vision and head are clearing. Everything looks the same as when I lost consciousness, though the dead spawn at the other end of the room has completely cooked down to a tarry, white-crusted mess that stinks like a tire fire. I listen for voices, but instead, I hear the distant buzzing of spawn in another room. The door beyond the dead spawn is shut, but the light above it glows green. I'm almost certain it was red and locked before.

I push through the door. It's almost completely dark inside, and I can hear the buzzing clearly. I cautiously step further into the room, and the door slams shut behind me as the lights snap on. I'm in a grey battleship interrogation room. The wall to my left is made of tarakium rigged to function as a one-way mirror. But there's no table or chairs in this room.

There's just the hungry, shuddering, bubbling spawn in the corner.

I realize I should have brought another cultivator or something to use as a weapon, and the realization makes me angry with myself, angry at this nightmarish simulation or re-creation or whatever it is, furious with the twisted psychs and brass who set me up, and absolutely enraged at the disgusting spawn rising in front of me, so I open my mouth and take a deep breath to scream obscenities at it–

And instead, I cough out a blue-black cloud of smoky particles that billow onto the spawn. The abomination flinches away, attack abandoned, its pseudopods and blistery multi-pupil eyes retreating into its gelatinous mass. It spasms, shuddering as if it's trying to sneeze. Surprised, I taste the powder coating my tongue, and I realize it isn't ash or soot. It's bitter, sweet, and the grains are sticky. Pollen, I realize, amazed. I've just coughed up a whole bunch of pollen onto the monster.

Each tiny coal-speck of pollen dissolves on its glistening surface, and the spawn is in visible distress. At first, I think it's an allergic reaction, a rash, but the nodules rising on its flesh burst open, and I see tiny rootlets sprouting. My pollen is fertilizing the cells beneath, and they're becoming my seeds. I am simultaneously repulsed, astonished, and delighted.

The seeds grow with a vengeance, sending spiny roots all through the monster. It stops buzzing and emits shrill fluting screeches as the roots spread like strangling kudzu through its bulk, impaling and crushing it.

"Not so nice when someone does it to you, is it?" I sit down on the floor to watch it die.

It takes an hour for my vines to utterly annihilate the spawn. When it's all over, there's something like a tree's root ball there on the floor. I think that if I could just find a nice, deep patch of dirt, something very interesting might grow.

One thing bothers me, though: I can still hear the buzzing. It's very faint, and it's extremely far away, but I can still hear the spawn. *All* of them.

I had forgotten about the one-way mirror behind me, but I hear the click of a speaker coming on and remember that I've been watched this whole time.

"Ms. Muñoz." It's Lieutenant Colonel Mercedes Patel's voice.

I stand and face the mirror but resist my urge to salute. "Yes?"

"I'm pleased to report that you have passed your final exam with flying colors," she says.

"Why did you decide to try this...experiment with me?" Dark pollen puffs like cigarette smoke from my lips. I'm still furious with her, but for now, at least, curiosity is an effective tarp on my emotions.

"That's largely classified, I'm afraid. But I can tell you that our researchers discovered that people like yourself who are long-term survivors of initial encounters with the spawn have particular genetic traits that, under the correct conditions, can produce interesting physical enhancements when they are exposed to spawn for a second time. We have implemented customized training and testing programs for survivors. And many of these uniquely personal trials have produced uniquely successful results."

I stare at my blue hands, which seem greener now. "How many have survived your tests?"

"That is classified. But know that you are not alone."

I clench my fists. I *am* alone. I'm supposed to help save humanity, but even if I succeed, I can't rejoin any human group, not even the other soldiers condemned to space, and that's a bitter leaf indeed. If Patel were in front of me, I'd punch her right in her face, but that's why there's a good thick tarakium mirror between us.

I throw up my hands instead. "You've turned me into a walking biological weapon. That's all I am now, isn't it?"

"You are a most effective *soldier* in our war against the spawn." Her voice is sternly corrective. "You are still human in all the ways that most matter. You are a tremendous asset to our forces, our nation, and our planet."

"What happens now?"

"You must stay here in deep space for a few more days, so the doctors can clear you for duty. Then, you will take command of one of our Shuriken-class vessels and a small tactical operations unit. Because of your condition, most of your crew will be remotely controlled android drones. We hope to assign you at least one living crew member, both for morale and for backup in case your other crew lose connection to their drone bodies."

"Someone I can't accidentally kill with my breath?"

"Yes."

"I want a laboratory," I blurt out, staring at the root ball. I'm feeling strangely protective of it, and I don't want it to dry up and die. "And a good greenhouse. One suitable for trees."

A pause. "I believe that can be arranged."

"And can we wrap this in some wet burlap, please?"

"Yes. We're just as curious as you are as to what's going to grow."

I rest my hand on the wrapped, dormant root ball as the autopiloted shuttle glides into the docking bay of the *USS Flechette*. We land with barely a bump, and the rear door slowly lowers. I unbuckle my flight harness and walk down the ramp.

It's chilly on the flight deck, which is fine. Extreme temperatures don't bother me as much as they used to. I just need to sit naked under grow lights for a few hours each day.

Six android drones stand at attention on the flight deck behind a human lieutenant. I blink. Is he human? He towers a head above them, and his skin is crocodile rough, blackened as if he's been charred by a fire. He's wearing a short-sleeved uniform, and his arms, neck, and face look as if he's been torn apart and put back together with steel staples. As I stare, trying to make sense of what I'm seeing, recognition dawns.

"Joe?"

His grisly face splits into a smile. "Yep, it's me. Good to see you, Bea."

"Good to see you, too. Not to be rude, but how did you survive all this?"

He gives a laugh like stones grinding together. "I didn't. But I'm here anyway. Well, let me introduce you to your crew..."

Each drone steps forward as Joe gives their name, rank, and a brief career resume. It's a good crew, competent and smart. The drones are all the same drab gray model, but they've each got a different color stripe around their torsos so people can tell them apart. They're not human enough to seem uncanny valley creepy; they remind me of crash test dummies even when they salute and address me in their pilot's voices.

After introductions are over, Joe sends a pair of ensigns for my cargo and dismisses the others. He steps closer. Joe stinks of death. I'm guessing they have the temperature turned down to keep his flesh from rotting. I don't mind the smell, and my pollen can't fertilize dead cells. I'm relieved that I'm no danger to him.

"Can you hear them?" he asks.

I know he's talking about the spawn. The buzz of monsters massing amongst the stars. "I can hear every one of them."

"Are you ready to go kill those bastards?"

"Absolutely."

In my mind, I see a thousand planets covered in my trees, and among them, I am never alone.

A Hero of Grünjord

Part 1: Outlanders

Vinca felt her stomach twist as the vast Outlander skyship, black as the night betwixt the stars, rose from the valley Rift. The winter sun shone harshly through wispy clouds and gleamed on the snowy mountains ringing that cursed chasm. But the ship reflected nothing. If it were not for the nauseating hum of its engines shaking her very bones, she would have thought the ship to be a catastrophic absence in the sky, like the strange, distant, invisible stars the monks argued over. "Black holes" some called them, but Vinca found that name unsatisfyingly prosaic. A hole was something to be filled, nothing more, and the word did not convey the planet-devouring danger the strange stars held.

Perhaps the Outlanders hailed from a world near one of those dark, hungry stars, and built their ships as homage to those world-eating celestials they worshipped as ravenous gods. Or perhaps the unrelenting darkness was simple camouflage in those cold star-reaches. Either way, if this lone ship made it past the defenses Queen Ahlgrena and her armies had raised, it would wreak terrible destruction across Erd's ten continents.

A century before Vinca's birth, the Rift first opened after Grünjord's most powerful wizard botched a spell intended to create a new freshwater spring. One of the Outlanders' ships had burst through and laid waste to kingdoms and nations as far south as the Qiimaha empire. Where the ships landed and the Outlanders spilled forth, those who met their blister-eyed gazes suffered seizures and madness and could not defend themselves. Hundreds of thousands died, mostly humans but dragons, too, and the ship was only brought down when the human kingdoms and dragon tribes pledged to set aside their grievances and work together. The land still bore blackened scars where no plants would grow and people who stayed too long inside their borders later sickened with malignant tumors. Queen Ahlgrena's great-grandfather took responsibility for his wizard's accident and pledged to the neighboring kingdoms to do whatever he could to keep all their lands safe.

"This one's bigger than Queen Ahlgrena's keep," Bhraxio said as he pumped his leathery wings harder to try to rise above the Outland invader. His voice sounded profoundly worried inside Vinca's mind.

She could feel the quiver of his wing muscles' strain through her sheepskin saddle. Fire-breathers like Bhraxio were inherently hot-blooded and could fend off the chill far better than humans, but this bright morning was exceptionally bitter. The extreme cold was taking a clear toll on the young dragon. The first breath of outside air had sent her into a coughing fit. If it were not for her magic-imbued flight helmet–which in her wisdom Queen Ahlgrena had commissioned for all the dragoneers–her face would have already frozen as hard and solid as a marble statue's.

"We can bring it down." Vinca leaned forward in the saddle and gave Bhraxio a comforting gauntleted scratch through the wooly fur of his neck. There were thirty dragoneers in the skies today; they'd be able to surround the ship and bombard it with grenades enchanted to home in on and cling to the hot places on the hull where the strange, tough metal that composed the craft's skin was weakest. It might take two hundred bombs to sunder the ship, but they had plenty of grenades and fliers with hand cannons. "We *will* bring it down."

"Try to bring it down in one piece," Captain Gunther *replied* through the enchanted helmet. "Sister Lutera told the Queen that the monks need an intact ship for defensive study."

Vinca blinked. Their tried-and-true bombardments couldn't possibly drop the ship whole. "That wasn't the course we plotted this morning."

"New orders from the Queen's captain," Gunther replied simply. "She told me only a moment ago. You're the first to know. I'll tell the others shortly."

"Are we to endanger the towns for the sake of bringing the monks a scientific prize?" Her voice was as sharp as her sword. Other dragoneers might have feared to speak to Gunther so boldly, but she and he had fought a dozen Outlander invasions together, drunk entire barrels of ale together, and sundered the springs of several beds together. Gunther, often grim and intimidating to his troops, was a surprisingly playful lover. Vinca was reasonably sure that she was only one of perhaps three people who'd ever heard the huge, bearded warrior laugh. If she couldn't speak her mind to him, then she could speak it to no one.

"No." Gunther sounded unruffled. "Endanger none if you can. But a whole ship's better than a burned wreck."

Life was precious in Grünjord; it had not always been so. But the constant Outlander threat had forced the kingdom to change and advance far beyond most other realms. Their King or Queen was no longer simply born to rule but had to be elected by representatives from every district. Grünjorders had become expert at waging war, but they also realized they had to build a country worth battling for. The kingdom was in a renaissance of the arts and sciences, and every child went to school to learn letters and numbers. Even the plumbing and heating in the average burgher's house was rare in neighboring kingdoms and an unheard-of marvel in more distant lands. Vinca had spent her first seven years in her father's keep in distant Coravia, and she could remember no pipes, only chamber pots and drafty latrines that opened to the polluted castle moat below.

"Our troops wait on the ground," Gunther said. "If you can bring it down within five leagues of the valley, the wizards will be able to slow its fall in the air, and our soldiers are prepared to clear the monsters inside."

"I spy it as being nearly five leagues away now," she replied. "Do you mark it so?"

"Aye," he agreed.

Then they hadn't a moment to waste.

"Rise!" she urged Bhraxio. "Get me well above the skyship! Keep pace!"

With a great press of wings, the dragon did as she asked, and Vinca quickly unbuckled herself, unsheathed her skyship-metal boarding axe, and gathered her legs beneath her to get ready to leap clear of his wings.

Based on the wrecked hunks they'd recovered, there would be a ring of wide round porthole windows above a room near the center of the ship. The monks believed the monsters steered the craft from that room. From outside the ship, the windows appeared as the same flat black as the rest of the craft, but while the metal of the ship was supernaturally tough and could only be cut with magic, the glasslike material of the portholes would shatter beneath the Outlanders' own metal.

Vinca's stomach churned. Many dragoneers had tried what she was about to attempt, and none so far had succeeded. Half had died, plunging to their deaths, smashed by the hull, or swept into the furnace blast of the ship's strange engines. The odds that the wind would simply blow her off the top of the craft were extremely high. But if there was even a slight chance of bringing the ship down, she had to try.

"Be ready to catch me," she said. "Pull up on my mark so I can get clear of you, and watch for my fall!"

"Aye!"

Vinca gripped her axe tightly and held her position until they were over the middle of the vast ship; she guessed they were maybe fifty meters above it, but the void of the surface made distances difficult to gauge. "Now!"

Bhraxio swept his wings in reverse, and Vinca used her sudden forward pitch to lengthen her jump. She vaulted over his muscular wooly shoulder and plummeted toward the ship.

She spoke a simple charm to safely soften her fall. The plunge was quick and disorienting nonetheless, and instead of landing on her feet as she'd hoped, she landed painfully on her hip and began to slide across the ship, nothing but shapeless dark all around her. Her booted feet hit a metal edge and blackness loomed in front of her: it had to be a porthole.

With both hands, she swung her axe into the mass. The glasslike porthole material shattered inward, huge dark shards falling into a room that at first glimpse was a dazzling constellation of red, blue, and yellow lights. Her second glimpse showed her a gray metal deck three meters below and grotesquely misshapen creatures recoiling from the plummeting shards.

Her mind swam when she saw the monsters below. They were like the bubbling scum that sometimes formed on stagnant ponds. No bones, no permanent limbs or heads that she could see, just roiling, shifting masses of colorless gelatinous flesh. No–they had a color. It just wasn't one she could name. Eerie green eyes boiled out of their flesh like pustules. There was no rhyme or reason to their forms, and they made terrible buzzing noises that bored right into her brain like parasitic worms trying to erase her thoughts and will to fight.

Vinca shook her head to clear the vile buzz. She gripped her axe in her left fist and drew her magic-forged skymetal broadsword with her right. Took a deep breath. Leaped down onto the glass-strewn deck. She began to swing at anything and everything, a whirling blade cyclone. Slashed panels sparked and smoked. The hideous outlanders emitted fluting shrieks and recoiled from her onslaught.

A tiny part of her was appalled at this indiscriminate brute force. Precise strikes based on careful foreknowledge of a foe's weaknesses were best. But the monks couldn't agree on what the different panels and gadgets might do. It seemed best to destroy as much of their ability to pilot their ship as she could while she could.

And she couldn't keep this up much longer. Her heart was pounding and her shoulders straining. Worse, the monsters in the room with her were recovering from their surprise, gathering together, melding into a huge, towering mass. She slashed at the looming monstrosity, but its jelly flesh seemed to heal itself the moment her blade passed through it–if these creatures had vitals, she could not reach them. At best she could pop a few of its vile eyes, but three more would blister open in its remains. Quicklime would melt an Outlander. She wished she'd thought to bring a bag of the white powder with her.

"What's happening in there?" Captain Gunther's voice was faint inside her helmet.

"Fighting," she grunted, slashing at the monster.

A light flashed near her, and she whirled and buried her axe in the panel with as much force as she could muster. A solid foot of the broad blade sunk into the metal and wires. Her shoulder and elbow ached sharply at the impact. A moment later the ship gave a lurch, and began to plummet downward.

"Ah, well done!" Gunther exclaimed.

Suddenly in free-fall, she and the monstrosity both rose off the gray metal floor. Vinca released her axe and kicked off from its stout leather-wrapped handle toward the broken porthole. The Outlander shrieked at her and lashed a gooey pseudopod around her ankle, trying to drag her back down. She slashed the fleshy snare off her boot with her sword and recited a levitation charm to take herself out to the bright blue sky and blinding sunlight.

The bitter wind slammed into her and knocked her breath away as it blasted her clear of the vast, plunging ship. The gale knocked her sword from her suddenly-numbed fingers. She cartwheeled helplessly, unable to speak a charm to slow her fall, unable to right herself enough to get her bearings. The wind was so loud against her helmet she wasn't sure she'd be able to hear the ship crashing if the wizards hadn't been able to catch it.

"Do you live? We can't see you," Gunther said.

She couldn't voice a reply in the thin air.

"Bhraxio, please see me!" she thought, praying he could hear her. Many dragoneers' mental connections with their dragons was only as good as their line of sight. If they couldn't see each other, they couldn't hear each other, either. Vinca had been able to talk to Bhraxio through castle walls, but they'd only been separated by a few yards. She had no idea how far the ship had traveled while she'd been inside it, or whether he had been able to keep pace.

"I'm almost there," she heard inside her mind. "Roll yourself into a ball; I don't want to break your limbs."

She hugged her legs to her chest and tucked her helmeted face to her knees.

A moment later, she felt Bhraxio's leathery talons close around her body. Then a rough guts-flattening jerk as he winged away.

She felt dizzy from vertigo and relief, and in the sheltering cage of his claws, she could finally take a deep breath.

"I'm alive," she croaked to Gunther. "Bhraxio has me. Have the wizards got the ship?"

"Yes!" he said. "Our ground troops are clearing it of Outlanders now. You've landed us a real prize! I reckon you won't have to pay for your own drinks for at least a fortnight!"

She smiled and massaged her sore shoulder. "I think tonight I'd rather have a hot bath and a rubdown."

He gave a sly chuckle. "I'm sure that can be arranged."

Vinca and Bhraxio were surrounded by cheering, ecstatic troops and townspeople the moment he set her down along the main road into the city. She scrambled onto his back, and the next several hours were a blur of cheering people and waving pennants and proffered goblets of ale and wine as the crowd led them in a parade through the villages outside the city wall, then through the gates and around the town square.

Queen Ahlgrena herself brought Vinca up to her address balcony and gave a rousing speech in honor of the dragoneer and Bhraxio, who'd flown to a sturdy iron perch beside the elevated stage. Vinca, fortunately, wasn't expected to do anything but stand steady and wave to the crowd below; that was enough of a challenge as she was thoroughly dizzy with drink by then. After three rounds of huzzah! the queen put an official golden medal of honor on a red satin ribbon around Vinca's neck. They all went downstairs to a fine banquet for all the dragoneers, wizards, and the men and women who'd slain the last of the Outlanders once the ship was grounded.

In the castle's ceremonial banquet hall, gilded statues of the old heroes of Grünjord gazed down upon them from alcoves ringing the ceiling. Half the alcoves were empty in anticipation of mighty new heroes. Though Vinca drank no more alcohol, her head swam at the realization that this day had earned her a place among them.

After a dessert of intricately frosted cakes that seemed nearly too beautiful to eat, Gunther took her aside and led her through several gilt-and-marble corridors and staircases to an ornate set of double doors in crown prince Stellan's wing of the palace.

"What are we doing here?" Vinca asked Gunther.

"As I recall, you requested a hot bath," he replied, smiling enigmatically. "Prince Stellan has one of the best soaking pools in the entire kingdom, which likely makes it one of the best in the entire world."

"But not *the* best?" she replied, half teasing.

"Well. It's a matter of opinion, isn't it? The bath is exactly as the prince desired it for himself, so he considers it to be the best. And he is an epicure of considerable taste and knowledge, so it has the best of all the options he prefers."

Prince Stellan was still young, just a few years older than Vinca. His mother likely had many more decades left in her reign, presuming she continued to please the voters of Grünjord, so he hadn't yet had to buckle down and prove himself as a leader and administrator. But unlike most responsibility-free princes who had lived and died in the many kingdoms of Erd, he was neither a rake nor a bully. A hedonist, certainly: he loved fine foods, and fine wines, and even finer clothes, the latter of which he maintained his figure for through tournament fencing and horsemanship. He advocated beautiful living, and had popularized makeup and fancy hairstyles for men and boys in the kingdom. But the queen had impressed upon him the importance of behaving like a gentleman, and though it was rumored he'd had a prodigious number of lovers, absolutely no one had whispered that he'd taken a girl or boy to bed against their will. Other royals in other kingdoms were said to rape for vile, predatory sport, and some openly bragged of it as a mark of twisted manliness. But that evil was abhorred in Grünjord.

So, Vinca knew she would be perfectly safe if Gunther left her to soak alone. Besides, she doubted she'd find a respectful advance from Prince Stellan to be the least bit objectionable. But that had to be pure fancy; the prince could charm nearly anyone in the kingdom that he desired. He was probably ensconced in his chambers with a lovely bevy of admirers. It was more than enough that he'd offered up his private bath to her.

"Are you staying, or leaving?" she asked Gunther, tracing a gilded vine decorating the doors with her index finger.

"That is entirely up to you."

She looked him up and down. He'd washed his face and combed out his long blond hair and beard before the banquet, but he still wore most of his battle armor, and his tunic was white with dried sweat. And darkly fuzzed with wind-blown dragon hairs. "You could use a wash."

He arched a bushy eyebrow at her and pursed his lips in disapproval, but the twinkle hadn't left his eyes. "Is that your way of asking me to stay?"

She couldn't keep from grinning impishly at him. "Yes. Stay."

"As you wish." He grasped the golden door handles and pushed them open.

The bathroom beyond the doors was a lavish work of marble and gold. Two round bathing pools were sunk into the floor, both tiled in ocean blue. Arrayed around them were benches and intricately-wrought hanging racks for clothes. Two fluffy white bathrobes hung from one of the racks. An assortment of fancy soaps sat in a reed basket by the rightmost pool, and bathing oils by the left.

"The pool on the right is for getting the grime off," Gunther said as he closed the doors behind them. "And the one on the left is for relaxation."

She gave him a look. "I do know how bathing works."

"Well, I hear that they only have rags and sticks in Coravia," he teased.

"Our castle had a tub, thank you very much," she replied as they approached the benches. "And my father, the king, insisted we bathe once a year whether we needed it or not."

"Ew," he laughed.

"Fortunately, having survived a filthy childhood there, hardly anything up here makes me ill."

"You were about seven when our scouts found you, weren't you?"

"Yes." Humans with the ability to bond telepathically with dragons were rare; Queen Ahlgrena had sent her wizards far across the continents of Erd to identify and recruit promising youngsters. "I was the fifth child of eight, and my father never looked so happy with me as the day he sold me to foreign strangers for a fat bag of gold."

Gunther looked at her sharply. "People aren't objects. You weren't bought. We don't do that here."

"Well, where I came from, people *are* things. My father most certainly saw the recruitment incentive as my purchase price."

"I'm sorry." Gunther awkwardly gave her a side-hug. "I didn't mean to bring up unpleasant memories."

"It's fine. And it's in the past." She forced herself to smile up at him. "I have a better life as a dragoneer here than I ever would as a princess there. And my father probably got to buy a very nice horse. It worked out for everyone."

"What about your mother?"

Vinca frowned, trying to sort through her hazy memories. "She wasn't happy about selling me off. But she had so many other children, and surely more to come. My absence probably made her life easier."

There came a loud knock from a different set of doors behind them.

"Yes? Who is it?" Vinca called.

The doors opened just a crack.

"May I enter?" Prince Stellan asked.

Her heartbeat quickened. "Yes. Certainly."

The prince stepped into the bath room and closed the doors behind him. He was barefoot and wore a white robe that matched the ones hanging on the rack. His curly hair was bound in intricate braids, and he wore golden eye shadow that looked gorgeous against his dark skin. She had certainly admired him from afar, but up close he was even more handsome, and she felt an unaccustomed electricity in her chest.

"To what do we owe the honor of your presence?" She wasn't sure whether she ought to bow.

"Oh, the honor is entirely mine." The prince smiled reassuringly. "You are our hero, and you deserve the finest that our kingdom has to offer. I wanted to personally make sure that everything here is to your satisfaction."

Vinca looked around at the pools and baskets and benches. "All this is wonderful."

"I also wondered," the prince said, "if I might join the two of you? I do want to make sure that you're well satisfied this evening."

It took her a moment to fully realize what he was offering. She felt heat rise in her face, and she looked at Gunther, partly for confirmation of what she was hearing, and partly to see whether he was upset at the prince's advance. Gunther merely smiled at her and gave a little shrug as if to say, *Why not? I'm game.*

"Yes," she told Prince Stellan. "That would be lovely."

Part 2: Inlanders

Vinca lay cozily sandwiched between Gunther and Stellan in the prince's silken bed. As comfortable as the rest of her was, her bruised leg was starting to ache beneath her. Gunther snoozed like a hibernating bear, but Stellan was gently stroking her bare hip.

"I need to shift a bit," she whispered over her shoulder to the prince.

He released her and scooted away on the bed. She rolled over to face him. His amber eyes were bright, and he wore an oddly thoughtful expression.

"Have you slept?" she asked.

"A little. I…would like to discuss something serious, if you don't mind."

Her heart beat faster. What could this be about? "No, I don't mind."

He traced the curve of her face with his forefinger. "Sometimes, ordinary people rise to their occasions and do extraordinary things. I don't think that's what happened yesterday. I think you are an extraordinary woman, and you will do more extraordinary things. My greatest worry about myself is that when you strip away my extraordinary circumstances, I'm not much more than a pretty face. But I hope that if I keep company with genuinely extraordinary people, they will give me occasions to rise to."

"You're asking me to join your court?"

"I'm asking you to be my queen."

Lightning once struck Vinca while she rode Bhraxio in a storm; this felt much the same, and for a moment she couldn't speak.

"Prince Stellan, I am deeply, deeply flattered..." She trailed off, not sure how best to phrase her profound concerns.

He smiled at her. "But we've only just met, and regardless of the intensity of our meeting, we hardly know each other well enough to pledge marriage. You believe I am probably suffering from lust-induced, harebrained infatuation. Am I close?"

She nodded.

He took a deep breath. "I do realize this sounds like madness. But hear me out."

"Of course."

"I *have* been trying to become a man of substance. I frankly lack the talent to become a proper wizard, but I have studied hard, and I do have some natural ability for prognostication. Prophetic dreams. They don't arrive reliably, but when they do arrive, they've been entirely reliable. Does that make sense?"

"I think so?"

"I know you're a woman who appreciates directness and honesty, so I should lay down all my cards, yes? I have dreamed of you. Of *us*. Standing together to lead this country. We're much older in my dreams, so I wasn't sure it was you, not until I saw you send down the Outlander ship. But now I'm certain. I also know that nothing I say will be enough to convince you right now, and that's fine. There's no hurry."

"Why me?" she finally asked.

She wondered if her mother had ever dared ask that question before she found herself bound to a life of royal obligation. Did marrying the King of Coravia seem like a fairy tale escape into luxury, at first? Vinca had witnessed but little of her mother's life, and she knew the gilded edges were cold and hard.

"We're excellent complements for each other," the prince replied. "You've skills I could never attain. You're a genuine hero of Grünjord, and people respect that. You're a genuine princess of Coravia, and that would satisfy traditionalists. And..."

"And what?"

"And I think I fancy you a great deal."

She finally gave into her urge to kiss him. "I fancy you, too. But this is a lot to consider."

"I know that. I also know that my proposal might seem like a golden cage. While there will be inescapable responsibilities, your life would be your own as much as possible. I wouldn't stand in the way of your other loves. I know you care for Gunther, and he cares for you. If the time arrived when you wanted to have a child with him, I would treat the boy as my own."

Vinca felt another lightning shock. "Your dreams told you I'll have a baby with Gunther?"

"My dreams were unclear. But our son seemed very…large. And rather blond."

"Oh." Vinca's whole body felt warm. She hadn't ever considered that Gunther might want to have children with her someday.

"Think upon this as long as you like." He kissed her, and slipped his hands around her hips to draw her closer. Suddenly her flesh was keening for his.

"May I take your mind off things?" he asked.

"Yes, please…"

Vinca groggily awoke to a steady *tap-tap-tap* at the prince's window. Stellan stirred beside her. Gunther snoozed on, oblivious.

"What's that?" the prince whispered blearily.

Vinca's eyes finally focused. "A bird. A crow. It's carrying something."

She and Stellan climbed out of bed and went to the window. The crow was perched uncomfortably on the sill outside, his scraggly feathers fluffed up to protect his scrawny body against the bitter cold. A small scroll was bound to his scaly leg with a leather thong. It eyed them beadily and let out a hoarse caw.

Stellan reached for the latch and opened the window. Vinca shivered at the sudden blast of frigid air as the crow hopped inside, eyeing her and cawing again.

The prince hurriedly shut the window. "Looks like the bird's had a rough time of it!"

The crow gave another caw and awkwardly held out its leg to her. She carefully untied the thong and unfolded the tiny scroll, which was handwritten in the trade language of the Southern continent. A dark lock of hair–Vinca's own, she realized–was sewn to the bottom of the paper.

Gunther, roused by the bird's noise, had lumbered out of bed. "What's happened?"

"This bird flew all the way from Coravia," she marveled. "No wonder it looks so ragged!"

"That's over two thousand leagues away," the prince replied. "My falconer will want to see this mighty bird."

The crow cawed at him and puffed out its feathers again.

"This is part of a finding spell." Gunther pointed at the lock of hair. "I didn't think the Coravians approved of magic?"

"They don't," Vinca replied. "But like anything else the church forbids, they'll resort to it if the need arises."

"What does it say?" Stellan asked.

"It's been a long time since I've seen this language...I'm still working it out." She tapped a stamp near the lock. "This was penned by a local scribe. But it's from my mother. It says, 'Dearest Daughter, I am dying. I would like to see you again. I wish we had not sold you. Please visit if you can. Bring this letter so the guard will let you in. If you cannot visit, know that I love you.' She's signed it with her mark. I remember it."

"Could this be a trick?" Gunther asked.

Vinca turned the seamed paper over in her hands. "I can't imagine why anyone would try to trick me like this."

"Unfortunately, I *can* imagine reasons for skullduggery here." The prince held out his hand. "May I take that to my wizards for analysis?"

"Certainly." She gave him the letter.

"If it's authentic, do you want to visit her?" Gunther asked.

"I...I don't know." Her mother had given her life. But had not protested very loudly when her father sold her. Did she owe her mother anything, now? And was seeing her one last time a matter of debt? She sometimes wondered how her brothers and sisters had fared. If she ignored this reason to go back, another was not likely to arise.

"Bhraxio could fly me there in a week," she mused. "Assuming he's willing to take me there. And assuming we're allowed to go."

"You may certainly visit your dying mother," Gunther said. "Of *course* you may."

"But before you settle on a course, let's see what my wizards and agents report," Stellan said. "I don't know enough about that quarter of the world to advise on whether it's safe or not."

The prince summoned her to dine with him that night, and they discussed his experts' findings over tawny port and roasted duck.

"The letter is authentic," the prince said gravely. "I am very sorry for your impending loss."

"Thank you," Vinca replied. "Bhraxio says he will take me to see her."

"Coravia regards dragons as devils. You'll need to travel under cover of an invisibility spell, and he will need to transform into a horse or dog when you arrive."

Vinca nodded. "I'll ask what he prefers."

"And it's such a long way that my wizards recommend he take a potion to increase his airspeed," the prince said. "It might make him feel a bit sick."

"Taking that would also be his choice."

"Another problem is that your father has not been the most...*diplomatic* ruler in the region. He's made threats against the neighboring Xintu kingdom, and our intelligence reports that both sides are amassing forces. Your father has fewer soldiers, and the Xintu leaders know this. War could break out at any time. Coravia is likely to be overrun. If that happens, your duty is to return yourself and Bhraxio safely to Grünjord. Your father made his own political bed a long time ago, and his problems aren't yours to try to fix."

Vinca pursed her lips. She wasn't surprised by any of this news. Coravia was founded by Northern seafaring colonists. They'd treated their indigenous neighbors poorly from the start, and that didn't change as the Coravians abandoned piracy for religious piety. The Xintu royal family still considered the Coravians to be land thieves even though they'd been there for close to a millennium. And, based on the dimly-remembered rants she overheard as a child, her father considered their neighbors to be degenerate savages even though the Xintus had superior art and better literacy and medicine. Despite the ages-old conflict, there was a great deal of surreptitious trade between the two kingdoms. For all she knew, her mother had enlisted a Xintu shaman to enchant the scroll so the crow could find her.

"I couldn't fix my father's problems even if I tried," she said.

"Wear armor, and carry a good sword. But not too much armor–tensions are high and you don't want to seem threatening. I'll make sure that Bhraxio's transformation can be reversed at a word."

Bhraxio opted to turn into a large mastiff, reasoning that they would be inevitably separated if he became a horse. It was summer in the southern continents, but even the warmer months in swampy Coravia tended towards a damp chilliness. Vinca wore a knee-length hauberk of light skymetal mail under a pale grey chemise and loosely-woven blue kirtle with enough decorative embroidery to look like a proper lady's outfit without seeming ostentatiously fancy. She carried a canvas-sheathed longsword strapped beneath her rucksack; at a glance, it wouldn't look like she was armed. None of the flimsy footwear popular with Coravian women was suitable for fighting or riding, so she opted for her regular boots and hoped they wouldn't earn her too many stares.

The hike from Bhraxio's landing spot to her father's keep was muddy and uneventful. They passed a few peasants and soldiers who gave her and Bhraxio curious looks, but none accosted them. As they approached the outer wall, Vinca realized that the keep was much smaller than she remembered. And it was almost gratuitously ugly, all rough-hewn squared granite angles and spiky wrought iron. Nothing about the structure spoke of grace or enlightenment. Positioned as it was on a steep rocky hill well away from the nearest village, it had never been built to provide protection for the common folk whose taxes paid for its creation. It was a physical assertion of ego and dominance in a sulky, undernourished landscape, the crude architectural equivalent of an armored fist beating against its owner's proud, skinny chest.

Vinca crossed the bamboo log moat bridge, breathing through her mouth to avoid being overwhelmed by the sewer stench of the filthy water below, and approached the guards at the castle gate.

"What is your business here?" one demanded.

"I'm here to see the queen. At her invitation." She handed the guard the scroll.

He looked at it upside-down, clearly not actually able to read it. "Who are you?"

"I'm her daughter. My name is Vinca."

The guard's eyebrows rose a bit at that, and he gave her and Bhraxio another suspicious once-over. "I'll let my Captain know. Wait here."

The sun hung low in the sky by the time the gruff captain of the guard arrived to lead them to her mother's chambers in the eastern tower. The castle yard was full of soldiers, all either too young or too old, and most with ill-fitting boiled leather armor and well-worn weapons. To her eye, some of the boys were as young as twelve or thirteen, not even old enough to wield a razor.

"A sad lot, indeed," Bhraxio thought to her.

"Soon they'll have to resort to training women," she thought back darkly. "Or die of pride."

"Is my father here?" she asked the captain.

"He is. He's attending to military matters."

"Does he know I've arrived?"

"He does."

Vinca waited for the man to elaborate, and when he did not, she asked, "Did he say if he was going to see me?"

"The King has much on his mind. If he wishes to see you, I reckon he will."

"Understood."

The captain's tone softened. "It's not safe to travel. If you need a bed for the night, your sisters can give you a place to sleep."

The sour stink of sickness in her mother's room was unmistakable. The Queen of Coravia lay pale and gaunt upon stained sheets and a sheepskin coverlet damp with coughed-up blood. She was attended by two women a few years younger than Vinca.

The captain rapped the butt of his spear upon the stone floor and stood very straight as he announced her: "Lady Vinca of Grünjord is here to see her mother, the Queen."

The two younger women stood, peering at Vinca nervously.

"Is it truly you?" the one with dark brown hair asked.

Vinca was mortified to realize that she wasn't sure of her sister's names. "Cathara? Camine?"

They both smiled, and Vinca was relieved that she'd guessed correctly. "Yes, it's me."

They rose to give her quick, awkward, but seemingly heartfelt hugs, and Vinca was surprised to discover that she loomed a whole head above them both. She wondered if the household had suffered from famine, or if the girls had been pressured to starve themselves when they were growing teenagers.

"Such a fearsome hound!" Black-haired Camine was staring at Bhraxio, who seemed nearly as large as she was.

"He won't hurt you," Vinca assured her.

"But this is a warlord's dog," Camine persisted. "What master would allow his slave such a beast?"

"Camine!" Cathara's voice was *don't be rude* sharp.

"Master?" Vinca laughed. "I have no master. I'm as free as you or your sister."

Her sisters looked genuinely shocked. Not just shocked, but dismayed.

"By the looks of things, your life has been considerably freer than theirs," Bhraxio remarked.

Vinca wondered if her father had used her as a threat: *Disobey me and I'll sell you to the next peddler!* What must it be like to realize that the sister they'd assumed had suffered a fate worse than death had instead survived and even thrived? By the expressions on their faces, it was a bitter draught, indeed.

"What ails our mother?" she asked them.

"She has the consumption," Cathara replied.

"Tuberculosis?" Vinca blinked. "But that can be treated. Cured."

"Nonsense," Cathara replied.

"Not at all! No one suffers from this in Grünjord."

"Those who allow sorcerers to tamper with their flesh go to hell." Camine's eyes were wide and accusing.

Vinca threw up her hands in exasperation. "It's an extract of bread mold! There's nothing sorcerous about it! You're worried about your mother going to hell? This, right here, looks an awful lot like hell to me!"

"Cathara. Camine." Her mother's voice was a papery rasp, but it still held undeniable authority. "Leave me with Vinca. I wish to speak to her privately."

"But Mother–" Camine began.

"Leave us!" The queen fell into a violent coughing fit and waved them off.

The two sisters obeyed, eyeing Vinca as if she might be a witch as they hurried from the chamber.

Vinca took Camine's vacated seat close to the head of the bed. "Mother, truly, this can be cured–"

The Queen raised a shaky hand and made a motion to silence her. "I don't want a cure."

"Why in the name of the heavens not?"

"I'm tired, Vinca. I have done my duty and I just want to rest. Forever. I think I've earned that."

The anguished ache in Vinca's chest told her that her heart was surely breaking. And from frustration as much as anything else. "If you won't let me help you…why did you want me to come home?"

"I wanted to see you one last time." Tears rose in her mother's rheumy eyes. "I wanted to know about your life. I wanted…stories of places far away from here."

So Vinca told her the tale of the Rift, and the Outlander invasion. She told her the story of meeting Bhraxio, and of the day they took down the vast dark skyship and were heralded as heroes by the Queen.

She had just started telling her about Prince Stellan when she realized that her mother's jaw had gone slack and she'd seemingly stopped breathing.

"Has she passed on?" Bhraxio asked.

Vinca pressed two fingers against the artery in her mother's fragile neck to check for a pulse. Nothing. "She's gone."

"I'm so sorry."

"Me, too." Vinca wiped at her eyes with the hem of her chemise. "Dammit. It was too late to save her even if she'd agreed to come to Grünjord."

"It was what she wanted," Bhraxio said.

Vinca gestured angrily at the shabby sick room and swore. "This is *never* what anyone wants. People convince themselves that death is a prize when they feel trapped and hopeless."

"Should we call for someone?"

"Not yet." Vinca felt too drained to deal with her sisters and their tears. Especially if the tears were just for show. "We came a long way to see her. I'd like to sit here a while longer."

The old lady's half-open eyes were filming over. Death looked nothing like sleep. Vinca gently closed her mother's lids. Was this what old age inevitably brought? Infirmity and regret after a life broken on the wheel of duty? What might her mother have accomplished if she'd had the knowledge to make good choices, and the power to live as she chose? But none except a few great wizards could scry the future; could anyone but them and those they held in confidence truly exercise free will? Prince Stellan had his prophetic dreams; what did she have besides an uncertain supply of grit and luck?

"I don't fear death," she whispered to Bhraxio. "But I surely fear the hopelorn decrepitude I see before me."

"This is not your fate," her companion replied. "Your mother may have been strong once, but you are far stronger."

She shook her head. "You can't be sure of that; you didn't know her."

"I know *you*, and I have met thousands of humans. I have yet to meet anyone stronger."

Vinca uttered a curse when trumpeted alarums blared in the distance and in the courtyard.

"Let's get to the roof and see what's happened," she told Bhraxio.

They ran up the stairs to the top of the tower. Sure enough, legion upon legion of soldiers with siege engines were marching up the castle hill, surrounding it on all sides. Their numbers were hard to gauge in the moonlight, but she guessed that the unready soldiers scrambling to get into their positions below were outmanned perhaps a hundred to one.

"You did promise the prince that we'd go home if this happened," Bhraxio said.

"They're going to be slaughtered. We can't just leave."

"What do you propose?"

"The Xintu wear bamboo armor, correct? That sounds flammable to me."

"I don't like killing humans."

"So let's be terrifying, and hope they have the sense to run off before we have to kill them."

Vinca shucked the canvas cover off her sword, dug her gauntlets and spell ingredients out of her rucksack, cut her dress so she could ride Bhraxio, and spoke the magic word to return him to his dragon size and form.

They screamed down upon the invading troops like a curse from the heavens. Bhraxio breathed great blasts of fire above the invader's heads while Vinca worked pyrotechnic magic she'd learned in their campaigns against the Outlanders. Blinding midair explosions knocked men flat and toppled their war machines. Some of the Xintu troops responded with volleys of arrows that missed their marks, but after a few blazing passes the invaders broke ranks and began fleeing for the cover of the forest.

Once the battlefield was cleared, Bhraxio swooped back to the castle and landed gracefully in the courtyard where the Coravian troops cowered fearfully.

Vinca didn't necessarily expect a hearty welcome of ale and huzzahs…but she also didn't expect her old, bow-legged father to come storming toward her, his sword drawn and an angry, profane rant about lost honor and sorcery spilling from his bearded lips.

Vinca slid from Bhraxio's wooly back and strode to meet her sire.

"How dare you!" the old king screeched. "This sorcery will bring the wrath of God upon us! You have doomed our souls! DOOMED OUR SOULS!"

He took an unsteady swing at her with his sword. She sidestepped the blade and punched him hard in the face. The King dropped like a sack of manure and lay on the filthy stones cursing her as he clutched his bleeding nose.

"How dare you!" A man a few years older than Vinca drew his sword and rushed at her. She drew her own weapon to parry his blow and when he inevitably overextended himself, she knocked the blade from his hand and kicked him square in the solar plexus. The air whoofed out of him and he sat down hard on the stones near his father, gasping. He was her eldest brother, surely, but in her rage, she couldn't remember his name. And she didn't feel the least bit badly about that.

"All right," she called to the men around her. "Would anyone else like to be an utter arsehole to me for the unpardonable sin of SAVING ALL YOU FLEABITTEN LOUTS FROM CERTAIN DEATH?"

The men fell silent as salamanders.

She stepped forward and addressed the king. "My name is Vinca, and I'm your daughter, gods help me. You sold me for gold when I was just a child. I can't say whether that deed marks you as the worst father I've ever met. But given what I've seen tonight, you are surely the worst ruler still living upon the ten continents. Whatever doom you face is the fruit of your own stupidity and incompetence."

She stepped to the side and addressed her brother, who still hadn't gotten his breath back. "If you're inheriting the throne here? Do better than this prideful jackass. Learn to hold onto your sword. For the sake of your people, make better choices. At least take a bath sometime."

She strode back to Bhraxio. "Let's go home."

As they winged away into the night, he asked her, "So, a change of subject. Have you thought more about Prince Stellan's proposal?"

"I think that when we get home, I'm going to learn all about economics, infrastructure, agriculture, and diplomacy. I'm no wizard. I might never glimpse the future except through Stellan's eyes. But I'm going to be the best damn queen anyone has ever seen."

"I wonder if this is the first time a princess has pledged herself to extreme competence out of spite?"

"It's not spite."

"It isn't?"

"The prince is delicious."

"Ah. So it's thirty percent spite, and seventy percent lust?"

She sighed. "Could we throw some civic-mindedness in there just so I don't sound like an arsehole?"

"Whatever makes you happy, milady..."

The Warlady's Daughter

Lulled by the steady swaying of the mule-drawn wagon, Elyria stared at the shimmering green sea of grass surrounding Oakengrove. It seemed to stretch on forever; a terrible, dull, oppressive expanse of green, relieved only by the occasional drab field of barley or wheat farmers had carved through the deep sod. Grass and grain, grain and grass! Would she ever get to see a real ocean? Would anything ever *happen* here?

Her miserable teenage reverie was broken by her uncle's voice: "Ria, are you listening to me?"

"Yes, Uncle Bevard." She sat up straighter on the wagon bench, then realized she hadn't any clue what he'd said. "I'm sorry; what did you say?"

He gave an exasperated sigh. "We're almost at the tavern. What's on their order?"

She spread the coarse, grass-pulp paper out on her lap. Its paleness contrasted prettily with the new purple skirt her aunt had sewed for her 16th birthday. Elyria had gathered a whole quart of pokeberries to make the dye, but of course her aunt had hidden the reason she needed them. The smooth fabric had come out a gorgeous, vibrant hue that made her think of royalty, which in turn made her imagine the traveling bards' tales of court intrigue and sword duels in the Northern palaces....

"Ria! The order?"

"Sorry, Uncle," she mumbled, forcing herself to focus on the dull list scrawled in his nearly indecipherable handwriting. "They ordered ten loaves of honey white, five loaves of dark rye, and five loaves of the nutberry."

He shook his head at her, his long rust-colored beard sweeping across the front of his plain work tunic. "Was that so difficult? We'd be finished already if it weren't for your constant woolgathering!"

She hung her head. "Sorry, Uncle."

"You told me you didn't want to be cooped up in the bakery all day." His frustrated tone made her want to jump out of the cart, dash into the shoulder-high grass and keep running until she got to the Amethyst Sea somewhere in the unfathomable Southern distance. "You *begged* me to let you come out here and help me with deliveries. Why can't you pay attention to what we're doing?"

A tiny, frantic voice in the back of her head wanted her to scream, *"Because it's all so bloody boring!"* But she knew saying it would be disastrous. Her uncle wasn't the kind of brutal man to backhand her for talking back to him. But he almost certainly would punish her with a month of scrubbing floors, chopping wood for the fires, and scraping ashes in the name of giving her a fresh appreciation for delivery duty.

So she meekly said, "I'm sorry, Uncle Bevard. You have been very patient with me, and I'm sorry."

"You need to spend more time in the real world and less time in your head." He pulled up on the mules' reins to halt them in the shade of the three-story public house at the edge of the town. The Iron Fist Tavern was built from clay bricks, thatch, field rock, plaster, and wooden beams secured with iron bands and huge iron nails with heads the size of a man's fist.

"Once you're married, your husband will expect you to be attentive to his needs at all times! If you turn out to be a poor wife, it will reflect badly on your Aunt Ruth and I, and you wouldn't want that, would you?"

It felt as though something inside her soul had been impaled on a spit and was being roasted, squirming and kicking, over a hot coal fire.

Don't say what you're thinking, she warned herself. *It'll be floors and ashes for sure!* "I...I don't think anyone will be wanting me as a wife, at least not soon–"

"Oh, nonsense!" He laughed. "You're a fine-looking female, healthy...you have the bloom of a girl who'd birth a fine, strong son!"

Oh, ye sweet and fuzzy gods, she thought. *Babies.*

Other peoples' babies were cute. And if cuteness were their sum, bearing them would be fine! But then there was the staying up all night with a crying infant, the endless dirty diapers, the colic. She'd been at Ruth's side when she gave birth to her little cousin Sky; her aunt had been in labor for two solid days. She nearly died of fever afterward! And to see the agony of a baby tearing through such a woefully small part of the body...oh no. She didn't know what malign curse the gods had put upon women to have to go through all that, but she wanted no part of it!

"There are plenty of lads and men who'd want a girl like you," her uncle continued, oblivious to her discomfort. "The blacksmith's son, what's his name?"

Oh gods, that brainless lunk, she thought.

"Corlis," she muttered. Being married to him would be like being married to an orc, except perhaps an orc might have better personal grooming habits.

"Ah, yes, Corlis! I've seen how he looks at you," her uncle sing-songed.

Have you also seen how he digs in his ears and eats what he finds? Have you heard how he can't pronounce words with more than two syllables? Elyria wanted to ask. She blushed, wishing the ground would open so she could tumble into a chasm and be lost forever.

"And there are right proper men in this community who could do well for you. *And* give our family's reputation a real boost in the bargain! Like Grainger Tevis; he's got at least fifty acres of the richest land around, and since his wife died last year, every woman in town seems to be trying to get his attention. I admit he's not much to look at...and he's a bit gruff...but that land!"

Grainger Tevis? He had to be at least fifty years old! She shuddered at the thought of his old, cold hands touching her in a marriage bed. It was just...just *nasty* for a man his age to want a girl her age. If Corlis was unappealing, Tevis was so many leagues beyond that she couldn't plumb the depths of her dismay.

"Well, it'll be at least another year before finding you a husband becomes a critical matter," her uncle mused aloud. "Wouldn't want you turning 18 and finding yourself an old maid, would you?"

"No. Of course not," she replied through gritted teeth.

He laughed. "Ah, we can worry about it later. The bread's getting stale while we sit here yammering!"

It took them another two hours to wend their way back to their family's thatched brick building in the center of town. The bakery and small rooms for the apprentices occupied the first floor, and Elyria and her family lived on the second floor. It had cost a pretty pile of silver to build, but her uncle had inherited a decent sum when Elyria's parents died. Their hard work at the bakery had turned him into one of the wealthier men in town. Not as wealthy as landed gentry such as Grainger Tevis, of course, but he did well.

"Stack the baskets and fold the linens, then wash up for supper." He unhitched the mules, and started leading them around to the barn behind the bakery. "I'll tell the apprentices to carry everything into the storeroom."

"Yes, sir." She set to shaking the crumbs off the cream-colored cloths and folding them into neat squares in one of the empty reed baskets.

She'd almost finished the last cloth when she heard a hubbub and the sound of heavy horses' hoofbeats coming down the thoroughfare.

Her mouth fell open when she saw a wedge of armored warriors atop huge black horses thundering down the cobblestones. Five, seven, nine...a whole dozen of them! With their fierce face paints and black swirling tattoos, they looked like something out of a fever dream. Where could such warriors as these have come from?

Elyria's jaw dropped further when she realized the warriors were all women! How was it possible? Girls simply weren't allowed to fight in Oakengrove. Her 12-year-old cousin Stone got into fisticuffs with the other boys all the time, but the *one* time Elyria had given a bully a well-earned kick in his nethers, she'd had to scrub floors for a week! And take endless manners lessons at Lady Stufflebeam's house! How had these mighty-looking women been able to take up arms, ride horses, and learn the arts of war? One look at their hard faces and battle scars told her that if these women had husbands, those men would dare not treat them as chattel.

And in fact, she saw no signs of wedding jewelry or other marks of marriage. If these women had avoided that dreadful fate, perhaps she could, too? Hope and fear swelled in her heart.

The warriors clattered to a stop in front of the bakery. A tall warrior with black braids curling from beneath her battered steel helmet dismounted and clomped forward in her hobnail boots.

"Bevard of Oakengrove!" she bellowed. "I am Radulla of the Nemain! Come forth and parley, or we shall drag ye forth!"

A moment later, her uncle came through the door into the courtyard, wiping his hands on his apron. His face was ashen, and he shot Elyria a worried, ashamed look that she didn't understand.

"I am Bevard." His voice shook. "What is your business?"

"Our lady Aetiane has sent us to retrieve her daughter. It is her 16th year, and it is time for her to join our riders, as you agreed when we left her in your care."

Daughter? Elyria wondered. *This must be a mistake. He doesn't have any girls in his care, except...*

Her whole world suddenly seemed to tilt at the realization of what this strange, amazing warrior-woman was saying.

"Ah." He paled and shifted his feet nervously. "Yes. Well..."

"Where is the girl?" Radulla stepped forward, scowling, and pulled off her heavy leather gauntlets as if she intended to beat or throttle him with her bare hands. "You were paid to keep her safe. If anything has happened to her–"

Her uncle took a step back, terror plain on his face. "No! No, she's fine...she's right there!" He pointed at Elyria, who felt as though she'd been thrown under a runaway cart.

Radulla turned and gave the girl an appraising up-and-down stare. Her dark eyes were disapproving and concerned. "You're Elyria?"

"Yes, ma'am." She gave the warrior a quick, uncertain curtsey.

"Let me see your hands."

Elyria held her hands out. The warrior stepped forward to scowl at her palms and knuckles.

"You don't have the proper calluses." Radulla sounded disgusted. "How skilled are you with the sword and bow?"

"Sword and bow?" Elyra stammered. "I'm...I'm sorry, but girls aren't allowed–"

Radulla whirled on her uncle with alarming speed. *"You have not trained her?"*

Bevard flinched and backed up against the brick wall of the bakery. "I...I didn't think Aetiane would come back. She's in such a dangerous line of work–"

"You had but one job to do! One!" Radulla stepped forward until she was right in Bevard's face. "You were to hire a weapons tutor from Castle Port and make sure that your daughter was properly trained when we came for her! Our lady gave you a handsome sum to ensure that!"

Daughter? Elyria wondered, blood rising in her face. *He's really my father? Why did he lie? Was he ashamed of me?*

Meanwhile, Radulla was still shouting, her spittle lashing Bevard's face. He cowered lower and lower under her tirade.

"I have seen *many* worthless sires in my time," Radulla snarled, "but you are by far the most incompetent. Even the most sodden drunks of the bowery know better than to cross the Nemain! We should make an example of you that none shall forget!"

The warrior's tone promised terrible violence.

"No!" Elyria shouted. "No, stop! Please have mercy on him. *Please.*"

Radulla straightened up and gave Elyria another appraising stare. "I have many qualities but mercifulness is not among them. You *will* be trained, and trained *properly*, and if anyone interferes, there will be dire consequences. Your mother will test you herself to be certain."

Elyria's throat suddenly went dry. "How will I be trained? Who will do it?"

"My lieutenant will stay behind to train you. Six months of *nothing* but training. If you have a beau, say goodbye to him this evening, because you will *not* be spending time with him after today."

She turned on her heel and pointed a stern finger at Bevard. "And *you* will provide our lieutenant with quarters, food, and anything she needs for your daughter's training. You will supply them without resistance or remark, and you will *not* interfere. Or your life will end in fire. Is this clear to you?"

"Yes." His face was ashen, and his voice was a broken whisper.

"Good." Radulla turned to face the other warriors, who had been waiting atop their steeds. "Korraine! Are you ready?"

"I am," replied a voice that rolled like a summer storm.

The other warriors reined their horses aside to allow Korraine through. Elyria's breath caught in her throat. Korraine was like a bouldered peak made flesh and poured into leather and chainmail, and she rode atop a mighty dappled gray warhorse that had to be at least 17 hands tall. And she wasn't human. Her features were coarse, and her dark skin had a strange greenish hue, like copper that had just begun to patina. Her neck and shoulders were corded with muscle, and her lower canines jutted up over her lip like small tusks.

"Baker-man," Korraine rumbled. "Have you a barn with a hayloft?"

Bevard nodded, looking miserable and embarrassed; several dozen townspeople had gathered at a safe distance and were whispering in each others' ears and pointing. "Around back."

"Good." Her golden eyes flicked to Elyria. "Tomorrow you shall also sleep in the barn. Find a sturdy bedroll. Some nights we shall sleep in the field."

"But my bed is right here above the bakery–"

"You must get your bones used to sleeping on the ground." Korraine's tone left no room for negotiation. "There won't always be fine linens or a hearth where you're going. Meet me at the barn at first cocks-crow and wear sturdy clothes. Spend the night as you prefer."

Korraine gave Bevard a pointed stare, her lip curling back from wolfish teeth. "I expect you have questions only *he* should answer."

Elyria finally broke the tense silence at dinner: "Why did you say you were my uncle when you were really my father?"

Bevard bowed his head and clenched the edge of the broad oak dinner table, his knuckles going white. Her cousins Sky and Stone–*no, half-sister and half-brother*, Elyria corrected herself–looked wide-eyed from her to their father.

"I..." Bevard's voice faltered.

"Just tell her." Her stepmother Ruth sounded and looked as if the weight of the entire world had fallen on her shoulders. "Just tell her, and be done with it."

Her father set down his fork. "Eighteen years ago, I and some friends travelled to the Orchard Festival in Castle Port. I was betrothed to Ruth, but because we had not yet married, her parents did not let her travel with us. Had they relented...well, they did not."

He cleared his throat, looking deeply ashamed. "My friends and I drank a great deal of cider and perry at the festival. I had sworn faithfulness to Ruth, but at a tavern I met a young warrior woman named Aetiane, and the drink made me forget my vow that night. I was still in a stupor the next morning; my friends carried me out of the inn, and I put what little I could remember out of my mind and focused on my love for Ruth. I returned to Oakengrove, and the next month she and I married.

"Then, ten months later, Aetiane and one of her lieutenants rode into town after dark. They carried an infant–you, Elyria–and they told me they were going to war, and that I was your father, and that I had to keep you and raise you. They gave me the money I used to purchase this bakery. Ruth and I decided that the best thing to do was to make up a story about a brother of mine who'd died and left behind an orphaned daughter. Such things happen all the time, and the townsfolk would not bring whispering shame down upon our house. Shame that I now cannot avoid facing."

Everyone was silent for several moments. Elyria tried to make sense of the storm of emotions and questions inside her. She'd been told she was an orphan when her own father was the one raising her. How could he be so ashamed of her? Why did the townsfolk's opinions matter so much more to him than being honest with his own child? He could have told her, and she'd have kept it a secret. Did he not trust her to keep their family's reputation safe? Did he not really love her as a father was supposed to love a child?

But then, her mother was still alive, too. Why hadn't she come to get her? Was she still off at war? Was she having some grand, dangerous adventure? Was *she* ashamed of Elyria, too, because her father wasn't even brave enough to tell the truth? Would Elyria ever be good enough for her, or would she look at her with dismay, as Radulla and Korraine had? How could she ever be good enough when her father hadn't prepared her to do anything but cook?

"Radulla said you were given the money to train me. And you didn't," she finally replied.

"But you were a girl!" her father exclaimed, as if this were the most obvious thing in the world. "Seeking a warrior's training for you would make people ask questions!"

He frowned, looking troubled. "Besides, to hear Aetiane talk, I expected she'd be dead on the end of an orc's pike within a year, two at the most. I *swear* I never thought she'd ever send for you, and that you would spend your life in Oakengrove. Ruth and I decided that we would raise you just as we'd raise any daughter of ours."

"But you didn't." Elyria felt a flush of anger. "I was always the orphaned niece. Not your daughter. You *never* would have admitted I was your daughter if they hadn't turned up today, would you?"

"Elyria! Don't speak to your uncle that way!" Ruth said, and then caught herself. "I mean, your father."

Elyria stared down at the rabbit stew and bread on her plate. *I am the daughter of a warrior woman,* she thought. Not just a woman; her mother had enough money to purchase a whole bakery. She was a warrior *lady*, the captain of her people.

"Apologize to your father," Ruth warned.

"I don't think I owe anyone an apology for speaking the truth." Heart pounding with anger, Elyria stood and picked up her plate and fork. "Good night to you all. I'll be in the barn."

"Don't you dare get up and leave!" Ruth's face was red with fury, but her voice was shrill with terror. "If you leave, you'll not be allowed back in this house!"

Elyria was too angry to care whether her stepmother feared the loss of her adopted child or was simply upset that she'd been disobeyed. She carried her dinner out into the darkness.

Korraine was on a folding camp chair beside a fire she'd built in the dirt in front of the barn. "That went as well as could have been expected." The orcish warrior's golden eyes gleamed in the firelight.

Elyria stopped short. "You heard us?"

The massive woman smiled and tapped her pointed ear; it reminded Elyria of a bat's. "I have unusual good hearing, thanks to my sire, may the gods devour his blackened, worthless soul."

The curse shocked Elyria. "What did he do to make you say such things about him?"

"He was an orc chieftain. I do not know his name, nor do I wish to know it. He captured my mother, Lady Ariale...she was your mother's sister. He tortured her. When the Nemain rescued her, she was pregnant with me, and her body was too broken to survive childbirth. Because there was no other family to take me, your mother and Radulla raised me on the backs of their warhorses. I teethed on arrow shafts and leather scabbards, and my first toy was a wooden dagger."

Korraine threw another log onto the fire. "It is my eternal regret that Radulla and Aetiane slaughtered my sire and his gang, because I would have liked that opportunity myself. I would have liked it *very* much."

"I'm...I'm sorry." Elyria didn't know what else to say.

"Sorry? There is nothing to be sorry about." Korraine stood and brushed off her leather tunic. "The Nemain saved me when any other humans would have burned me with my mother's corpse, or left me on a hillside for the wolves. I have never known children's games or had a beau take me to a town dance, but I have known a mother's fiercest love, and I have learned everything I can about fighting and surviving. And I am respected by our sisterhood; the Nemain look to me to train daughters whose fathers have failed them, and I do that as well as I possibly can. I live, so that you and your cousins might live."

Elyria stared into Korraine's campfire for several moments. "I have a question," she finally asked.

"Yes?"

"Do I have a choice? About training to become a warrior, I mean."

Korraine gave her a sidelong glance. "I know you'll be expected to marry soon if you stay. I got a good look at the lads here on our ride through the town, and if they have any outstanding qualities at all, they *must* be hiding them beneath their trousers. Do you really prefer to become a scullery-slave wife to one of these grassland bumpkins instead of seeking fortune and glory with your mother?"

"No," Elyria replied, blushing. She paused, trying to figure out how to voice the turmoil in her mind. "But Radulla didn't speak as if any of us here had a choice. If this is something I'm forced to do because my mother paid my father money, I'm still a slave, aren't I?"

Korraine laughed. "Few of us get to do exactly what we wish! Even the most powerful kings and queens are born into duty. But your mother would not want you to be forced into a dangerous life that doesn't fit you. Radulla...spoke *strongly* to aid your father's comprehension and stir his sense of urgency."

"So if I decide I don't wish to do this…?"

Korraine spread her scarred, calloused hands. "I was sent here to train you. That's the only duty I have right now. I have trained girls who were eager students, but I have trained girls who resisted and whined and feigned injury. I much prefer willing students! But I will not simply forget my duty in the face of your reluctance. Besides, you cannot know what life with the Nemain might be like until after I've trained you, can you? So why not learn what I have to teach you?"

"All right. That sounds fair." Elyria paused. "Have you never trained boys?"

Korraine shook her head. "Almost never. The Nemain only conceive girls, but every once in a while a girl decides she'd rather be a boy. And even more rarely, a boy wants to join us after he sees his father's daughter in training. The boys are welcome; it's handy to have some bearded chins around when we negotiate with clans that don't respect females."

Elyria frowned in confusion. "How is it possible that the Nemain only have girl children?"

"The story is that long ago, a princess named Nemae was married to a proud war king who got into a quarrel with a powerful wizard. The wizard, instead of attacking the king directly, decided to cast a spell upon Nemae so that she could bear no sons who could be heirs to the throne. The king discovered this after his twin daughters were born. Though it was entirely the sorcerer's doing, he blamed his wife. He planned to have Nemae arrested for witchcraft so that she would be executed and he could remarry. Nemae learned of the plot and fled in the night with her daughters, swearing that she would never again be at the mercy of a king's good will. She raised her daughters in the wilderness and taught them to fight, and our tribe grew from there."

"The Nemain don't marry?"

"Sometimes they do. Love is powerful, and leaving a child behind to be raised by strangers is by far the most difficult thing any of the sisters must do. Some do marry and leave us to raise families; some later return to us. Some fall in love with warrior men and women who join us for a few months or their whole lives." Korraine shrugged. "To me, the Nemain are all the family I need, and I see no reason to leave."

The next morning, Korraine took Elyria through a battery of lung-bursting calisthenics at the barn and in a nearby fallow field until the girl lay gasping in the dirt.

"You did better than many," Korraine said cheerfully. "You can't climb a rope or pull yourself up onto a branch, but you can press a good-sized log overhead and your balance is excellent. We'll work on the rest until you're fit. Now, let's go over to that orchard, and I'll show you how to care for a sword."

"Is...is it this hard for everyone?" Elyria gasped.

"At first it is. Everything gets easier with practice. Particularly the killing."

Elyria felt a chill. She sat up. "I...I don't like hunting," she admitted. "What if I can't kill?"

"Is it the blood and guts you dislike, or do you simply dislike hurting doves and deer and other gentle forest creatures?"

"I don't mind handling guts. And I certainly don't mind making sausage... but I just don't care for the killing part," Elyria replied, thinking of all the times her mother had told her to go wring a chicken's neck for dinner and the nearly-equal number times she'd given Sky or Stone a sweet biscuit to do it for her. "It seems...cruel."

"It's different when you look into a goblin's yellow eyes and see the violence it wants to commit upon you and your sisters. I think you'll find they're *quite* killable."

"But–what if I don't," Elyria pressed. "What if I'm rubbish at it?"

"Well, you must learn how to fight properly, first! And then see. But if it turns out you just don't have the spirit for killing, well. We always need sisters to care for the horses and tend to the sick. I can't train you in those arts, but Galetta can."

Korraine leaned in and spoke in a conspiratorial tone. "And frankly our cook Venia only knows how to make stew. Her biscuits are best loaded into the catapults and flung at the enemy. If you were to replace her, few of us would weep."

Elyria smiled despite her doubts.

Korraine slapped her on the back, nearly knocking her into the dirt again. "I'm turning black as a kettle out here, and I feel like I might boil. Let's go under the trees and put some sword-lore into that questioning head of yours…"

That night, Elyria collapsed into her bedroll in the hayloft, utterly exhausted. She thought she would surely pass right out...but falling asleep just seemed too difficult, somehow. The bedroll was lumpy, and the hay smelled musty. So she just lay there in a daze with her eyes shut, hoping that Nature would eventually take its course.

Meanwhile, Korraine's lantern was still lit, and the orcish warrior was digging around in her bag, making rustling noises in the straw. Elyria cracked open an eye and turned her head. In the flickering light, she saw Korraine threading tiny, brightly colored beads onto a length of sinew.

"What are you doing?" Elyria asked.

"Jewelry." Korraine held up the half-finished piece. The beads glittered, colorful as a field of summer flowers. "It'll be an anklet for me, if I keep it. Probably a necklace for anyone else!"

"You...make jewelry?" Elyria's tired mind couldn't seem to wrap itself around the idea that this hulking, dangerous warrior would spend her time creating dainty baubles.

"It's an ugly world, so I like to make something pretty at night. It helps me rest." She paused. "Someday, maybe, if we can help the other clans defeat the orcs and goblins once and for all, we can lay down our swords for good. And spend our days creating beauty instead of destroying evil."

The next two months were a blur of training, eating, and sleeping. Korraine spent a great deal of time teaching Elyria different forms of unarmed combat, some she'd learned from the fabled mountain monks whose god forbade them from shedding blood when they defended their libraries of ancient knowledge. When she wasn't studying fighting or armor-making, Elyria had to run or climb ropes or lift stones. She quickly got used to being sore, bruised, blistered, and filthy pretty much all the time. Neither her father nor her stepmother visited her at the barn. Stone and Sky were practically mute when they brought out the food and house supplies at Korraine's command, refusing to meet their half-sister's gaze, and speaking only to give short, terse answers to questions.

"This happens," Korraine said sympathetically as they both watched Stone scamper back to the safety of the bakery as if a wraith was chasing him. "They might feel differently later."

"And if they don't?"

"Then it will be all the easier for you to leave this place when the time comes." Korraine slapped her on the back. "Fetch us some water from the pump; let's get cleaned up, and I'll buy you an ale at the tavern."

They departed the bakery just as the sun was starting to set. Elyria wasn't prepared for the dirty looks the townspeople gave her and Korraine as they walked down the main street towards the tavern.

"Orcish filth," an old man growled, and spat at their feet. "Mingers!"

Elyria felt a surge of anger flush her face, and she'd half-turned, fists raised, but Korraine grabbed her elbow and smoothly led her on down the road.

"Let it go," she whispered, looking calm as a windless lake. "He'd just bleed all over your good boots."

It was only after Korraine spoke that Elyria realized the insulting old man was Grainger Tevis. So much for her father's plan to marry her off to the old bastard.

The tavern wasn't as crowded as it was on Aleday nights, but a good fifty men were seated at the round oak tables or standing at the bar. Everybody turned to stare at them as they pushed through the swinging doors.

"Two pints of dark ale, please." Korraine slapped two silver pieces down on the lacquered bar.

The bartender met Korraine's gaze as he polished a pewter mug with a rag. An unspoken conversation based on pointed looks seemed to move between them, and Korraine's hand casually dropped to the hilt of her sword.

"Two ales, coming up," the bartender replied. His eyes turned to Elyria and he smiled uncomfortably. "Your uncle farin' well?"

"Well enough," she replied.

"Ain't this a pretty sight," announced an alcohol-slurred voice to her left.

Elyria turned. The blacksmith's son stood there with a frown of distaste. He wore a sleeveless leather tunic that showed off the corded muscles in his arms and shoulders; no doubt he'd been strutting around town trying to impress girls most of the day. He was sweating as if he'd already had quite a lot to drink, but his legs were steady.

She nodded in cautious greeting. "Corlis. Good to see you."

He grinned at her unpleasantly. "So, I hear this *mudbeast* is showin' ya fightin'. Ya shoulda come t' me instead. All a girl needs to know is how t' swallow a sword."

He grabbed his crotch in an exaggerated, obscene gesture and hooted at Elyria. Half the bar laughed along with him as if he'd just told the cleverest knee-slapper of a joke they'd ever heard. The other half sat back in silence, nervously eyeing Korraine, whose expression was a studied blankness. She might have been bored, or sleepy, or calculating how to slaughter every man-jack in the tavern. It was hard to tell.

"Oh, Corlis. Always so witty." Elyria smiled sweetly at him. "*So* nice chatting with you."

She turned to get her drink at the bar, but Corlis roughly grabbed at her shoulder. She easily shook him off.

"I wasn't done with you, *bitch*."

"I'm quite sure I'm done with you, though."

"No fighting in the tavern!" the barkeep bellowed at her. "Take it outside!"

"I'm not fighting," Elyria shot back, annoyed.

"What, you scared?" Corlis sneered at her and gave her shoulder a shove.

In a well-practiced move, Elyria grabbed his outstretched right hand and yanked hard. He weighed a good three stones more than she did, but Korraine had shown her how to use what mass she had for excellent effect. Her quick yank jerked him forward onto his knees, and then he sprawled onto his belly with a curse of surprise. She twisted his wrist up and back, and pressed down on his elbow until he cried out and beat the floor with his left fist.

"You'll stop being a jackass and let me drink in peace?" She pressed harder on the sensitive nerve bundle at the base of his trapped elbow for emphasis.

"Yes, ow, goldamn, yes!"

She flung his arm down into his face. "Next time you try to put your hands on me, I'll break your bones."

Swearing, Corlis crab-crawled backward until one of his buddies helped him up. Nobody else stepped forward to challenge her.

"Oi, fightin's against the rules," someone in the back complained loudly. "Throw 'em out!"

"That *wasn't* a fight." Elyria glared at the crowd, unable to see who had spoken.

"The lad put his hands on her and that's not proper," the bartender said. "I don't see that she broke any rules teaching him some manners. They stay."

Korraine pulled out a nearby stool and sat down at her drink, a smile playing on her lips.

Elyria frowned at her. "What are you grinning about?"

"You're certainly your mother's daughter!" Korraine toasted her with the pewter mug and drank deeply.

The cold bite of autumn was in the Restday air when Elyria's morning of testing arrived. One of her mother's pet crows arrived two hours before at first light, heralding their impending arrival in a squawking monotone. That gave Elyria time to bolt down a quick breakfast, do some exercises and stretches to warm up, and get her gear on as her mentor stood by offering calm encouragements. Elyria tried hard to not think about what would happen if she failed: namely, that she'd have to stay in Oakengrove and make some kind of peace with her family and the disapproving townsfolk. The prospect of being stuck here, friendless and without prospects, seemed nearly worse than death.

"You can do this," Korraine said. "Just keep your head about you. Always defend yourself; easy openings will be traps."

Elyria stood on the cobblestones in front of the bakery dressed in leather armor Korraine had showed her how to craft herself. A wooden longsword she'd made from a fallen oak branch waited inside the scabbard at her hip; if she did well in her test, her mother would gift her with live steel. Her hands quivered inside her heavy leather gauntlets, and she vainly tried to still them. A steel helmet Korraine bought from a traveling vendor fit her only slightly better than a bucket; the extra padding she'd added muffled her hearing and made it even heavier.

If anyone was still sleeping when the Nemain rode down the main street, the war cries, clop of hooves, snort of warhorses, and clank and jingle of armor surely awakened them all. Korraine had told Elyria that the Nemain usually rode quietly as a spring breeze, but they could thunder in like a hurricane when they wanted to make their presence known. And clearly this morning they wanted all of Oakengrove to know they had arrived. There were at least three times as many warriors as had come to deliver Korraine, and Elyria saw a few male faces as well as massive orogs and fey-looking folk she guessed had to be elves.

And at the front, a proud-looking warrior in fine plate armor fit for any queen. Was it Aetiane? Elyria scanned her features, looking for any resemblance. It was possible–the curl of hair escaping her helmet was the color of hay, the same as Elyria's, and her eyes were the same river green. But the warrior queen looked directly at her–practically looked *through* her–and showed no sign of recognition.

Don't think about it, Elyria told herself. *Put her out of your mind. Just focus on the fight.*

Townspeople, some still in their nightdress, trailed after the warriors like the tail on a kite, but all kept to a safe distance. Above, Elyria heard the shutters of her parents' bedroom creak open. She didn't look up.

The Nemain pulled up and fanned out in a big half-circle around the front of the bakery. There was perhaps thirty yards between Elyria and the nearest warrior.

"Elyria of Oakengrove!" Aetiane called out. "Do you stand ready for the test of combat?"

"I stand ready," she called back, heart pounding.

A tall warrior in leather and scale armor dismounted and pulled a wooden sword from a scabbard strapped behind her saddle. Elyria flipped her visor down, drew her sword, and took a ready stance.

"On your guard, apprentice!" The warrior came in swinging, her wooden blade a blur.

Elyria parried the blows before she'd even had time to think. The crack of wood on wood echoed down the streets. Korraine grunted approvingly.

The warrior swung hard, seemingly trying to knock the sword from Elyria's hands, but Elyria's muscles were strong after Korraine's training, and her body easily absorbed the shock of the blows. They soon fell into a violent, fast rhythm of strikes and parries. Anything the warrior tried, Elyria found she could parry. Elyria thoroughly enjoyed it, even as the battle started to wind her, and she could see frustration gleaming in the warrior's eyes.

"I *know* you saw that opening!" Korraine barked. "This isn't dance class! You're faster; take her!"

Elyria parried hard, knocking her opponent's sword wide, and lunged in hard and fast, jabbing the point into the padded leather over the warrior's ribs. The warrior swore loudly and fell to one knee.

"Hold!" Korraine shouted.

Elyria stepped back, keeping her sword at the ready.

"Goldammit, I think she broke me rib," the warrior complained.

"I mark that as a killing blow, were this a match of live steel," Korraine called to the Nemain. "What say you?"

"I mark it as but a flesh wound," came an amused reply. "And your apprentice dragged things out so long that reinforcements have arrived!"

Two new warriors in leather armor dismounted and charged Elyria. She braced herself for the impact of her new opponent's heavy wooden weapons. The one on the left was fleeter of foot, and would arrive first–

Crack! Elyria parried the first blow, pivoted and drove her shin into the warrior's midsection. She heard the air whoof out of the warrior's lungs and she raised her sword again to meet the second warrior, but she couldn't lift her weapon quickly enough and the other tackled her and threw her to the cobblestones. Her helmet took the worst of the impact, but sparks still bloomed in her eyes like festival day fireworks.

When her vision cleared, she saw the two warriors standing above her, the points of their wooden swords inches above her throat.

"What happens now?" Elyria asked.

"Step aside and let her stand," Aetiane ordered.

The warriors fell back, and Elyria climbed to her feet, back and neck aching.

"Did...did I pass?" she asked.

Aetiane smiled and called out to the thronged warriors around her: "What say you, Nemain? Does this girl belong with us? All in favor, say 'Aye'!"

A thunderous *"AYE!"* arose.

"And so she is one of us!" Aetiane declared. "Welcome, daughter!"

Elyria suddenly felt light as a magician's balloon.

"Come forward and claim your prize," said Aetiane.

Elyria stepped up to her mother's warhorse, and Aetiane handed her a sheathed longsword wrapped in a fine belt.

"It's a good solid weapon," her mother said. "No doubt you'll find something finer on your adventures, but it won't fail you."

"Thank you, ma'am." Elyria buckled the sword around her slender hips. Her very own sword! She'd have never imagined that this could really happen. "When do we leave?"

"Just as soon as you gather up your things; we have a few extra horses, and you can choose whichever you prefer."

"Elyria, wait." It was her uncle's voice. Her *father's* voice.

She turned. Bevard the Baker stood there in his Restday best, but his hair was still mussed, as if he'd quickly awakened and dressed in a hurry.

"Yes, Father?" she asked uncertainly.

He looked from Elyria to Aetiane, a thousand emotions playing across his face. "I...I'm sorry. I failed you. I failed *both* of you. I was a fool. And I wasted precious time."

"Make it up to her when she visits you next year," Aetiane said.

"I'm coming back here?" Elyria asked.

"Just to visit," Aetiane said. "And only if you want to."

"I...I think I'd like that," she said.

The Nemain crested the dunes above the cove, where the *Dawn Fortune* awaited at anchor. Beyond the clear blue waters of the bay, the Amethyst Sea rippled like a vast, endless expanse of cerulean satin. The ocean! Elyria's heart soared. She'd dreamed of seeing it ever since the first traveling bard entertained her and the other children with pirate tales.

"The sea's not usually this calm," her mother remarked. "I take it as a good sign."

"There's a thousand kingdoms out there," Korraine said. "The minions of Endroren want them all. Are you ready to stop them?"

"I'm ready," Elyria replied.

Her mother smiled. "Then let's go…"

About the Author

Lucy A. Snyder is the five-time Bram Stoker Award-winning author of the novels *Spellbent, Shotgun Sorceress, Switchblade Goddess,* and the collections *Soft Apocalypses, Shooting Yourself in the Head For Fun and Profit: A Writer's Survival Guide, Orchid Carousals, Sparks and Shadows, Chimeric Machines,* and *Installing Linux on a Dead Badger.* Her writing has been translated into French, Russian, and Japanese editions and has appeared in publications such as *Apex Magazine, Nightmare Magazine, Pseudopod, Strange Horizons, Weird Tales, Steampunk World, In the Court of the Yellow King, Shadows Over Main Street, Qualia Nous, The Library of the Dead,* and *Best Horror of the Year, Vol. 5.*

Lucy was born in South Carolina but grew up in grew up in the cowboys-and-cactus part of Texas. She currently lives in Worthington, Ohio with her husband and occasional co-author Gary A. Braunbeck.

Lucy has a BS in biology, an MA in journalism, and an MFA in creative writing and is a graduate of the 1995 Clarion Science Fiction & Fantasy Writers' Workshop. She has worked as a computer systems specialist, science writer, biology tutor, researcher, software reviewer, radio news editor, and bassoon instructor. She currently mentors students in Seton Hill University's MFA program in Writing Popular Fiction.

If genres were wall-building nations, Lucy's stories would be forging passports, jumping fences, swimming rivers and dodging bullets. You can learn more about her at www.lucysnyder.com and you can follow her on Twitter at @LucyASnyder.

Publication History

"That Which Does Not Kill You"–*Looming Low,* Dim Shores, August 2017.

"Sunset on Mott Island"–*Shadows Over Main Street, Vol. 2,* Cutting Block Books, October 2017.

"The Gentleman Caller"–*Return of the Old Ones,* Dark Regions Press, February 2017.

"Executive Functions"–*You, Human,* Dark Regions Press, December 2016.

"The Yellow Death"–*Seize The Night,* Gallery Books, October 2015. Honorable mention, *Best Horror of the Year, Vol. 8*

"Santa Muerte"–*Streets of Shadows,* Alliteration Ink, September 2014.

"Fraeternal"–*Gamut Magazine,* October 2017.

"A Noble Endeavor"–*Steampunk Universe,* Alliteration Ink, January 2018.

"Blossoms Blackened Like Dead Stars"–*Ride The Star Wind,* Broken Eye Books, September 2017.

"A Hero of Grünjord"–*Hath No Fury,* Ragnarok Publications, July 2018.

"The Warlady's Daughter"–*Champions of Aetaltis,* Mechanical Muse, April 2016.

CPSIA information can be obtained
at www.ICGtesting.com
Printed in the USA
LVHW031415161218
600665LV00004B/608/P

9 781947 879089